THE GIRL HE NEEDS

AN ENEMIES TO LOVERS ROMANTIC COMEDY

KRISTI ROSE

Vintage Housewife Books

Cover Design © 2022 Qamber Covers

The Girl He Needs/ Kristi Rose. *-- 2nd edition*

ISBN: 978-1-944513-37-5

Previously published by Kensington Lyrical with the same title.

THE GIRL HE NEEDS

Three reasons I'm getting in a car with a stranger
by Josie Woodmere:
1. My piece of crap car is on fire on the side of the highway.
2. The guy in the truck doesn't look like a murderer... in fact, he's hot.
3. Even if he tries something, I'm confident I could take him.

Hottie in the truck, Brinn McRae turns out to be straight-laced and so not my type. Plus, I'm not looking for romance. I have to find a job and my estranged brother.

The universe must have different plans because the first job my Daytona temp agency sends me to is Brinn's flight school. And if I thought we weren't compatible before, working in his small office makes me question my feelings. The only problem is I'm not sure if I want to loosen his straight-laces or choke him with them.

I don't know if he's man I want, but I'm positive I'm ***the girl he needs.***

ONE

KARMA IS A DIRTY HAG.

Here I am, an hour out of Beaufort. It's hot, I'm hungry, and my car is a piece of shit. It's gone and called it a day. Black smoke pours out from under the hood and the stench of something burning could *almost* make me lose my appetite. Almost. If I wasn't a stress eater. To make matters worse, when I got out of the car, my phone charger got caught on the seatbelt and fell, landing between the door and the seat. I noticed it as I was slamming the door, using all my fury in the push, and effectively crushed the charger, leaving bits of black plastic littered on the ground.

I grab the flower I have tucked into my hair, throw it down, then stomp it into the pavement before I move to the passenger side door and jerk it open.

After removing the title from the glove box, I sign the car away. It's someone else's problem now. Then I dig in my bag for my phone, ready to search for a charity to donate the car, but once I pull it out I find the battery empty.

Karma. I knew it would catch up with me, eventually. A

girl doesn't live like I do without accruing some bad juju. Since walking out on my fiancée, Max, two years ago, I've dumped guys via text messages, ended a second engagement by changing my Facebook status, and just today I dumped a Marine by leaving a note on his house door.

For additional kicks, I quit my job as a hotel desk clerk this morning with no notice whatsoever. It's only right that my car would shit the bed, too. In all fairness, it's not that I set out to be a cold-hearted bitch. I just don't do long term. I'm up-front with all parties involved, but this is my life and I don't plan on living it for others. Nothing sounds worse to me than working the job, monogamy dating, and not experiencing anything new. I've been there, done that, and burned the T-shirt in a campfire ceremony in Small Town, Texas where "Josie Woodmere, a rising phoenix" was launched.

When I woke this morning, and the plan for the day ahead of me was best described as familiar rut, I tossed my personal effects into the few bags I own and left the hotel, steering my 2000 Saturn hatchback—affectionately termed Freckles because of the sheer volume of Bondo patches that comprise my paint job—toward the southbound interstate, stopping only at Nick's house to leave the farewell card.

It's the least I can do, say goodbye and wish him luck in his future endeavors, thanking him for teaching me how to shoot a gun, for showing me a good time, and for being a friend. Though karma's probably right, I should've taken the time to tell him in person, but I'm a girl on a mission to move on and friendly farewells tend to be long, drawn-out affairs. Especially when the guy in question is getting far too attached, asking me to leave clothes at his place and calling me at work just to say hello. Not that there's anything wrong with that. It's sweet really, but not for me.

Jerking my rolling suitcase from the trunk, I swing my tote and mat across my back and pull my sunglasses from atop my head. The last road sign said the next exit is nine miles away. It's going to be a long walk, so I might as well get to it. Had I known what sort of day I'd be facing, I certainly wouldn't have worn my wedge heels and long maxi skirt. The only smart item on my body is my tank top, and I'm fortunate that I've pulled my long hair into one equally long, fat braid.

Cars speed past me, kicking up small pebbles and sand, some pelting me on the arm. Some jackasses honk, wolf whistle, or call out obscenities. Others just hang their asses out the window. I reach into my bag and touch the .38 Special Nick gave me for my birthday. It's times like now that I'm glad I pack heat. I'm debating switching out my wedge shoes for my runners when a four-door truck pulls onto the shoulder ahead of me. It's an expensive one that's made for towing and comfort, and the placard on the tailgate advertises Alliance Aviation, Daytona Beach.

Have I caught my first break?

It backs up toward me and stops ten feet away. Cautiously, I walk to the passenger door, hand in my purse on my gun. The window is down and some guy hangs out his head.

I place him immediately. Suite 501. Last night.

The one with his head out the window is the younger brother of a much larger, and if my eidetic memory serves, unbelievably hot guy. An incredibly serious, must-have-a-corn-cob-up-his-ass, straight-laced, only-has-eyes-for-his-smartphone hot guy. If you like that sort of thing.

I don't.

"Reckon that's you broke down back there," baby brother says matter-of-factly. Must be a Mensa member.

At the window, I see the hot guy inside, his forearm resting on the steering wheel, looking at me over his brother's shoulder.

"Is a tow truck coming?" the driver asks. Mac something. My memory scrolls through the last names of the guest register from last night, taking a moment before locking on to the information. "No, that car and I are parting company." McRae, that's his name.

"Do you need a ride back to the hotel?" McRae asks as his eyes flick down where my rolling suitcase sits.

"I quit this morning. I'm actually headed to Florida." A van pulls off onto the shoulder about two hundred yards behind us.

"It's a long walk to Florida," McRae states.

I shift my attention back to the brothers. "I'm aware. I thought I'd get to the next town and either rent a car or catch a bus."

"You going down for a visit?" the younger brother asks. His brow knits together and I assume he's trying to puzzle me out.

"Something like that. I'm moving there." I gesture to my bags. It's none of their business that I've not only been on a quest to figure out my shit but also searching for my older brother, William. Who, with a simple three-lined email sent yesterday, spurred me into moving on earlier than I planned.

I'm glad you like the South. You should try to spend some time in Florida. You'd love it. It's great and why I choose to live here.

For two years I've been searching and it's my first clue.

"That's all your stuff? Hell, I thought that's what women took when they went away overnight." Younger brother laughs and turns to older brother. "Right, Brinn?"

I smile slightly at the joke, my attention on the van rolling toward us. It's not one of those pleasant minivans, sure to contain a family and seats sticky with juice box spills. It's an old utility van with painted-out black windows. I take a step closer to the truck and the brothers. I have my gun, but I never really thought I'd have to use it and certainly not an hour after I broke down.

"Look," I say, switching my hand from my gun to my phone and pulling it from my purse. "My cell is dead, I know the next exit is another nine miles, and I'm willing to compensate you for the gas." I nod my head toward the molester mobile coasting to a stop several yards behind the truck and raise my brows in question.

"Hell, we're headed to Florida, too. We can at least get you to the state line," little brother says. He's got a pleasing southern drawl that's more noticeable on certain words. He jumps out of the truck, opens the back door, and throws my suitcase in. He gestures for me to follow and I don't waste a second. McRae is pulling out as his brother's closing his door.

"Thanks," I tell them. "How lucky we met last night and you guys remembered me. My name's Josie." I'm grateful for the ride.

The younger brother laughs and swivels in his seat to look at me. "I'm Vann, this is Brinn. I don't think it's possible to forget a girl like you."

I give him a closed-lip smile. I can only guess what he means by that.

I look over to find McRae watching me in the rearview mirror. He's a hulk of a guy, tall and thick. Solid. His green eyes were the first thing I noticed about him last night and they capture me again today. He's Florida all in one bundle. Sun-bleached blonde hair, sand-chafed skin, and murky green eyes the color of the everglades. His clothes are freshly pressed and speak of how he plans the day to play out, with comfort and business. I dress for my mood and how I *hope* my day will go.

"You ever been to Florida?" Vann asks as he opens a laptop.

"When I was a kid." It hits me suddenly. The memory of the celebratory Caribbean cruise my parents took us on. I was starting college and Will law school. He was increasingly forgetful and overly stressed; the time away did nothing to improve his mood. It was the last place three young adults wanted to be, though I do think my younger brother, Stuart, experienced his first chick action on that cruise. Poor, unlucky girl.

How could I have forgotten? It had been such a tense trip and the first time in my seventeen years I'd felt like maybe I didn't know Will at all. Not twelve weeks after we returned, Will was gone.

I force myself to try picturing something other than Will's face on the day he left, to remember something more than the anger and fear of that day.

When I look up, baby brother is watching me.

"You ok?" Vann asks.

"Sure. Just catching my breath." McRae cuts his eyes to me and I switch the subject. "You came up for a Marine Corp graduation, correct?"

Vann slides his laptop onto the center console and turns

to me. "Yeah, this guy we knew as kids. He doesn't have much by way of family so Brinn wanted to come up and show him some support."

"Becoming a Marine is a big deal. Especially for Markus." McRae looks at his brother and his tone is similar to that of a parent using the conversation as a teachable moment.

"His mom overdosed a while back and his brother went to prison. He used to be a student of Brinn's. That's what probably got him this far," Vann tells me.

I nod though I understand only half of the statement. "Student of what?"

"Brinn teaches—"

"I'm a flight instructor," McRae says. "If he can keep his head down and eye on the prize, Markus will go far in the Marines."

I choke back a laugh at the eye on the prize remark. How many times have I heard my father say precisely the same thing to Stuart? Will and I never had trouble keeping our eyes on the prize. Our parents set a goal and we met it. Usually exceeded it. But what these last two years have shown me is that "the prize" is different for everyone and should be quantified early on. Had I known the prize was living a life resembling my mother's, with charities, the country club, and Junior League, and that striding toward said prize made me feel empty and lonely, I'd have eyed a different one earlier.

"May I borrow your phone?" I ask. "I should have someone collect my car."

Vann hands me his smartphone and I quickly search for a charity that will take my car and make the necessary call, effectively ceasing the small talk. He turns back to the computer and appears to be working on creating some graphics, or simply staring at the screen, as I haven't seen him do anything yet.

"How's it going?" McRae asks, tapping Vann's screen.

"This is stupid. I already built you a really great website. It's a waste of my time to do it again. It's not like you're paying me," Vann says with a huff.

"I don't want 'really great.' I want amazing. Perfect. And I've asked the right man to do the job."

"You hired out? Great! I'm off the hook." Vann slaps the laptop closed and makes like he's putting it away.

McRae laughs. "Get to work, smart ass. I'm paying you with opportunity and experience," he says while shoving his brother in the shoulder.

Vann returns fire by pushing back and the two have a brief shoving scuffle where McRae wins by pinning him to the door.

"All right," Vann says with a laugh and flips open his laptop, returning to his free labor.

The miles pass by with only the sounds of the radio, Vann clicking on the keyboard, and the continuous pinging of McRae's phone filling the space. It's hard for me to sit idle, and watching the miles speed by is mind-numbing. I stare at my dead phone and curse it, because without it I can't search the net. I'm desperate for something to do. I dig up a small notebook from my messenger bag and start making a list of what I'll need to set myself up in Florida, starting with jobs I wouldn't mind doing temporarily. I've done this enough times, after all, change is my niche, so I really don't need a list, but I do it nonetheless.

Vann swivels in his seat, resting his arm along the headrest, and asks, "What part of Florida you headed to?"

I picture the map of Florida in my head and place Daytona. Since my stay is temporary and my goal to reconnect with Will, I plan to settle in the top portion of the state first and move south if my search yields nothing. Daytona is a great place to start.

"Funny enough, Daytona. Talk about coincidence." I don't want to creep them out so I smile and give a nonchalant shrug. McRae cuts his eyes to me in what I'm sure is suspicion.

I dig out a book—a thick science fiction piece I've read so many times the spine of the book has a deep, permanent crease that allows the book to lay flat when open.

"Hey," McRae says to his brother and taps the laptop screen. "Focus."

He could have been saying that to me. The words of the book are lost as my attention continues to stray to McRae, who drives with one hand on the wheel, drumming his fingers to the beat of country music playing on the radio. His shoulders are broad, forcing his shirt to stretch snug against him. I notice the cuff of his sleeve gets taut as he moves his arm, his muscles flexing, and there's something so manly about him I have the crazy urge to run my hands across his shoulders and down his arms to feel the ripple of muscles. If he weren't such a stiff I'd consider proposing a one-nighter. Silent guys like him have deep fires that burn wildly once tapped.

I see the way he inspects the henna-created vines of leaves and flowers decorating my arms, and every time he glances at me, his gaze goes inquisitively to the diamond stud piercing below my lower lip. He's interested. And, wow, to get lost in this intoxicating pull of magnetism might very well be mind-blowing. If only the circumstances were different.

The ringing of a phone breaks the quiet and shakes me from my thoughts. It's coming through the Bluetooth of the car. The screen on the dash says Alliance Aviation is calling. McRae answers it on the second ring.

"Uh, Brinn? Can you hear me?" The voice sounds young.

"Yeah, you're on speaker, Smitty, so watch your mouth."

"I'm sorry I called, but we've a problem here."

"What kind of problem? Can't Becky handle it? She needs to learn how to deal with administrative issues."

I look at the book in my lap, pretend to read, and provide some semblance of respecting his privacy.

"That's one of the problems. Becky just up and quit. Walked out and—"

"What! She did what? She was just texting me with questions. She's only been with us for two weeks. What could have gone wrong?" He sighs heavily, pushing his hands against the steering wheel. His knuckles whiten.

"Yeah, she got called into Mark's office; when she came out she cleaned off her desk and left."

"You sure he didn't he fire her?" He bangs his hand against the steering wheel.

"No from what *I* could hear, he just chewed her out. But we've got other problems."

"Like what?" McRae's tone is clipped.

My attention is drawn to his jaw and the popping of muscle that tells me he's clenching and unclenching his teeth.

Hell with reading, I totally tune into this drama.

TWO

"WHAT OTHER PROBLEMS DO WE HAVE?" The car accelerates and the energy in the truck shifts from curiosity to urgency, and the budding sexual tension gives way to anxiety. I close my book.

"That pilot the boss hired didn't show up today," the kid, Smitty, whispers.

Static comes across the line and for a second I wonder if the connection is lost until it sounds as if the phone is being fumbled. Muffled voices break through, and McRae groans. I'm sure he's figured out what's about to rain down on him.

"Brinn?" a man says, clearly holding the phone too close. Brinn's name sounds garbled.

Vann looks at me over his shoulder and mouths, "His boss."

"Dammit. What the fuck is going on here? You said you could handle this business. If you want any part of it, you'll figure this out ASAP. How am I supposed to sell part of it to you when shit like this happens? Don't fuck anything else up. You understand me? You are zero for two." The words reverberate off the walls of the truck and blend together.

The rate of twitching in McRae's jaw increases. I wonder if he counts to ten to calm himself or if his ability to yield easily comes naturally.

"Listen..." McRae says.

I admire that his voice is more resigned than pleading, as one might expect in an ass-chewing situation. The fumbling sound returns and the kid comes back on the line.

"It's me," Smitty says. "Just a second." There's a pause. "Ok, he's gone." Smitty breathes a sigh into the phone.

McRae glances at me in the mirror, and I'm unable to look away. I know I should but I just can't, and it has nothing to do with those avocado-colored eyes.

His glance darts back to the road and he continues the conversation.

"We have Becky quitting and the pilot not showing up? Do you happen to know why not?"

"I called him, and he said no one provided any information after the big boss called and offered the job," Smitty squeaks.

"Motherfu— Is that all, Smitty?"

"Well, I guess it's a good thing the pilot didn't show up because no fuel's been delivered yet and we don't have enough for the lessons schedule today. Not that there'll be any lessons, so there's that."

McRae groans. He leans back into the driver's seat and tries to loosen the tension by shrugging his shoulders, but just as soon as he lets them relax, they tighten back up and the vein in his neck pops back out. Poor sap. If only he'd recognize there's a different way to live. I give a silent thanks to whatever higher power or universal force helped me see the light when I did. Maybe this guy will catch a break too.

The conversation continues as the miles speed by. "Did you call the fuel company?"

"I did, they said nothing's been scheduled and they won't be able to get to us for another two days. I'm guessing you want me to start calling the students and canceling their appointments."

"That sounds about right. Thanks, I appreciate you stepping up." McRae thumps his hand against the steering wheel in frustration. At least he doesn't take it out on the messenger.

"Brinn." The timid voice comes across the speakers, and I sit up. The bottom is about to drop out, and I can't help but bear witness.

"Judas Priest, what now?" McRae growls.

"Mel walked off the job. Said something about calling his union."

I tap Vann's shoulder and he mouths, "Mechanic." With a nod, I sit back and wait. There's no purpose in hiding my interest. I can smell potential legal issues a mile away, an inherited trait, and this train wreck is an ambulance chaser's wet dream.

"Is that it or did the building burn down, too?" McRae's grip on the steering wheel is so tight I wouldn't be surprised if he ripped the wheel off the column and threw it out the window.

"Nope, that's it. Anything special you want me to do?"

"Nah, just finish canceling the appointments. We should be there in about two hours."

"Roger that, boss." He disconnects the call.

Wow. *Boss.* Of what, I'm not sure. Today it must suck to be him.

"I told you that you were taking on too much." Vann snaps the laptop cover closed and smiles smugly at his brother.

McRae punches him in the arm, causing Vann to flinch and rub the spot on his bicep that took the impact.

One simple interaction—a sentence from one sibling to another—and I'm left feeling a loneliness I've managed to push aside for the last two years. I was never close with Stuart but Will... I drop my eyes to my lap and remember how Will made everything wrong in my life right. It was Will who covered my back and got me through those terrible middle school years, who made me feel normal and not like a grade-skipping freak who had no business existing, much less messing up the grading curve.

The sound of a phone being dialed grabs my attention. Pushing aside the constant ache for what I'd lost seven years ago when Will left, I wait, dare I say excitedly, for the dumpster-fire drama happening before me to continue.

The call goes straight to an answering machine and at the beep, McRae starts in. "Mel, it's Brinn. I just heard from the office that you walked out. I'd like to talk to you about it. I don't think there's anything that requires union involvement. I know you've been unhappy with the work schedule and—"

"Hello," Mel says over the line.

"Mel, it's Brinn."

"Yeah, I know. Listen. There's nothing you can say that'll make me change my mind. I'm gonna file a grievance."

"For what?"

"My list is endless. Work place conditions, heck, it's

almost like harassment." Except he says harassment like hair-s-ment.

"Harassment?" McRae looks at me in disbelief, as if I have any clue whether that statement's valid or not.

"My wages are a disgrace; my last performance evaluation was a farce—"

"None of that's harassment, Mel."

"But it's discrimination. Against an old man who's close to retirement. You're trying to chase me out instead of doing the right thing."

"How so?"

"Giving me grief about my doctor appointments. Asking me if I thought the work would be too much when you brought in the other pilot. For what it's worth, I ain't nobody's Pops and I'm offended y'all call me that. I asked you to stop."

"Now listen here, Mel. This is bullshit and you know it. Don't be a dumbass."

It's clear McRae's about to get on a good roll and light into this clown, but before he can continue I lunge across the console, reach across his shoulder, and disconnect the call.

"What in the hell? Why did you do that?" He twists in his seat, his glare swinging between the road and me.

"You were saying *way* too much. You need to shut up and involve the company lawyer, quick." I sit back in my seat and pull the seatbelt across my body before producing a notebook from my purse. Funny, mother wasn't lying when she said geometry wouldn't come in handy with my day-to-day life, but my Yale law degree would. Score one point for demanding, cold-hearted mother and zero for wayward, disappointing daughter.

"I don't see how this is any of your business," he shouts, before looking back at the road.

"You're right, it's not." He watches me in the mirror and I meet his gaze. Usually the winner of all stare downs, I relent, instead concentrating on what I want to get on the paper, only looking up briefly when the truck shifts into the other lane and bears down on an exit. He's totally going to ditch me.

"There's no company lawyer. Wouldn't getting one make things worse with Mel?" Vann asks as he turns and I feel his attention on me.

Writing furiously, I answer without looking up. "Mel already has a lawyer. I'd say things have already taken a turn for the worse."

"How could you possibly know that?" McRae asks.

I know he's bright. I know he's running a company, maybe second in command, and it has gone to shit on him in only a handful of minutes, probably because of his intransigent and controlling nature. Getting him to see what I've figured out takes one level stare, his eyes meeting mine in the mirror. I can almost picture the gears in his head working. It takes a second, but he puts it together.

"He was recording the call." His eyes shift back to the road but he leans toward the wheel and rakes a hand down his face before giving a weary sigh. "How do you know he was recording?" Vann asks.

I let McRae answer. "He let the answering machine pick up first. Jeez, what did I say?" He mumbles the last part to himself.

"How does any of this make sense?" Vann asks.

I lean forward coming to rest between the two front seats. "If he's documented that he's asked repeatedly to not be called Pops without success, that's harassment. If your performance evals reflect the time off he's taken as negative to his job performance and he's got clear medical issues, that's a case for discrimination."

"I knew you were spreading things too thin," Vann says before shifting closer to the door. Apparently, a whack to the arm is a small price to pay to get in another I-told-you-so dig. He turns to me. "I told him hiring old friends who needed a good job didn't mean they were gonna do a good job. You'd think after two other failures with a personal assistant, my brother would get smart."

I hand McRae my notes.

"What's this?" He glances between the paper and the road.

"That's everything you said. You'll need to show it to your lawyer."

He shoots me fleeting glances. As if he can't wrap his mind around the fact that I may have just done him a solid. I don't want to be annoyed, but I am. It's something I've become all too familiar with, this impatience with people underestimating me. They see what they want to. Having an overly large chest doesn't help my plight, either.

"Uh, so... I owe you something more than a thank you, but I can't even think of a way to repay you," he says. His drawl is as subtle as his brother's and charming. He gives me what looks like a shy smile. Or one that shows he isn't familiar with accepting help.

"We can call it even. Giving me this ride...so...thank you." Our eyes meet and we smile at each other. I get the impression from the way he shifts awkwardly in his seat that he doesn't like being in debt to anyone, either.

I can't stop myself from asking and change my attention

to baby brother. "What did you mean, Vann, about hiring friends?"

I wonder about McRae's intentions. The picture being painted is one of a genuinely nice guy. But I've yet to come across one in my travels, and I need assurance that my sense of people's character hasn't taken a sudden cliff dive. That the road isn't making me too jaded and cynical. I could have stayed home and achieved that with far more comfort and luxury.

Vann turns to look at me, and I glance at the eyes watching me in the mirror. McRae does an eye roll before looking back at the road. "Brinn has this idea that he can help some friends from the old neighborhood. Friends who are capable of working but don't. What my brother doesn't understand is not everyone is as driven to change their lives as he is. They think they're getting a free ride but this guy"—he cocks a thumb to his brother—"makes a workaholic look lazy and a taskmaster gentle."

McRae chuckles and shakes his head.

If I ask the next obvious question, I will be prying for sure and I'll forever know things about these brothers I'm not sure I want to know. I'm not looking to play twenty questions and divulge anything more about my life. So I keep it simple. "Oh, I see."

Perception of his character—intact. It's a relief to know McRae may be the worst businessman ever but at least he has a bleeding heart to balance it out. Oh, how my father would cringe at the thought.

"What are you hoping to find in Florida?" McRae asks, glancing between the road and his ever-chiming cell phone. Business never stops for him.

It's an odd question. Usually people want to know what brings someone to a destination.

I want to find my brother. I want to know why he cut me from his life. I want to know why I can't connect with people, why leaving is so easy. I want to know what it is I want. But what do I say to this stranger?

I hesitate before deciding on my fondest wish. "I'm reconnecting with my brother." If I say it enough maybe it will come true.

"So where can I take ya? I have to swing by Daytona Beach first and check in with the shop, but after that I can take you anywhere. It's the least I can do." I'm pulled in by his soft southern drawl and the way he says "ah" for I.

"Actually, Daytona Beach is perfect. No need to take me anywhere else. Just drop me off at a motel that's close to food and shopping. I need to get a charger for my phone."

"The Sleep Inn in Ormond Beach is perfect," Vann tells us.

"We should be in town in thirty minutes," McRae says over his shoulder. "Are you sure you want a motel? It really isn't any trouble to take you anywhere. To your brother's or something?"

I recognize his need to provide. He's a control freak, just like my father, like my mother for that matter. He wants to manage me, either to ensure he's done the right thing or because I'm a loose end to him. The difference between this guy and my father is that if I were to end up dead in my hotel room, McRae would probably feel he shouldered some of the responsibility, even if he never saw me again. My father would *never* go that far.

"No, thank you. The Sleep Inn will be fine."

"There's a Walmart across the street and lots of food," Vann says.

"Perfect," I say and smile. I'm starving.

As we're pulling into the motel parking lot, I take in the convenience of its location. I can easily get by without a car for a while as I try to get organized. I know I have to watch my budget, but I've done a good job of being frugal over the last two years. Selling off my BMW Coupe when I set out on this journey was the smartest move I made, hands down. I've been able to find enough work along the way to avoid dipping into my emergency funds, and I want to keep that momentum going.

McRae idles for a minute before he turns off the engine. His eyes flick to the clock on the dash and then to me. I'm sure he's anxious to get to his business. "I don't feel right leaving you here," he says.

I'm already pushing open the truck door. I reach for my rolling suitcase and toss it out of the truck. Both Vann and McRae leap out and come to stand by my door. Vann takes my suitcase and pulls up the handle. McRae reaches out and takes my tote, yoga mat, and purse. He offers me a hand to help me out of the truck, but I slide out on my own.

I smile at the brothers as I take my bags. "I'm fine. This is perfect."

"Here's my business card. It has my cell number on it. Don't hesitate to call me if you need anything." McRae passes me the small stiff card. I give it a quick glance, taking in the blue tones he used, but purposefully don't look at the information. I don't want my brain to store any of it.

"Thanks. I appreciate the ride. Good luck with Mel and all that business." I don't want to give him any of my information, though I know I should in case they go to court. I'm a witness to the conversation, after all. But intuition tells me I haven't seen the last of these two. Twenty-four hours ago, I certainly didn't think I would be riding to Florida with them. So I say nothing and turn away. I look back once, give a wave, and don't look back again. When I get into the motel lobby, I toss the card into the trash and walk to the front desk.

I check in, renting the room for a week. Today's plans include walking to Walmart, lounging by the pool, and Italian for dinner. Every new adventure starts somewhere and mine begins here, with my first actual lead in finding Will, and shockingly provided by him. Something good waits for me here. I can feel it in my bones.

THREE

SUMMER IS OFFICIALLY in full swing and the weatherman is talking about this season's hurricane names. Families from all over the world are visiting the beaches, the Mouse, and partaking in the awe that is Florida, and I just looked at a room-to-let that left me desperate for a shower and looking over my shoulder.

It wasn't the girl renting out the room who had me mentally running through my self-defense moves; it was her boyfriend. Being skeeved out was no longer my chief worry, as is the usual with rooms to let. Some are dirty, others, eh, just not the safest of environments. But this place offered a boyfriend who embodies creepster. Guys eye girls, that's a fact, and generally I know what they're thinking. This dude? His once-over gave off a vibe that he was formulating a plan likely involving duct tape, a plastic tarp, and possibly a concrete block. After I'm safely in my rental car, I scrub my hands over my body as if it might wipe away the heebie-jeebies.

Discouraged that I haven't found a place to stay and that

my attempts to draw out my brother have failed, I'm left feeling more deflated than a flat balloon. I cleave to my one success, landing a job at a local British pub called the Fox and Hound the second day I was in town. I stopped in, hoping for some fish and chips and mushy peas, and started chatting with the lovely woman who owns the pub about what we missed most from the United Kingdom and her hometown of Oxfordshire. Within twenty minutes, I became their new bartender.

With a cheerful chime, my phone indicates new emails. I'll be honest. I check it a lot. After I emailed Will to tell him I was in Daytona, I thought and, said-a-prayer-before-I-pressed-send, hoped, I'd get an immediate response. By immediate, I was willing to accept within the same day. It's been a week, and I refresh for new email so often I believe my smartphone can anticipate it now.

I suck in my breath when the screen indicates an email from Will. The time stamp is eight minutes earlier, when I was trying to extricate myself from Creepy House.

Room to let? I don't know how or why you do it. Sounds too revolting and not something I'd like to experience. Good luck with that.

That's it?

It's hard not to be frustrated with the lack of progress in my attempts to make headway with Will. All I want to know is why he walked out. Why he cut me from his life. He'd been there for every single important moment in my life, and when he needed me the most he walked away. And never looked back. The first two years after he left, he never responded to a single email I sent. Now I cling to the bits and pieces he gives me. But frustrated or not, I want to know. I want him to tell me to my face, and more than anything I want to know him again.

But apparently that's not going to happen if I'm living in a room-to-let, and I can't carry the cost of a hotel indefinitely, considering the pace at which Will moves.

In a stroke of what I hope is genius, I pull up a popular vacation rental site and scroll through the options. Granted, the expense will burn through my cash faster than I'd like, but I can try to offset it by getting a second job. It's only temporary, after all. I'll tackle that obstacle when I have to. Hopefully, my extended stay will appeal to a landlord instead of the day-to-day gig, and I can negotiate a better rate.

"Please, please, please let there be something," I whisper as I scroll through the list, hoping my luck can do an about-face, grant me a lucky break. At the bottom, I see the perfect rental.

It's for a one bedroom, over-the-garage apartment. The description says bright and airy and that alone makes me feel warm from the inside out. I haven't stayed in a space larger than twelve by twelve since I left home. Once I even lived in a yurt. The few pictures make me eager to see inside.

No roommates? More than one room?

This appeals to me on such a deep level I think it's talking to my soul. Couldn't I indulge myself just a tad with this apartment? Without giving it anymore thought, I type out an email and wait anxiously for a reply.

Instead of driving back to my hotel, I drive to the beach and construct an email to Will while I wait. I've sent a series of these light but slightly probing emails over the week that I've been in town.

Hey, sure love the beach. Everyone says I should see the Gulf Coast beaches, but I'm pretty happy with the sands on the Atlantic side. It beats Connecticut :). You live near the beach? I'm still looking for a place to stay. Have a lead on an apartment. I know, going nuts here. Fingers crossed.
Hope you're well,
Jo

No sooner do I send out Will's email than one from the rental place comes in. The landlady, a Mrs. Cramer, invites me to see the place today and I quickly respond with a resounding yes, using lots of exclamation points. The address she gives me is only minutes from the beach where I sit. The drive there is down a lovely street, lined with giant oaks and ficus. I can see the Halifax River on my left and hear the ocean on my right. A second chime from my GPS prompts me to turn left into a driveway leading to a large stucco house with rear views of the Halifax River.

I've worn an apple-green T-shirt with long black shorts and paired the outfit with simple flip-flops, a plain belt, and braided my hair down the back. I'm trying for a conservative look. The henna on my calves is fading and if this place pans out, I might be able to squeeze in some time to do some more artwork before my next shift. I've gotten pretty good at creating various patterns and enjoy doing my stomach and legs the most.

The front door opens before I can ring the bell and what looks to be the sweetest older lady stands before me. We're dressed almost the same except her T-shirt is white and black polka dots. Her hair is teased out and sprayed stiff, as if she's just come from having it done and set.

"Hello, dear. Are you Josie? I'm Eleanor Cramer." She extends an evenly tanned, manicured hand.

"Yes, ma'am." We shake hands and her grip is firmer than I imagined. She makes me think of those southern-born ladies who belong to the Daughters of the American Revolution, and I imagine somewhere in her house a map of her lineage hangs.

"Well, it's like I said in the email, I'm very open to a longer stay than a few days or a week." She places a warm hand on my arm. "I have to admit. I was not keen on this idea. It was my son's. He kept saying it's a wasted opportunity, but I'm the one, not him, that lives here and will have to deal with the revolving door. So your inquiry suits us both. Please come in." She steps back to give me room.

"I'm glad you're open to the possibilities. You have a lovely home," I say, looking around. I expected it to be decorated Florida retirement-home style with a beach theme and white wicker furniture. I don't know why. But it's not; it's French country with creamy leather couches and toile and checkered pillows and curtains in vibrant reds and yellows. My eyes settle on a painting hanging over an antique oak table in the foyer. I step closer and gasp.

"Is that an original Frederick Remington painting?" I stare at the work. "It's extraordinary."

"Yes, my husband loved all things Remington." She stands next to me as we look up at the painting of *The Soldier*.

"My father does as well. He has several original bronze statues. He's made it his life's hobby to try to collect everything he can. If he knew a private owner had this, he'd never give you a moment's rest. It's a nice piece."

She shrugs. "I like landscapes myself. Not paintings of cocky men."

We laugh together.

"Let me show you the apartment. Like I said, it's over the garage, but you'll have a separate entrance and one of the garage spaces is for you. I certainly don't need three spots." She leads me through the house, where I see several landscape paintings. Through the French doors off the living room, I catch a glimpse of a pool. The backyard is fenced, offering privacy, but a gate in the back opens to the dock on the river. I cross my toes and hope the pool's included.

"What brings you to Daytona, Josie?"

"I thought I'd come and try to spend some time with my brother."

"Does your brother live close?" Following a quick smile, she leads me through the kitchen, stopping to pull a set of keys off a holder by the backdoor before going outside. Across a breezeway is a side door that opens into a well-lit garage. Stairs are tucked along the side wall.

I don't want to lie, but I'm not sure how to explain the situation with my brother without sounding crazy.

"Are there two entrances?" There's an additional set of stairs outside her backyard fence with access from the driveway.

"Yes. One to the front of the apartment and this one is private. If you decide you want it, I'll include the pool. Since it's just you. It is just you, correct?"

I can't contain my smile. "Yes, it's just me."

"The rent also includes all utilities, cable, and I've a dock to the river if you have a boat." She leads me upstairs.

"I love the idea of a pool. I'm originally from New England so weather for pool opportunities is limited."

"The pool will be happy to know it. My grandkids come on holidays only, they're at the age where hanging out with their grandma isn't cool, so aside from their visits and my morning swim, it rarely gets used. New England, you say?" She pauses a few steps up to ask.

"Yes, ma'am. Stamford, Connecticut."

"Oh, I've been there. It's lovely. Lots of big houses. McMansions, I think they're called."

I stifle a laugh because the first time someone called our house a McMansion my mother nearly lost her mind. "That they are."

At the top of the stairs, she fits a key and swings open the door to present a small but functional laundry room. Painted a soft blue with two small white cabinets and crown molding, the space is large enough for a full-size washer and dryer and holds an abundance of character. I clutch my hands together in delight and to contain the rush of hope and fear. I can't afford to fall in love with a place I'll be leaving. That's why renting a room was always the smartest option.

"The apartment comes furnished and that includes the washer and dryer. Some of my children lived here while they were in college though my mother was last to live here before she passed." She turns and places her hand on my arm. "But I don't want you to worry. She didn't pass here."

"I hadn't given it a thought," I say, which is true. I'm completely captivated by the place and if need be would share it with a ghost. Sold by the simplicity of a laundry room. When I entertained the idea of an extended vacation rental, I never imagined I'd get so lucky.

A pool? My own laundry room? In the last two years I rarely had both if either at all.

"We're coming in at the center of the apartment so I'll

take you to the front and we will work our way back." She turns right out of the laundry room and walks down a bright hallway into the living room.

It's small but larger than any place I've stayed since I started my journey. The ceilings are high and large solid planks of wood, stained a dark espresso, make up the floor. The apartment is tastefully furnished like her house. It runs the length of the garage and is longer than it is wide with the front door centered on the end wall and large windows on both sides of the living room. One set of windows allows for views of the river.

"Is that the ocean?" I ask as I point toward the blue horizon out the opposite window.

"Yes, it's only three blocks from here."

A delightful sigh escapes. I can easily live here while I wait.

I head into the kitchen and look out the window over the sink. It's a view of the pool and the river. I run my hands over the full-sized fridge. I can buy a whole gallon of ice cream and store it without worry. The kitchen is painted a buttery yellow and reminds me of my mother's. I can almost smell the cranberry scones my mother's chef bakes every fall.

"It's just the one bedroom but it's large. The apartment includes all the essentials. Such as a TV, internet, a five-piece kitchen, and full bath." She leads me down the hallway. The bedroom has French doors that open out onto a small balcony and a simple but elegantly made queen-sized sleigh bed. I imagine staying in bed all day reading a book. I imagine making dinner for Will and catching up as we sit on the balcony or even the dock. Once I have that vision, I can't imagine anything else.

It's more than I dreamt, or dared to hope for.

Suddenly, I'm afraid she'll turn me down. I look up at the ceiling and the fans that turn slowly, trying to steady my racing heart. Standing here fills me with a sense of coming home that I don't want to lose. Part of me screams to run away as fast as I can but another part, the one that's done without for two years, stamps down the screamer and convinces me to stay.

"I love it," I tell her. "I would love to fill out an application. I can pay for six weeks upfront. I know I'm young and maybe not your ideal tenant"—I gesture to the henna that covers my legs and arms—"I don't do parties. I like to keep to myself."

I want this place, admitting that scares me. As I take in the space around me, I push back a longing to customize it by buying throw pillows for the couch in chevron patterns with funky colors. I want to buy a giant bottle of detergent instead of the little boxes from the vending machine. For the first time, I experience pangs of angst knowing the last two years of my life do not scream reliable or dependable.

"Let's go down to my kitchen and write out the agreement over a glass of iced tea," Mrs. Cramer says.

"Thank you." I take her hands in mine. "Thank you," I gush.

I want to say more, to let her know she's safe taking a chance on me. I want to hug her. I open my mouth but struggle with the words.

She pats my arm. "I've good instincts about people, my dear, and I believe we'll be a good fit. After all, how many people out there know Remington did paintings? Most just know about the bronze pieces."

The first thing I'm going to do after I move in, besides buy a car, is sit on that balcony and watch the sunrise with a cup of coffee. Then, because I've now committed to a large expense, I'm going to find a second job.

I follow Mrs. Cramer down the stairs, back through the garage, and into the house and it dawns on me. I'm filled with such a sense of peace and contentment that surely I must be doing the right thing. I look around one last time, excited to make this place my home. Temporarily.

FOUR

I EASE the beer tap back and pour a perfect draft, lost in my thoughts of the simple luxury I found this morning as I walked around my apartment. Alone. Not a roommate, a fear of spycams, or loud neighbors. Just me, my T-shirt nightie, and a cup of coffee. A week of living there and I'm still awed by my luck. It's glorious.

Having arrived at work between the happy hour and dinner shifts, I found Jayne, the bosses' daughter, sitting at the corner of the bar with papers spread before her. According to her, she's been at it for over an hour. Apparently, this is her alternate office. She's always here.

Her normally well-groomed appearance is offset by the fact that she's chewed off all her lipstick. Her chin length ash-blond bob looks windblown and a pencil pokes out from a small knot she's made. She stops to look at me when I deliver her dinner order, but I don't think she sees me. She jolts out of her reverie before scanning the half-full restaurant. The dinner rush is over and the bar is in that state of rest as we wait for the families to leave and the partiers to arrive.

"I think I blacked out and lost time," she says as I slide the plate of fish and chips next to her ledger. "My only hope is that this accounting was masterfully completed while I was having my fugue. If not, there may be violence."

I shrug an apology because I'm one hundred percent certain the fugue state she thinks she experienced was just a small daydream. "If the guy at table three pinches my ass one more time when I pass to use the restroom, there'll be violence," I tell her. "Must be that kinda night."

She reaches over the top of the bar and pulls out a bottle of malt vinegar from the shelf below. After dousing her fish and chips, she shoves a handful of fries into her mouth then returns to beating her calculator to death with the eraser end of her pencil.

"Buggering bloody bollocks. These numbers! They refuse to balance. If I can't get this worked out I'll commit an act of cruelty to my own person." It's hard gauging the severity of her words because she's English and seriously, what sort of act would she commit? Their cops don't even carry guns. She stabs at the calculator again and takes a long swig of her wine.

The last few nights I've worked, Jayne's been on the same stool, her business books spread before her. Try as I might to avoid developing anything further than a superficial friendship with her, as this tends to be the easiest for all parties, Jayne makes it hard. She's warm and as welcoming as her parents, and even though she successfully runs her own clothing boutique, she can be found helping out when there's a shortage, without complaint. She's comfortable in her own skin and has a dry, self-deprecating sense of humor I understand. A large portion of my time at the bar is spent chatting with her, laughing about some of the patron's antics, and discussing our common interest in Graham Norton, who we both binge watch whenever possible.

Making friends with girls has always been difficult for me. Maybe because my only real friend was Will and perhaps because of that I relate better to guys. Either that or Jayne's different.

"Just a thought, but it might not be a numbers issue but more a you've-had-too-much-to-drink issue and this place is distracting. I can see from here that you've miscalculated column two."

She groans and stares at the numbers. I touch my finger to the set where she went awry.

"It doesn't help that you've been making eyes at tall, blond surfer over there." I place a glass of water next to her wine.

"You're a buzz kill," she says in a bang-on American accent. Usually so posh with her Oxford English, it cracks me up when she does her American speak. She pushes the water back toward me. "You should put this away and relax."

I tap her papers. "When do you do that? Relax?" She's here every time I am and I imagine she's here when I'm not.

She purses her lips. "Quite right. I haven't relaxed in a long time. A good shag would fix that right up."

I lean against the bar and rest my elbows on the top. "Is there a Mr. Jayne?" It's my attempt at making casual girl-friend talk even though it feels intrusive.

She snorts. "No boyfriend. I've been casually seeing this guy, Brad, who, it would seem, is really just a scheduled shag when he's driving through town. Which is about every other week. Clearly, not enough." She smirks and nods toward the blond surfer. "How about you? You're fairly new here, and if you tell me you've got a steady I might simply lose it. Not that I don't want you to have someone but the reflection back into my own wasteland of a sex life...well." She waves her hand dismissively.

Bemused, I laugh and roll my eyes. "I don't have anyone, and I'm not looking for anyone either."

"You say that with a firm determination. You just out of something serious?" She pulls the pencil from the knot on her head, places it on the counter, and then begins to massage her scalp.

"I've managed to escape something serious twice now." I give a half shrug, feigning nonchalance, but the truth is Jayne is the first person I even hinted about my past too. Maybe I'm curious as to how she'll react or treat me.

"Ohh, that sounds like a story." She stops her massage to pick up her wine. "Do tell."

I go for broke. "I was engaged two years ago and left him at the altar."

She coughs on her wine and looks at me with large eyes. "You're joking! I've never met someone who ditched at the altar." She leans forward. "That took courage."

She doesn't know the half of it.

"Was he a creeper? Found out he was boning his dog or something?" She replaces her wine glass with more fries, still eating them by the handful.

I can't contain my laughter as I try to picture Max, Mr. Lawyer Extraordinaire, getting cozy with his mother's Labradoodle, Lord Byron. But as quick as I am to laugh, I'm just as quick to sober.

"He was all—what do you English say, broody? For one of the law clerks in his office." I confess for the first time.

"Every time he looked at her he got this stupid, sappy grin on his face. He'd get all nervous when she was around. It would have been cute if I wasn't the girl in the office wearing his grandmother's engagement ring. If people didn't always give me looks of pity." If I had someone who looked at me like that. Just once, even. "It was obvious he wanted her more than he wanted me."

"Filthy bastard." She pours more malt on her fish before breaking off a bite.

I nod in agreement. "But that's not why I left. I mean to say it wasn't the initial cause for why I left. Truth is, I wasn't in love with him either. He was...familiar. I've known him since our mommy-and-me playdates."

Jayne grabs her napkin and begins to wipe her hands. She sits back and stares, studying me. "What made you leave?"

I look around the bar. The steady stream of people coming in. The groups gathered in sections laughing and getting rowdy. I return my attention to her. "You ever been in a room like this, full of people, and felt utterly alone? As if you were invisible and weren't sure you even existed out of the mold someone else created for you?"

Jayne shakes her head and quietly says, "I've often felt alone in crowds like this but never invisible."

"What made it worse was the crowd of people was my family and the guy who was supposed to love me forever but didn't even see me."

Jayne covers her mouth, following it with a slight head shake. "I would've never guessed. Do you still feel that way?"

"Invisible? No," I lie. Well, partially lie. I don't often feel that way anymore. Only where Will is concerned.

It's a heavy bomb to drop on someone you're getting to

know, so I try to ease the weight. "That and I thought about sex with this man for the rest of my life, and I couldn't stop yawning. He doesn't like to be sweaty."

We laugh together.

"What about you? Any skeletons in your closet?"

Jayne holds her wine glass between her hands, a large smile on her face. "Not me. I don't do anything that spans past a month. Six weeks tops."

"Seriously? Even if you really like them?" I lean against the bar, anxious for her to share.

"I try not to pick guys that I could really like, that makes it hard to leave. But I really don't have space in my life for anything more than casual, and I've found that after a few weeks casual becomes familiar. Men generally don't like a successful woman. At least the ones I've found don't."

She glances at surfer guy. "Truth is, once I stand up and men see how ghastly tall I am, they either back off or come at me like they're hunting giraffes and I'm a conquest. They want to see if their face lines up with my tits."

"Does that actually happen? Guys begging off when you stand up?" She's certainly tall but not freakishly tall. More like model tall.

"More than I care to count. I suppose I shouldn't complain." Her shrug expresses an indifference I'm not certain is real.

I tap my finger on the bar in thought. "Hmm. Men are assholes."

Jayne laughs. "We should go out sometime. Someplace other than here, where my mum is not so quick at hand."

I shrug, hoping she doesn't recognize it for the lack of commitment it is.

"Give me your phone," she says, holding out her hand, her fingers wiggling.

"How do you know I'm not some crazy single white female or something?" I pause, my hand on my back pocket, fingertips on the phone.

"I have a radar for crazy women. My cousin's mum is a true nutter. Learned early with her. Hand it over."

After pulling out my phone, I slide it across the bar.

She picks it up and, I presume, adds her number to my contacts before texting herself. She hands me back my phone then fidgets with hers.

"There. We're BFF's now." She giggle snorts and covers her mouth, surprised. I laugh as well.

"I don't think I've ever said that before without being sarcastic."

"I'm sure I've never said it unless I was teasing my brother," I say and slide my phone back into my pocket. I return to what I'm supposed to be doing. I fill more drink orders and refill Jayne's water glass. I'm reaching for her wine glass when she snakes out a hand and stops me.

"Are you cutting me off?"

"Do you think you need another drink?" Neither of us moves our hands.

"I think I'd *like* another drink." She presses her lips together to keep from laughing.

"I think you'd also like to get your bookkeeping completed, accurately. Don't look now, but here comes surfer dude." I clear any extra dishes from the space around her and she waves away her nearly empty dinner plate. She flashes me her teeth and I give her the thumbs-up; she's clear of all food particles.

"Hey," Surfer doll says, leaning against the bar. "I

couldn't help but notice you noticing me." He sounds like a cliché. His words are slow, deliberate, as if he's thinking them up on the spot and it requires a tremendous amount of brainpower.

Jayne and I glance at each other and look away before we both end up laughing.

"I do apologize," Jayne says. "I wasn't noticing you as much as I was staring at the space over where you were."

Jayne motions to the wall along the far side of the bar where a sign proclaiming Hard Work is the Path to Success hangs.

"I'm doing my accounting and the sign is motivation to not pack it in." Jayne's hand rests on the leather books spread before her.

"But you're noticing me now, aren't 'cha?" He leans forward, or more sways forward.

I pull the table number up on the computer and see that for a table of three guys, they've ordered five pitchers of beer. Catching Jayne's eye, I hold up a pitcher and five fingers.

"I'm not, actually. Without a doubt you are in my space and I see you, but I'm not noticing you in the way that you'd like." She pushes him back and he burps in her face, blowing it out.

"Sorry," he says and waves the air between them.

"Mmm. As am I," Jayne says but the sarcasm is lost on him.

I laugh and turn away so surfer guy can't see. Jayne convinces him to go back to his friends without causing any sort of commotion, an art I admire.

When he's back at his table getting what I'm sure is a ribbing, I return to Jayne and smile. "Nicely done. Maybe next time you do your books and need to concentrate you should keep your gaze downward."

She smirks then giggles. "Perhaps you're right. Too bad he was a bit dim. Is it wrong to assume he'd be that way in bed as well?"

I shrug and shake my head. "Not worth the risks or effort."

"Agreed." Jayne hiccups loudly and covers her mouth in surprise. "I've had too bloody much to drink. Which is good news for my ledger but shitty news for me because now I need a ride home and you know what *that* means?" She holds out her wine glass, tipping it to let me know she wants it refilled.

"You'll be taking a cab?" A glance at the clock tells me her parents have left for the night.

"Worse, I'll end up calling my cousin, Pippa."

"Pippa? Come on, with a name like that she can't be too bad." It's a weak argument and not one I'd use in a court of law.

"I told you her mother was mental. Pippa though, she's lovely. In small doses. Very small doses. Miniscule." Jayne's thumb and index finger are a hairsbreadth apart.

I refill her glass. "Seriously?" If it's as bad as she says, she deserves a drink.

"Bloody right I'm serious. Pippa will probably want me to meditate before she lets me out of the car."

I arch a brow.

"She's a nutter for yoga and all things like it. Moony." She clasps the wine close to her chest.

"If you want to wait until closing, I can take you home," I offer with a shrug of one shoulder.

"Bless you," she says and grins.

"If she's such a pain, why do you hang out with her?"

"Because the American government continues to cock up and issue her tourist visas and because she's my family and the one friend I've had my entire life."

I nod in understanding.

We don't get to finish our conversation as the bar's patronage picks up and I'm slammed with drink orders and helping out with the occasional table delivery.

I scan the crowd. The bar is filled with a mix of die-hard locals still in their work clothes, names sewn across the pocket of their shirt, bikers with their leather chaps and helmets resting on the floor, and college know-it-alls. They wear smug smiles and tight clothes; at least the girls do. Every garment is chosen to show off their tan, and as a flock of them pass headed for the restroom, the telltale aroma of coconuts and sunshine lingers behind them. I watch them with eyes that now have experience.

"Josie, I really have to pee. Can you take this order to table fifteen and check in with seventeen?" Sara, a bouncy college junior, pleads. She's a hard worker so I do her a solid and wave her off but not before warning her of the pincher at table three.

I come from behind the bar with Sara's notepad and pull up the tray I'd just loaded with a pilsner and a cosmo. Seriously? Cosmos are over and usually the person ordering one is attempting to reach a coolness they've only witnessed on TV.

"Here you go," I say and place the cosmo in front of a blonde wearing a black short-sleeved sweater set accented with a long strand of black and white beads that she's twirling around her fingers.

"And for you." I put the pilsner in front of the guy who's

face deep into his smart phone. When he glances up, my eyes clash with the swampy green ones I've seen before. The same color as the new cashmere throw I indulged in when I moved into my fabulous apartment.

We both gasp and I give a short, quick laugh.

"We meet again." I wink.

"You work here?" McRae asks. The phone in his hand chimes.

"No, I'm sitting at that table of guys and saw you all were without your drinks, so I thought I'd pitch in." I point to a random table behind him. He looks at the group of frat boys then back at me and laughs.

"You're working, I see." I nod to his phone.

"How long you been here?" He slides the arm he was resting behind the blonde back from the ledge of the booth and places it on the table where he flips his phone face down and begins to toy with it.

"My shift started a few hours ago." Hoping to contain my smile, I pull on my lower lip with my teeth. Don't want to be too obvious with my pleasure at seeing him again. "This is the end of my second week."

My body begins to vibrate; my nipples pucker under my shirt simply from being in the same space as him. Holy Hades, McRae is hot.

"You two know each other?" The girl asks, looking between us.

"Yes," he says, his eyes never leaving mine.

"No," I say at the same time. Then add, "Sorta. Not really."

I'd like to get to know him. The charge of attraction sparking between us is intense and just as strong now as when I felt it in the truck on the drive down. Only now we're in a setting where it's common to hit on people and we're a little less strangers. Which is the stupidest rationale in the world. Clearly, we're still strangers. I don't even know if this is his wife next to him and he's the sort that doesn't wear a ring. Though I have a hard time imagining the tailored blond to have the skill set to keep his attention; she's more concerned with herself than anything else.

"Josie is..." He cocks his head to the side, maybe trying to find a way to define me. How he knows me. *Josie is the girl I picked up on the side of the road.* If that's not a public service announcement for crazy, I don't know what is.

I throw him a bone. "Sara, your waitress, will be around in a flash to see if you need anything," I say, hoping to let the subject drop. His eyes dart to my chest, my exposed midriff, and my legs before bouncing back up. "Have a good night."

I move to the next booth, and the four guys turn their attention to me. The big one on the end gives a wolf whistle. He's clearly the ringleader by the way he monopolizes the larger portion of the bench and is leaning away from his friends while they lean toward him.

"What can I get you boys?" I don't lean on the table or act coy. My woman's intuition has kicked in and all thoughts of McRae and his blonde are gone. I remove the three empty pitchers of beer as fast as I can and stand back so they know I'm ready to take their order and nothing else. The metaphorical pad is out and pen is poised. Experience has taught me to be leery of the sort of personality the ringleader seems to embody. I'm always hopeful I'm wrong.

"I could use a tall glass of you," the oaf says and I detect a slight lisp. My kid brother, Stuart, has one and years of speech therapy have taught him how to get around it.

The asshat grabs the knot at my waist where I've tied my

Oxford United jersey, and tugs, trying to get me to step closer, his fingers purposefully grazing my exposed midriff. He lets go to trace a knobby finger along the painted henna vines that scroll across my belly.

I bat his hand away. "Keep your mitts to yourself unless you want me to break them. Consider yourself warned." I'm glad I decided on my heavy Doc Martins, whose sole purpose is to inflect lasting pain when kicking the shit out of someone.

I gesture with the empty pitchers and wait patiently for an order, refusing to engage further. Dumb-dumb continues to leer, his fingers drumming against his leg. Another guy, in what I assume is an attempt to steer the conversation away from me, asks the oaf which draft he thinks they should try. But oaf boy is not so bright.

"How 'bout you let me show you my man skills?" He snakes out his hand, trying to grab my waist, but I quickly side step.

"Are you going to place an order? Because I'm moving on." I look him square in the eyes. The busboy passes by and I dump the empty pitchers in his bin, freeing my hands.

"Yeah, Rolling Rock, draft," he says. His lips press into a thin line.

"OK, Sara will have those to you soon and will take your food order then." I walk one step away and the stupid fuck slaps my ass with a fat hand. He ends the slap with a full-handed cupping of my butt cheek and a squeeze. I swivel on my heel. McRae is glaring and starting to get out of the booth when I catch his eye and wave him off. He hesitates a second before slowly sitting down, his fist clenched at his side.

I plant my hands on the table and lean toward Mr. Grabby. Conversation around us stops. Guys like this lout are the sort of drunk whose creepiness and pervy ways come out the more they drink.

"You think it's OK to put your hands on me?" I ask. Some people shouldn't drink. Ever. Yet, I don't care how much he's had to drink. Manhandling someone is not OK.

"Honey, you know you wanted it, and you want me to do a whole lot more." He reaches out, cups my breasts between both his hands, and leans toward me, in what I presume is an attempt to place his head in my cleavage. To motorboat.

If I was angry before with the ass cupping, this sends me over the edge. Feeling at the mercy of another person is a button I no longer stomach being pushed. I've long since replaced the accustomed fear with anger and control.

Snatching his hair at the scalp with both my hands, I pull his head up. When he's looking at me, smirking, I snake my right hand out to grab his left, placing mine over the back of his hand to pull it from my breast. I position my thumb so that I'm pressing his back, resulting in his wrist and thumb being at an awkward angle.

"Stand up," I say and twist his arm, forcing him to get out of the booth.

"Let go of my hand, you stupid bitch," he snarls and leans toward me. Three moves. Ears, head, groin.

"Apologize." I give him one chance. Three seconds, five max, and this fuck stick will be writhing on the floor.

"I said to let go." He does a mock lunge toward me and the training I received in Texas kicks in.

In a flash, I drop his hand but grab his ears and twist, bringing his head forward. He cries out in a mixture of surprise and fury, and I use the shock to my advantage as I slam his face into my knee, busting his nose. He calls me a name so vile it's sheer instinct that drives my foot to connect with his crotch.

All the men in the room groan, reflexively covering their dicks. The jackass is down, on the floor writhing and calling me a stream of names I haven't ever heard used in mixed company.

I lean forward and whisper, "Want to stick your face in my chest? Perhaps you should ask next time. Touch another woman like that when I'm around and I'll break your dick."

When I straighten up my eyes meet McRae's. He's half out of his booth ready to be a white knight, my Sir Lancelot, but I ease his duty toward chivalry by squeezing his forearm in silent thanks as I walk by.

Yes, it felt good to take down that clown, but the second after I did it, I was mentally calculating the consequences of my actions. Knowing they could result in a lawsuit for both my employers and myself. I'm well aware that I may just have royally screwed the pooch.

FIVE

TWO THINGS I can't stop ruminating.

First, how fortunate I was with the bar incident. It was no surprise that the idiot had a prior record for assault, which trumped my actions. So when given the choice, neither of us pressed charges and he walked away with an ice pack on his nose while blubbering and swearing to keep his hands to himself from here on out.

Second, I think I need to return the new cashmere throw I bought. The one I simply had to have even though it was beyond expensive and a luxury I haven't allowed these last two years and is the exact same color as McRae's eyes. A lovely shade of freshly sliced avocado and mojito mixed. Every time I look at it, I think of him. I re-experience the zing of pleasure I got when I leaned across him, and I want nothing more than for him to touch me. On all my girly parts. More than once. Until my body is numb from intense satisfaction.

It's insane how charged the air was between us. The

epitome of instant attraction, I suppose. I bury the blanket under the pillows I bought and return to my task. Hoping it'll provide the distraction I need. Besides, he'd likely show up for sex with schematics and a time limit.

With the Sunday paper spread around me, I sip my coffee and try to ignore my phone. Refreshing my email app will not make one from Will appear. No matter how badly I want one to. We had a good email exchange there for a few days. Mostly me telling him about finding a place in Daytona and getting a job, trying to draw out any tidbit he might give me to indicate where he lives.

Who am I kidding? It was four years of email exchanges before he dropped the Florida hint, so chances are awfully slim I'll get another clue anytime soon. I'll be old and gray before I get the chance to reconnect with my brother.

Frustrated with the truth in my thoughts, I push my phone away and peruse the want ads. If I keep thinking like that, it'll do nothing but bring me down, send me into a wasteland of confusion, anger, and hurt. Instead, I focus on what I can control.

I like my bartending job, but I also like eating and considering tips are what carries my pay and the rent on this apartment is higher than I planned on paying, I'll be getting a second job. I figure something administrative will help me keep up my computer skills. I spot an ad with bolded letters ADMIN ASSISTANT NEEDED. Like a beacon in the night, it seems this was meant for me. Providing little information other than requiring standard computer and people skills, the ad's phrase "organizational genius," a skill I possess in spades, makes me commit the address to memory with a plan to visit first thing tomorrow.

Without giving it further thought, knowing I'd talk myself out of it, I take a chance and email Will to ask if he wants to meet up sometime. I include my new address. One thing I've learned, to press him is to shove him away, but I miss my brother desperately. The only way I can live with not ever seeing him again is knowing I tried everything, and I hope the tone of the email is light and non-threatening enough that he doesn't feel put off. Not that I know what put him off in the first place.

I hit send and toss my phone at the couch. It hurts to know he doesn't want to see me as much as I do him.

Frustrated, I decide to take Mrs. Cramer up on her offer to use one of her bicycles to explore my new neighborhood and get in some much needed exercise. It'll help clear my head. The Florida sun, the sea breeze, a day off from the bar, and exercise, it's the perfect combination. Tomorrow, it's back to the grind of Internet searching for Will and stopping in about that job.

Under my T-shirt and shorts, I wear my bikini. In the bike's basket, I pack a bag that includes a paperback, water, sunscreen, a towel, my cell, and granola. The path I've plotted makes my trip to the beach a mile, which isn't much, but today is about relaxing more than making my exercise quota. I start out at a slow pace but that feels like cheating so I step it up. Rising, I pedal fast to a count of thirty before I sit and do another thirty count, rest for fifteen count and start the cycle over.

Palm trees line the landscape to the beach. Of all the places I've traveled, this one fills me with a sense of coming home. Maybe it's the beach lifestyle that I like so much.

I'm standing up, pumping the pedals and counting,

when I see the runner coming toward me. I recognize him instantly. McRae. Maybe it's the way he moves his body, which is solid with his sinewy chest and arms. Or it's the way my body vibrates when he's nearby that tips me off. He's running without a shirt; sweat glistens off his pecs. My mouth goes dry, I lose count, my foot slips, and I sit, pedaling backward while I let out a long, even breath. It's crazy, but I think my uterus just started pulsing. His shorts fall mid-thigh, and I watch the powerful muscles in his legs contract and relax, all in harmony with my heartbeat.

Ear buds dangle and connect to a band on his upper arm and I can't stop staring at his form. Just thinking about wrapping myself around him and feeling those arms holding me nearly causes me to crash the bike. When he sees me, he stutters in his stride, pulls the ear buds out by yanking on the cord, and briefly opens his mouth before slamming it shut.

I smile, glad I tied my tank into a knot that rests above my belly button because his eyes wander to my waist and follow the new vines of henna downward. McRae feels it too, this pull, I'm sure of it. Seeing the emotions flash across his face gives me pleasure. Is it as strong for him as it is for me? Is he the positive to my negative? With a flash of clarity, I know what I want. McRae. With muscles hard enough to cut a diamond. I want to experience him unfettered, unchained, with no attachments or obligations. I want it so badly I can barely breathe. For one night, I'd be willing to give his schematics a go.

I'm not overly modest by any stretch of the imagination, not anymore that is. I like sex. I like it a lot. It's energizing to experience the press of a man's body against mine, to touch them and learn their shape. When with someone intimately, you learn more about them and see them in ways you never could with an arm's length between. Like peeking into their soul. I want a glimpse into this guy's soul. His green eyes, straight nose, and his day-old beard make me want to know him in the biblical way. I've never been so fucking attracted to someone in my entire life.

When he's got a full frontal shot, I stand to pedal once and lean forward to expose my cleavage. It's a cheap shot, but I'm a girl on a mission now. I cruise the bike slowly past him.

"Hi," I say as I roll by, coming to stop at the edge of the boardwalk.

"Hey," he calls from behind me.

I twist, looking at him over my shoulder. He's stopped running, has turned to face me, and is leaning against a weathered post. One hand rests on his hip, his chest rising and falling with each deep inhalation.

"You live around here?" he asks.

"Yeah, right down that road." I wave in the direction of Mrs. Cramer's house. McRae follows my finger, which indicates the area of larger, more stately homes, and looks back, puzzled.

I laugh. "I have an apartment over the garage."

He pushes off the post before walking toward me, flipping the ear bud cord over his shoulder. "So you're settling in?"

"For now." I lower the bike's kickstand then climb off and meet him half way.

"Do you live around here?"

"Yeah, about a mile up the street." He motions behind me where older, smaller pre-war houses make up the neighborhood.

Wow, knowing he's close makes my pulse skip excitedly.

"That was pretty bad ass what you did to that guy at the bar." He leans down and reties his shoe but glances up at me. A car drives by slowly. I never saw or heard it coming until it was upon us. I'm so completely honed in on him.

"You've got quick reflexes. Like a Kunoichi." The admiration in his voice warms me. When he stands, he comes a step closer.

"Ha, I'm hardly a female ninja, but that's a compliment I'll take." I force myself to look at his face and not his chest. The last thing I want to do is openly drool over him.

It's obvious McRae doesn't know what to think of me. I've seen him watch me, a curious and puzzled look on his face. On the ride to Daytona, I'm pretty sure he was going to kick me out of the truck until he realized I'd saved his ass with the phone call. I get that he's having a hard time seeing through my exterior, but the quick snapshot of something more he's had impresses him enough to pique his interest and that pleases me. Usually guys aren't all that interested in what the inner Josie Woodmere is like. Not that I'd give them a chance to find out.

I don't give a rat's ass about the tightly wound types and their haughty opinions but there's something else about McRae that I like. Maybe it's the light smattering of chest hair or the way his shoulders are wide but his waist tapers. Or maybe it's the way he is with his brother or that it bothered him to leave me at a hotel. I lick my lips and look up at him. Without heels, I'm small enough that he could rest his chin on the top of my head comfortably.

I try to stay on topic. "I don't think I can afford to not have quick reflexes. All women should know a little of what I know."

"I guess it could come in handy on occasion." He nods

while stretching each arm behind his head. His pecs jump and give in to the long stretch. I meet his gaze and try not to lick my lips.

"Occasionally? Ha, try frequently. It doesn't matter how a woman dresses or what she's doing. She could be a target simply by smiling at the wrong person. I work from a premise that I might always be a target, so I've prepared myself to know how to handle any situation."

"You've had that happen to you before?"

"Pricks like that are everywhere." That's an under-statement.

His brows shoot up and I know it's at my word choice. I've seen the type of girl he likes. She's the type who pretends to not use profanity, but give her a strong drink and a room of her girlfriends and it's a whole different story.

"You headed to the beach?" he asks, indicating with his head to the water that waits just past the boardwalk.

"Yeah, you?"

"Yeah, I like to cool off in the water."

"Well if we stand here any longer you won't need to cool off." I take several steps back and stretch my hand out, reaching for the bike's seat and something to ground the elec-trical current sparking between us, yet am unable to pull my eyes from his.

"I can watch your stuff for you," I say in a breathy voice.

"What?" He blinks several times.

We're shrouded in a cloud of lust, and the palpable air and erratic, loud beating of my heart makes sound muffled. It's good to know he's experiencing it too.

"Your phone and shoes. If you're going for a swim I can watch those for you."

"Got it." He gestures for me to precede him.

I lock up the bike with clumsy fingers then scoop out my bag of stuff from the basket. When I pass him the energy around us crackles.

I find a spot on the beach, kick off my flip-flops, and drop my bag on top of them. After laying out my towel, I shimmy out of my shorts and pull off my T-shirt, leaving me standing before McRae in nothing but a skimpy red and white polka dot bikini.

He stares at the art across my belly; his gaze travels along the path then dips below the top of my bikini bottom and holds. "OK, I'm ready," I say and his pupils dilate.

If there weren't a smattering of families around us, I'd jump him right here and now. There's little doubt he'd stop me.

"I beg your pardon?" he asks, his eyes jerking back up to mine.

"For your stuff." I sweep my eyes across his finer-than-fine form. "I'll put it with mine. In my bag."

"Right," he says and gives a small shake of his head. "My stuff like my phone and watch."

I nod and step back to my towel, where I lower myself down and stretch out.

He kicks off his shoes, drops his phone on my bag, and jogs to the water, diving in when he hits the spot where the waves break. Knowing his attention is on his swim, I fan myself. Embarrassed that such a simple exchange of words combined with his presence could make me weak in the knees.

After the third buzzing from his phone, I turn it off.

By the time he's done with his swim and coming out of the water like some Adonis kissed by the sun gods, I've moved on to a paperback, but I've read the same paragraph three times. My attention was focused on him. I slam it shut and clutch it tight, using it to steady me. "Have a good swim?" I ask as he reaches for his things.

"I did. That a good book?" Beads of water evaporate off him. Others rest in the hills and valleys of his defined chest, occasionally breaking free to streak downward and drip onto me. My body is already past inflamed, so it wouldn't be a surprise if the drops began to sizzle.

Is this a stupid conversation? Yes, it is. We should stop tiptoeing around what we really want to say and get down to business. But I don't suggest that; he'll need some priming to abandon control. Instead, I answer his question.

"It is a good book. I've read it before. Several times actually. It's my favorite." He leans in to look at the cover before he bends to put on his shoes. "Science Fiction. Looks heavy. I wouldn't have figured you for the sci-fi type."

I shrug and go for broke. "Maybe if we run into each other again we can get to know each other better."

"Maybe. Chances look good, seeing as how we're neighbors now." His eyes drift to my henna.

"I imagine I'll be spending most weekends here if I'm not at the bar," I hint.

"I always run by here on the weekends."

"This is a good time. Not too crowded." I watch him over the rim of my glasses. "Yes, it is." He lifts his delectable mouth and produces a crooked smile. "Well, enjoy then. Thanks for keepin' an eye on my stuff."

"No sweat." I lie down and adjust my top before wiggling back into my spot. His phone buzzes and a soft expletive escapes when he looks at the screen.

"Work," he says. "I gotta run. So, again?" He gestures to the beach.

"Yes, please," I say and meet his gaze.

With a curt nod of his head, he heads back to the boardwalk.

Lord, that man.

I fall back on my towel, a quivering mess.

SIX

THE ADDRESS for the job I found in the classifieds takes me to a portion of the business district that's not based on the International Speedway but instead aviation. The building is really a hangar housed in a row of hangars within a stone's throw from the Aeronautical University and the international airport.

A large neon number hanging over the door lets me know I have the right building. Outside, a crew of guys are building up a post from which I can only assume a business sign will hang. There's nothing on the door to let me know the company name or specific business. The hangar is constructed from the typical gray aluminum and behind it sits two planes, a Cessna 152 and Cessna 172. The hanger door is ajar and inside is a Beech Sierra and Piper Seneca. If it didn't look legit, with the crew outside and the planes' noses sticking out the hangar door, I'd have turned around and left.

The planes make me think of McRae, specifically his hot

as hell body. Scanning the parking lot, I don't see the truck that brought me to Daytona.

I come face to face with a freshly scrubbed-face kid with bleached out hair. He's tall enough to be confused for a basketball player but is so thin it's a wonder he can defy gravity and remain upright.

"How's it?" he says, wiping his hands onto a towel. It's as if he's used to seeing me every day and this is our customary greeting, no response needed.

"Hey. I saw an ad in the paper for an administrative assistant. Is this the place?" I smile at him and relax my shoulders. This kid doesn't scan me up and down or stare only at my chest. He looks at me with no never mind whatsoever.

"Yeah, this is the place. You're looking for Mark, the owner."

"Is he here?"

"He's through the door and down the hallway. That's where all the offices are." He nods toward a door on the far wall that's labeled Employees Only.

"Great, thanks. I'm Josie by the way." I stick out my hand and wait. When he shows me his still greasy hand, I shrug and take it.

"I'm Zach, Zach Smith, nice to meet you. I sure hope you stick around. You seem all right and we need that around here." He does an eye roll and offers me the rag to wipe my hand.

"Fingers crossed." I hand the rag back. "Nice to meet you," I say with a backward step. We smile at each other before I turn around and stride through the doorway.

The layout makes sense to me now. When I pulled up I saw

the doors that lead to the office portion of the hangar but they were on the side of the building and out of sight of the parking lot. It's a quirky design to say the least. Through the main door is an outer office and waiting room of sorts. The desk is piled with papers lying askew and some have fallen to the floor.

Thin floor-to-ceiling partition walls divide the space into three rooms, all sitting behind this one. I consider waiting patiently on the faux leather couch that rests against one wall but it's unlikely this Mark character, who I'm assuming is the man I hear yelling at someone from the far left inner office, will even think of looking out here.

I walk up to the door leading into the inner office and give a closed-lip smile. The man is tall and wearing the typical man clothes: a golf shirt and shorts. Unfortunately, he's paired it white socks and Crocs. He takes off his baseball hat, uses it to wave me in, then scratches his head before he puts the hat back on.

"Fine. I'll pick up milk," he shouts and slams down the phone. "My wife. She stays home all day. Why she can't get the freaking milk is beyond me. Please tell me you're here about the job. Please don't be a half-wit. I'm Mark Thompson. I own this mess." He plops down into the large executive chair behind his desk.

"I'm Josie Woodmere and I'm pretty certain I'm not a half-wit." I don't offer my hand because he has no interest but instead pass him my resume. He's given me the once-over, twice, but he's at least making an effort to not stare. He scans my resume, which excludes my Juris Doctorate but includes my business management bachelor's, and the name of my alma mater. I've found omitting my education altogether works in my favor. But this job is for an administrative assistant, so I figured having a degree in business might work to my advantage.

With brows raised, he looks between me and the paper in his hands. "Yale? Well according to this you're either pretty damn smart or the biggest half-wit I've met to date."

"My father's a very active alumnus." I catch myself mid eye roll.

"Any particular reason you're not out putting that Ivy League education to good use?" He puts a cigar in his mouth.

"I'm here because I want to be, not because I have to be. I'm here because this is what *I want* to do."

"You sound just like my daughter," he mumbles before leveling me with a stare, sizing me up presumably.

He chews on the butt end of a stubby cigar and I continue to meet his gaze. "Take a good look around, lady," he says, tossing the cigar onto his desk. "We've got nothing but foul mouth men here and horny college boys. Someone's going to say something obnoxious or crude. Definitely disrespectful and I can't stop them. You think you can handle that without running out of here in tears?" He pulls out a fresh cigar from his desk drawer and taps it on his desk.

"I can handle myself." I sit back in the seat, folding my hands in my lap. I can bring him to his knees in three or fewer moves.

"I sure hope so because if you can't you'll need to leave now."

"What exactly are the job duties?" I ask.

"Whip this place into shape. My oldest, a girl, graduates college at the end of summer. She has yet to find a job and if she doesn't she'll be coming in here as the office manager. This job is until then. That's all I can offer."

"That's fine. September is a long way off. I don't make plans that far out."

"It's three months."

"Exactly. I'm pretty good at whipping things into shape. I might be able to get it together sooner than the end of summer." Clearly this place is up and running. It'd be a different story if they were dead in the water. All this place needs is some organization and streamlining.

He nods in appreciation. "You manage that and I'll give you a bonus. I'm trying to spend more time on the course, like to get involved in some other business ventures, but mostly I want to spend less time here. I have a GM, but look how that's working out. This place needs someone who can organize it."

"You have a GM?" From first appearances it looks like the GM is pretty useless, but I hold my tongue. This time.

"Yeah. He's new at the GM stuff. He's my instructor. Whip him into shape too," he says with a chuckle.

"You want all this done today or can I do some tomorrow?" I smile.

His laugh is a short bark. "I like you. You can start right now." He hands me a stack of paper to fill out.

"Any chance we can keep quiet about where I went to school? I've found people tend to...treat me differently when they find out."

"Listen, this is the south. We only care about your college's football team. It'll work to your advantage to keep it mum where you went to school. Have they *ever* been to a bowl game?" He guffaws and slaps his hand against his desk. "Call down to the kid if you need any help." He tosses the new cigar into his mouth and chews on the end. He picks up the phone, dials a number, and nods for me to leave. Clearly we're done.

I walk out to the desk and throw my purse onto the chair. I pull open the drawers and find them in worse shape than the top of the desk. I decide to get the lay of the land first. Other than the waiting room and front office combination, Mark's large office, a smaller office, and a storage area make up the last two spaces. The storage area is poorly organized with filing cabinets, a folding table, several five shelf racks, and a box of office supplies and forms thrown haphazardly into the space. The other office is sparse, as if it rarely gets used but there's an inbox tray, pencil holder, and a computer on the desk. A fine layer of dust coats the entire area and not a potted plant can be found.

I know nothing about running an aviation company, but it appears this place has grown with little attention to the administrative aspect. It's a wonder they make money. What I do know is how to put this place back together. I'm exceptionally good at doing that. I clasp my hands together with anticipation. I love a good challenge.

I enlist Zach to help me pull out the folding table and set it up behind my desk then I stack all the loose papers on top. We move the filing cabinets to the far wall of the storage room so we can access them easier and I pull all the papers out of those as well. It's lunch before I realize and I stop briefly for a taco and a large iced tea. The room looks as if I've made it worse, not better, but inside the storage room looks amazing.

I love this shit. More importantly, I'm good at it.

Zach found me a stepladder and I'm stacking old files and forms on top of the shelves, feeling pride at my achievements, when I hear the GM come in.

"Mother of all that's holy. What the hell has happened here?"

"In the storage room," I call and try to push the box onto the shelf.

I know he's come into my space when his hand reaches over mine and shoves the box into place. "Just what in the hell do you think you're doing?" he says.

I turn on the ladder and come face to face with McRae.

He's in dark cargo pants, a white T-shirt, and a dark navy flight vest that stores a small notebook, pens, and I'm guessing whatever else he uses when flying. Aviator shades hang from his front collar and his hair is mussed. In a surprising response, my knees buckle from the impact of immediate attraction and I lean against the file cabinet for support, half sitting on the top of the ladder. The space is small and narrow and I'm very aware of how he fills it completely.

"McRae. We meet again." I let the smile come.

There's no use fighting it. Something warm fills me; I like seeing a face I know. Especially his. I totally cyber stalked him over the weekend. After seeing him walk out of the sea, water streaming down his body, I became so hot for this guy it seems obsessive. I've yet begun to understand any of it.

Of course, he has virtually no online presence other than his LinkedIn profile and a reference to him being an adjunct professor at Emery Riddle University. His résumé is impressive. But hell, not as impressive as watching him swim the ocean. If I was the creepy stalker type, I'd have stolen a picture of him on my phone, but I'm not, so I'm stuck trying to visualize how his shorts clung to his muscular thighs when he walked back up the beach toward me. He looked powerful, a total alpha male whose domination would be a welcome gift, and I wasn't the only one watching him. He's the sort of guy who could take care of a girl during a zombie apocalypse. There's a depth to his eyes that tells me he's lived and seen things, and flesh eaters wouldn't faze him a bit. He's a survivor and I find that makes me antsy to put my hands on him.

"What's going on here, out there?" he asks sharply, waving to the outer office.

"I'm the new administrative assistant." I tuck my hands behind my back and meet his gaze.

"The hell you say." Bracing one hand against the wall, he runs the other through his hair. "I wish Mark would've run this by me." He says the last bit to himself.

"Well, it was run by the owner, so I'd guess that's sufficient enough." I try not to take his reaction personally.

"I don't like it," he says, as he surveys the newly organized shelves.

"You don't like being organized or you don't like me?" Honestly, at this moment I'm betting it could go either way. McRae at the beach is not the same as the one I'm staring at.

"I don't like being out of the loop." He tries to frown down at me. "Have you ever worked in aviation before?"

"No."

"How do you know if you've done all this correctly? Maybe you've wasted your time. Then I'll have to fix it all and I'm pressed for time." He gestures to the shelves. Ah, so that's the real problem.

"Don't be such a douche. I've had"—I glance at my watch—"nearly seven hours of uninterrupted time to work on this. You'd have gotten this far, too. Rest assured, it's done to a standard even you would find acceptable. It's not that hard to file gas receipts with gas receipts and flight logs with flight logs. Funny enough, I'm pretty good with the alphabet and sequencing items numerically. I can also read and reason." I shrug as though it's a crazy notion. "You could say hi, you know."

His brow is furrowed and he opens his mouth as if he's going to say more on the subject but instead pauses and the crease between his eyes relaxes.

"Hi," he says with a smile. "Small world."

"Isn't it?" I grin back.

His smile is so genuine I can't help make my own wider.

"Looks like you're settling in. I admit I'm surprised by that," he says.

I like McRae. I like the fact that he doesn't always stare at my chest and talks to me like he talks to everyone else. Often men come at me with one objective, to get me out of my clothes, and I'm OK with that. I have hormones, too. But don't talk to me as if I'm too stupid to know the agenda.

"Really?" I ask softly. "Why are you surprised?"

He shrugs. "I suppose I *assumed* you'd find Daytona a little too sleepy." The way he emphasizes assumed is more a jab at him than me.

"I find Daytona to be just right. Odd how our paths keep crossing."

He nods. "Yeah, the bar, the neighborhood—"

"And now here." I laugh, touch his arm, and almost jerk back as sparks tickle my fingers. Goodness, he emits testosterone. There's something seductive about a man in charge who isn't waving his cock around to prove it's big.

"So you plan on staying in the area for a while? I kinda figured you traveled around, preferring not to be pinned down anywhere."

"Oh yeah? Why so?"

"Well, at the hotel your badge said you were from Washington. You sound like you're from up North, not the Pacific Northwest." He gives me a skeptical look. "And you moved down here with what...four bags? Strikes me as someone living on the fly."

"More like someone just trying to experience life before I settle down."

"I get that." He nods, briefly lost in thought.

"So you're the GM *and* the flight instructor?" That explains why this place is in the state it's in. The owner is distracted with everything outside of his business and this guy's carrying the load of two jobs. Maybe more.

"Yeah." He rubs his palms over his eyes and stretches his shoulders back before he returns to brace himself against the wall. "I contract with other schools as well. Or I use to until this grew."

My mind flashes back to the beach and it's as if I have x-ray vision as I imagine his muscles rippling under his clothes.

"Well, now you have me here to help. I aim to please." It's a simple line that has no secondary meaning until I look from his green eyes and a muscle in his jaw jumps.

Drawn from my current reality, I go to a fantasy place where we take off all our clothes and try to steam up this little space to the point where it rains inside. He stands there all cocksure and large, his strong arms corded with muscles. Even his large black aviator's watch turns me on. His white T-shirt stretches tightly across his chest, hinting at what I know is underneath.

"So, ah, you want to show me what you're doing here? I mean, about all this." He pushes off the wall and gestures to the reorganized storage area.

"Sure, and if you have a minute I'd like to schedule some

time with you to go over the books. There're some things I don't understand."

"There are lots of things I don't seem to understand," he mumbles and crosses his arms over his chest.

"Well, let me show you." I turn back on the ladder. Using everything I have in reserve to not go primal and jump him, I channel the energy into showing him how I've organized the old files and stored them overhead. Inside the cabinet, easily obtained, are all the current records needed at a moment's notice. I've also inventoried the office supplies and am keeping a running list on the computer stationed at my desk as well as a purchasing calendar. No more running out of fuel while I'm in charge.

"Wow, I don't think this company has ever been this organized. What about the mess out there?" He points to the outer offices before he steps back and gestures for me to precede him. The space is small enough that I have to turn sideways to get past him. When I do, our fronts brush against each other and I place my hands on his biceps.

"Excuse me," I say. Even in heels, my head reaches only slightly above his collarbone, and when I look at him, I see McRae in a whole new light. Perhaps he won't need as much priming as I first thought.

Maybe it's because I'm satisfied from all of today's organization or because I really like this town. Maybe it's how studly he looks in the flight gear or that he looks driven. Whatever the reason, I want him not because he's cut from the cloth of gods, but because there's loneliness in him I identify with. How his smile doesn't always reach his eyes or that he thinks happiness can be found in a sweater-set-and-pearl-wearing socialite who's likely been conditioned to climb the social ladder. A lifestyle like that never brought me happiness, and McRae is disillusioned if he thinks it will bring some to him. He's got too much depth for the vapidness of pageantry.

He stares down at me and his green eyes wander to my piercing. His lips twitch. The sound of his vibrating phone breaks whatever was passing between us.

Rolling my eyes, I move out into the main office and see why he was so shocked when he first arrived. The place looks ransacked. Paper is everywhere, boxes thrown around the floor with recycling or shredding flowing out of them. I turn to make a joke about the mess but he's totally engrossed in his phone, thumbs flying madly across the screen.

"Holy crap. I've never seen a phone be so busy as yours. Any of that business I can help with?" It's annoying as hell. I want to snatch the phone from his hand and stomp on the screen. He'd definitely thank me later. Once he got past the shock and withdrawal.

"It's mostly all business. We've always been short on office staff, so I sent all the calls to my phone as well as the emails. Some of it's from my job at the University."

"All the calls?" That explains why the office phone is so quiet.

"Yeah, students, other schools looking for instructors, you name it."

"Give me your phone." Palm out, I wait. After he hands it over—reluctantly I might add—I repress the urge to smash it, instead set about loading some apps. "I've put everything on an online calendar and can send you daily emails with the following day's schedule. I've also set up reminders about when orders need to be completed. Like jet fuel." I give him a knowing smile and hand back his phone.

He scans the screen. "It all looks good, I'll give you that," he says and I catch his eyes darting away from me.

I pick up the office phone. "What's the code to stop forwarding the calls? It's my one mission to make that thing shut up." I nod to his phone that, coincidentally, hums with vibrations.

He types in the code and for a moment it's blissfully quiet. I take advantage of that silence and send all the calls to voice mail, as it's quitting time soon.

"This calendar is really nice," he says, the app open on his phone.

Stepping close, I tap some empty space highlighted green. "There's some free time on Thursdays that's not accounted for. Anything I can put into that time?"

He shakes his head. "That's my time. I don't work for Mark then, so you can't schedule me for anything."

"OK. Very mysterious." I wag my brows.

"Same for my time at the college. My office hours there are not flexible. I've a chance to land a full time teaching job if I apply for my Ph.D."

"How can you possibly manage all that with all this?" For added emphasis, I push over a pile of papers and let them slide across the table, stopping when they collide with the next pile.

"I just will," he says with a shrug. "I don't have to take the position, but it's a great contingency plan."

"And here I thought this place was your lifeblood."

"It is."

"Then why would you need a contingency plan?" I toss that zinger out, not expecting an answer.

We stand in silence for four beats.

"How's your brother?" I ask, conceding the point to

McRae. I used to have contingency plans for my contingency plans.

"Fine. Busy with school."

"What's happened with Mel?" I sit on the corner of the desk and start swinging my foot, glad I painted my nails a fire red last night.

He licks his top lip and clasps his hands in front of his crotch.

"Mark and I got a lawyer involved right away like you suggested. Mark was pretty resistant at first. But we've managed to contain it. Thanks for the advice."

"My pleasure."

"Hey," Zach calls as he comes into the room. "You two doing all right in here? I guess you've met already, but I thought I'd come to see if everything was going well." He stands in the doorway, his hands tucked in his back pocket, his eyes bouncing between us.

"Yeah, we're good," I tell him while McRae steps back.

"You two aren't fighting or anything, right?"

"Why would you think that?" I ask.

"Because I feel like I interrupted something." Zach shrugs.

"No, it's all good." McRae tells him.

"You're Smitty, aren't you?" I ask, putting together the pieces of the phone call from our trip down.

The kid ducks his head and says, "Yeah, that's what all the guys call me. You can too if you want." When he looks at me, I can tell how much he really wants me to call him Zach.

"That's OK. I'll stick with Zach."

"Good," he says with a nod. "I mean, good that y'all ain't fighting. I'm heading out then." He points to the door and gives us a wave as he leaves the office.

"Your Smitty is your best employee," I tell McRae over my shoulder.

"I reckon he is," he says.

Having exhausted all aspects of polite conversation, with the exception of the weather, I resort to fidgeting with the ancient computer I found on the desk I've claimed.

"I'll be in my office if you need me." He gestures to the smallest of the three offices.

"OK." I bite my lip and stare down at the word QWERTY.

Holy hell, if we keep dancing around all this sexual tension, one of us is going to become unhinged. Likely me.

SEVEN

I ARRIVE EARLY TO WORK, excited to spend the morning organizing the papers in the main office. I can see it coming together. By the end of the day, I'll have most of the office set to make everyday operations more seamless. Then I'll tackle the books, set up some spreadsheets, and map out how everything is restructured so McRae won't get his panties all bunched up and complain about being out of the loop.

Staying busy keeps my mind off the limited communication I've had from Will. I've dreamt of hiring a computer hacker to search the Florida driver's license system for him, but I don't have the money or access to a hacker. Nor do I want to spend time in jail for a felony. I have no leads. No idea what he could be doing for a living. Apparently he never finished his family-mandated law degree, as his name doesn't pop up on any school website nor has he taken the bar exam.

Pushing aside my anxiety regarding my brother, I force myself to focus on what I can control, the organization of this office and my desires for McRae. At least I hope I can control that. Good luck if he shows up today looking all Top Gun.

I carry the files of past accounts receivable and payable to the storage room and tuck them into a box, label it correctly, and rest it on the top of the filing cabinet so I can climb the stepladder and store the box overhead. I sense McRae come into the room before I hear him, so I turn and smile. He looks like he's just landed a badass fighter plane and my pulse sprints off on a mad race.

"You're early." I wasn't expecting him for another hour.

"Yeah, my student cancelled. He's home with the flu. You need any help?" He nods with his head toward the box I just pushed on the shelf.

I climb down a rung and lean against the ladder, resting my hip on a step and look up at him. I can't stop smiling. "No, I'm all done in here."

"Where is everyone?" He indicates with his hand to the hanger that lies beyond the storage room door.

"Zach went home early. Something about a study group with a cute girl, and Mark called. He's in Arizona. You're in charge. That happens a lot doesn't it? You get to be the boss without really being the boss?"

He narrows his gaze at me. "Mark's grooming me to buy into the business. This is just his way of doing it."

I'm pleased that I managed to swallow my snort of disbelief. It's easy for McRae to go into a tailspin; I've found that to be common with all anal-retentive people.

He shifts and looks over his shoulder. "So it's just us?"

I can't tell if it's because he's nervous or concocting a plan. Does he think I might seduce him? Well, I suppose that's a high probability. All it'll take is one crooked grin from him.

I spent a large amount of time over the last few days thinking about McRae and my need to touch him. The more I consider the options, the more certain I am about my solution. One thing for certain is dating him would be senseless. He's the sort who'd date with intentions toward the long haul. Long for me is measured in single digit weeks.

Besides, it's not like I'm the sort he'd want to date anyway. I don't even own a cardigan, and I left my pearls in Connecticut.

But this man. McRae. Brinn. With eyes that speak of a depth I'm not sure I'll ever understand. He's far too serious for someone his age and from what I've observed and what others have said, he's extremely giving. Hiring people from the old neighborhood, wherever that may be, or driving up to attend a Marine Corp graduation when he barely has time to sleep. I've seen his crazy work schedule. This is a guy who carries the weight of the world on his back and I would wager, and probably win, thinks of others before himself and that makes my desire to give back to him ping something fierce.

"You had anything to eat?" he asks and rolls his head, stretching his neck. I immediately think of ten ways to relax him.

"Mmm, no. Not yet. You hungry?" I lick my lips and scan the length of him.

He's dressed similar to yesterday. Sticking his hands into the front pockets of his jeans, he leans his left shoulder against the wall, his head dangerously close to knocking against the shelf that encircles the top of the storage room.

"Yeah, I'm hungry." He watches my mouth.

"You should get something then. Takeout, perhaps."

"That's a good idea." His eyes dip to my chest and jerk back up.

"You look tired. Is there anything I can get you?" I sit on the top step of the ladder, letting the slit of my skirt fall open and exposing my thigh, which shows the new art I did.

His eyes fixate, traveling up the design. "What did you say?" He brings his eyes slowly back to mine.

"I asked if you wanted me to get you anything." Like me for example, can I get you a helping of me?

"Is that new?" He's staring at my leg.

"Yeah, from Sunday. You like it?"

"How big is it?"

The skirt I'm wearing hides nearly half. "Well, it goes up and across."

I show him the area, moving my hands up my thigh. When I reach my hip, I spread them out toward my butt and stomach.

"It reaches the one I have on my stomach." I place both hands over my lower abdomen and spread them wide to show the space the art is taking. With his eyes still on my hands, I run them down, across my thighs, and slide them off my legs. I don't bother pulling the opening of my skirt together. Being near this guy makes me feel naughty. I like it.

"You let some guy do all that over your body without knowing him?"

It takes a moment for me to realize he asked his question with a touch of judgment, and my attraction flickers when my anger flares.

"It's not like we fuck afterward. It's art."

McRae's eyes drop to my mouth and his nostrils flare slightly. "You just say whatever you're thinking, don't you?" He licks his lips and steps closer.

"Why not? Is it offensive?" I sit up straighter and lean toward him. It's the craziest flirting I've ever experienced.

"I guess to some it can be." His eyes rise to meet mine and the air in the closet is sucked out, the temperature climbs, and I resist the urge to fan myself.

Instead, I tap my index finger once to my lower lip. "Are you offended by this mouth?"

His eyes follow my finger. He pushes off the wall, pulls his hands from his pockets, and leans toward me, placing his left hand against the wall over my right shoulder.

"No." It comes out a raspy whisper. He reaches out with his right hand and rubs his thumb over my lower lip, gently caressing my piercing.

We come together like stars colliding, in a clash of sparks and fire. It's not a simple kiss, two lips meeting and exploring. It's an impact driven by need. He presses me against the stepladder and filing cabinet and I clutch his vest, my fist pulling him to me. Our tongues unite, and the exploration is about dominance, being the first to claim the other. He cups my ass and we can't get any closer with clothes on. His other hand is inside the waistband of my skirt, his thumb on my hipbone.

"Sweet mother of God," he says when we part to breathe. But only two breaths pass before we press our lips together again. It's as if they've just found their perfect half and can't bear to be apart.

Kissing him is like nothing I've ever known. My lopsided and crazy world straightens and rights itself. The blurriness clears and my insight becomes crisp. I want him desperately.

"Wait," I say. "Close the door." Just in case someone comes in. Our faces are a breath apart, both of us gasping for air. He hesitates, lets go, and backs up to the door, watching me as he moves. Slowly, he pushes the door closed and walks back to me.

"Listen, I'm sorry about that—" he starts.

"Are you really? Because I'm not." I step off the ladder and stand in front of him.

"Well if you're not then I guess I won't be either." His smile is just a twist of the lips, but when our eyes meet, it opens. I smile back at him. "But this can't happen again. We work together now, and I have too much invested in this job to throw it away."

"Yes, that's a sticky situation. But you're not my direct boss, and I'm going to be moving on soon. I'm here for a few months, max. Just enough time for us to dabble. Before you know it, I'll be a memory." I shrug one shoulder. "Besides, I'm certain my background and credit checks came out OK. I don't have any prior arrest, any outstanding lawsuits, or a history of them."

"I didn't see it, but Mark said you aren't a whack job."

"I have an idea." I place my hands on his chest and play with the zipper of his flight vest.

He doesn't say anything but raises one brow. I take that as a sign to continue.

"I'm attracted to you. Simply put, I want to sleep with you. I'm going to assume you're not put off by the thought of sleeping with me. Filthy mouth and all that." I give a quick laugh. My lips still burn from his kiss and they feel swollen and full.

"I wouldn't put up a fight." He picks up a strand of my hair and twists it around his palm.

"I'm going to make you an offer, but you have to accept it or decline it right now. No maybe. No time to think about it."

He stops twisting my hair. "What kind of deal?"

"Nope, you get no information except that it includes us having sex together."

He winces. "Yeah, but that's not fair. I have a lot at stake here, and maybe this includes me dressing up or includes me, you, and animals or something I'm not into."

I stop pulling his zipper. "You really think I'm different, don't you?" I know he does, it's apparent in his hesitation when he's talking with me, but when we kiss all that hesitation is lost.

"No, I don't know you. I have to be practical here."

"OK, fair enough. It's straight up, ordinary sex. Just you and me. The reason why I'm making you decide now is because you're *so* practical. You need to let go a bit. Step off the path. So, what's it gonna be? You want to do me or not?"

He twirls my hair without tugging it, all while our eyes never leave each other. He brushes his thumb over my piercing. I tug his vest zipper down an inch and wait.

"And you think this is a good idea? Because I'm not so sure."

"Yeah, look at us. It's clear we have a mutual attraction, and until we burn it off it's going to be there. Making work awkward. I'm not here long—"

"I want us to get along."

"But if we don't address this tension, it's going to make working together really uncomfortable."

"And you think if we have sex it'll fix everything." He gives me a half smile that tells of his skepticism.

"It can't make it worse. We're both adults. If we know the deal up front then there should be no issue. You in?"

I watch his face, looking for some sort of expression to let me know what he is thinking, but the guy has an amazing poker face.

"If this goes tits up then at least you'll know I'll be gone at some point. Worse case, Mark's daughter starts in September. Bye-Bye, Josie."

He searches my face before saying, "OK. Yes."

I meet his gaze, excitement coursing through me. "Are you sure? Don't waffle on me. By saying yes, you need to be all in. I'm not talking a relationship. I'm talking sex. No strings attached sex."

"Can girls even do that?" He drops my hair, wrapping his hands around my waist instead. The press of his palm spans my lower back. It's the craziest notion, but I feel supported, as if he's got me and no matter what the weight, he'll carry it.

"Mmm. Why don't you find out first hand?" Our bodies get closer.

"OK, I'm in. It's a firm yes." His voice is low and husky.

As I press against him, his arousal pushes back and I stroke the length. "Yes, yes it is." I pop the button on his jeans, pulling the zipper down, exposing his white briefs.

He lowers his head. "Shall we seal the deal with a kiss?"

There's no need for a response other than to bring my lips to his. I stretch and he bends. His vest slides off, and I run my hands up under his T-shirt and around his waist.

"Rule number one," I say when we separate. "It's OK to date other people. We aren't dating. This is straight up sex. Booty calls are not only OK but also expected. We accept this for what it is. Chemistry."

"OK."

All sense of reason is gone. We're riding the high our impulsivity provides. He backs up to the ladder and lifts me, setting me on the middle step.

"Rule number two is we leave it out of the office," he murmurs before kissing the space below my ear.

"After this time, of course," I tease.

"Of course." His hands slide up my shirt.

"This is crazy," I say.

"Like flying upside down. Nothing about this makes sense."

"You mean this is a thrill ride?"

He pulls back to look at me, a wicked smile on his face. "Yeah, definitely a thrill ride. Could be a train wreck."

"Let's find out. Take this off." I pull his T-shirt up at the hem, tugging it off quickly before he reaches for my shirt.

"Holy shit," he says when I'm standing before him with my bra the only fabric between his hands and my breasts.

"These are incredible." With one hand, he lightly traces the fading henna down the valley between my breasts before sweeping up and over one breast, the nipple beading beneath his palm.

"Look who's talking. Where did you pick these up?" I run my hands down powerful arms, caressing the high and low of his muscles.

"Life," he says and dips his head and places a soft kiss on my collarbone.

"I like a guy with a little chest hair."

"I'm glad I could provide." His voice is deep and raspy and a tad thin. It tells me our pace is about to amp up.

"Rule number three. Anyone can back out at any time without consequences. When you're done, you're done." Touching him everywhere has become my singular purpose.

He's traveling his lips along my neck when he chuckles.

I pause my exploration. He looks up, our faces a breath apart, his eyes hooded from desire.

"I laughed because I think I may be the luckiest bastard on the planet. Like I've been given the keys to the holy land. You talk about an eject button and I'm feeling like a Powerball winner. Eject from what?"

"You're good with this deal, then?" I ask in a whisper as I wrap my arms around his neck and my legs around his waist.

"Better than good. I've heard tales of these things, urban legends. But I thought they were myths. Now I know they aren't, and sirens do exist. I'm all in."

"My skirt unties at the side," I say and gently grind against him. He slides his hand up my thigh, leaving a wake of goose bumps behind.

Clothes fall to the floor, my shoes stay on, and we press together closer than two bodies can get without him being buried inside me. I don't wonder where he found the wherewithal to pull out the condom from his wallet, but I'm glad it appeared. If I was in a less than frenzied state, I might have remembered to mention one.

The light from the high wattage bulb is nothing but a glow, as I can't see past him. He fills the space around me and all my senses are attuned to him and him only. The world shifts or pauses or shudders or maybe all of them when he presses me against the filing cabinet and slowly slides in. Life becomes hazy and I give myself over, letting go of everything that doesn't matter at this moment. Because the only thing that does is McRae and this connection I feel right here and right now.

Our timing is in sync. Our release leaves me quivering in his arms. He breathes warm air against my neck and all I can think about is getting more.

"You're bad news, Josie," he whispers and kisses the lobe of my ear.

"Holy shit." I shudder against him one final time. "This was the best idea I've had. Ever."

His grunt is half laughter, half moan. "You're not gonna hear me disagree."

I'm propped between him and the cabinet and when he moves our skin separates like new Velcro.

"Do you always carry condoms?" I rub my hand over my cheek and jaw line.

"Yeah. I'm a single guy in hopes a moment like this might happen. I can't believe it actually has."

"We should make it happen again sometime."

"I'd like that," he says, his thumb caressing my jawline. "I'm sorry about the beard burn." He kisses it gently.

"I like this scruffy-faced you." I trail small kisses over his five o'clock shadow.

There's easiness between us and not the awkward moment that usually accompanies sex with a near stranger.

"What do we do now?"

"We pat ourselves on the back, get dressed, and go about our business." I push away and we're no longer joined. He eases me into a standing position and watches me dress. He tugs on his jeans that ride low on his hips and I consider having round two right here and now. I meet his gaze and he pauses, his hand on his fly.

A phone rings out in the office and we both jump.

"I'll clean up in here," he says.

"I'll meet you in ten minutes in your office to go over the books." I pull my hair out from beneath my shirt. "Oh, and maybe we should exchange numbers. You can text me if you want to do this again." I swirl my index finger in the space between us and give him a salacious wink.

"So you're serious about this...no-strings thing?" He looks

like a child who might have his favorite toy taken away at any moment.

"Are you waffling? A little intimidated?" I step close and once again have the feeling of being sucked into space or an alternate universe. Everything around me blurs.

"No, not at all. I'm just making sure we're on the same page."

I cup the back of his head and bring it down for a kiss, nipping his top lip before breaking away. He makes a low, deep growl and on a giggle I quickly turn and walk out.

"Judas Priest," he says behind me.

Mother of all things good and holy, I'm going to need divine intervention because my appetite for him has just been whetted.

<h1 style="text-align:center">EIGHT</h1>

BEING in the storage closet with McRae was oddly enough like swimming in shark-infested water, exciting, breathtaking, and dangerous. Oh, so very dangerous. I thought one taste might do the trick, but that one sample left me wanting more. This must be what addicts feel like. I can see why they're surprised to find themselves at the mercy of their drug of choice. McRae could easily become mine.

I cut out of work a few minutes early. It's not until I'm a mile away from the hanger that I clasp my hands to my cheeks and laugh. A deep, effervescent laugh that originates from my core and is a mixture of teenage giddiness, sultry dominatrix, and plain and simple pleasure.

My word, McRae is something else.

If it weren't for the reminder in my phone, I'd have forgotten to go by the Fox and Hound to get next week's work schedule. When I pull into the lot, I spot Jayne's fire red coupe and check my reflection, looking for any signs that might tip my hand as to what McRae and I have been up too.

The beard burn has faded to a soft pink that I manage to conceal under powder.

Entering through the back, I wave to the staff that I've started to know, as we seem to share many of the same shifts. Jayne comes out from the back storage room carrying a large bag of flour. Her aquamarine Lily Pulitzer shift dress is dusted with a fine coat of white powder.

"Bloody mess I've made in the back room. Bag exploded when I accidentally dropped it." She plops the large bag onto the steel counter, creating a plume of white, before brushing fine flour particles from her dress.

I pull the work schedule from the wall and take a picture with my phone. It's charming how her folks still do things old school like paper schedules and time off request sheets. Nothing automated here.

I picture Jayne sitting at the bar with her ledgers. "Have you thought of automating your books? No more pencils and calculators."

"Yes, but I'm terribly unlucky with electronics. They always malfunction. Usually of the smoke and popping variety."

"I see." Even though I really don't. I itch to help her organize but I hold back, waiting for better timing. "Do you need help cleaning up?" I point to her once lavender but now grayish-colored shoes.

"Yes, please, and you can tell me all about what it is you've gone and done." She gives me a knowing smile.

"I have no idea what you're talking about," I say before turning on my heel and escaping to the storage room.

Another large bag lies upside down on the floor with a flour field spreading out in at least a ten-foot radius.

"I'm talking about your smile," Jayne says from behind me.

"Is there something wrong with it?" I toss my phone on the counter before I pull down a broom from where it hangs on the wall.

"No, it's lovely. It's blinding and seems to be stuck in that position."

"It's nothing." I turn away, hoping to conceal the grin.

"Right. Nothing. Nope. Pull the other one. Come on, Josie, tell. This is what girlfriends do, they share. I promise to squeal the proper amount."

With what I hope is a serious expression, I face her, but her sanctimonious smile makes my efforts fruitless, as I really can't contain my own. Oh, what the hell.

I drop the broom to the floor and clasp my hands together excitedly. "OK, guess what I did?"

Jayne gives me a bored look and says in a flat tone, "You got more henna." She points to my stomach.

"I did. You like it?" I raise my shirt to show her the entire piece. "But that's not what I'm talking about."

"Right. OK. You shaved it all off. You have a bald bird." She leans against the wall.

"What? No! Why would you—? No." I shake my head. "I slept with McRae."

"I figured you slept with someone." Jayne stands up. "McRae? Isn't he your boss?" Her eyes go wide.

I wince. "Well, no. Technically, the owner, Mark, is my boss."

"Right. So he's just another employee?"

"Um, he's second in charge." I put my hand on my hip and dare her to say more.

"Don't just stand there, give over." She gestures for me to continue.

I step closer to her so the conversation is between us. "It's just sex, no strings. I established that up front and he agreed."

"Of course he did."

We both laugh. I once dated a guy who told me women could rule the world, if only they knew how much power they wield. After today's experience, I totally get what he was saying.

"Yup. I'm in. I'm out. I'm gone."

Jayne picks up the broom and hands it to me before reaching for a second one.

"What if in order to reestablish your relationship with your brother you have to stay?"

I shake my head. "Being here has nothing to do with my brother. I can live anywhere and have that." I'd spilled my guts about my brother a few nights ago when the bar traffic had been slow.

Jayne clasps her hands over mine. "I hope you're right. Are you going to tell me what it was like?"

I stare at her, blinking, as I try to find the words to describe what I experienced with McRae. The grin still carves my face.

"I see," she says and smiles. "At least tell me *something*."

"He's got an incredible body. All tone. If I were to take a piece of paper, lay it on top of him, and rub chalk against the paper, the outline alone would make you drool. The real thing is...."

"Extraordinary," Jayne answers for me.

I nod and wag my brows.

My phone buzzes on the counter and Jayne reaches for

it. After a quick glance at the screen, she says, "That comment about location not being key to knowing your brother, are you sure about that?"

"Positive. Why?" I take my phone from her outstretched hand. A glance at the screen shows a text from Will. The first text I've ever received from him.

"Because in two years of searching, you've had only emails. Three weeks here and you're getting a text message. Coincidence? Perhaps."

Air leaves my lungs as I swipe the screen to read the message. What I see makes tears spring to my eyes.

"Is it awful?" Jayne asks.

I shake my head and try to steady my shaking hand, but the quiver in my voice tells everything. "He wants to meet."

I look around the room and try not to lose it. This moment. This is what I've been waiting for. I close my eyes and my mind takes a crazy tangent. Why now? There's been no more increase in communication than before. Nothing's really changed other than me being in the same state.

"Go, I'll take care of this." Jayne dismisses me with a wave of her hand. She knows it's been seven years since I last saw my brother. She knows how much I've missed him. That I hate myself for waiting so long. I didn't have to tell her that. She figured it out.

I give her a quick hug. Our friendship may not have logged in hundreds of hours, yet, but there is an honesty and sincerity to Jayne that I appreciate. A kinship that I'm certain time would only strengthen.

"Let's talk tomorrow," I say, walking backward out of the storage room, my phone pressed to my chest.

"Yes and I want to hear all the details."

I laugh and hurry out of the building, high on the afterglow of sex and friendship and the feelings of fitting in. Once outside I text Will that I most definitely want to meet and wait for a response.

OK is all he texts back.

OK?

And just like that I deflate. I reread his message and realize he never said when he wanted to meet. I just assumed he meant now. I rest my head on the steering wheel and rein in my disappointment. I can wait. I'm good at it.

"I *can* wait," I whisper with determination. I've waited this long.

My mind circles from Will to McRae while I make the short drive home. Once I pull into the driveway, all thoughts are forgotten.

A large black Harley Davidson motorcycle is parked in front of the garage. It's built for long trips with large saddle-bags hanging over each side. It's totally badass.

When I step from the car, a tall, bald guy rises from the stairs. His jeans sit low on his hips and fall over heavy motor-cycle boots. His T-shirt is plain orange and sleeves of tattoos cover each arm. A large thick scar runs across the top right side of his scalp, over his ear, and comes to rest above his right brow. I'm about to inquire if this stranger needs help when I meet crystal blue eyes identical to mine. I burst into tears, covering my mouth to keep in the sobs.

"Aw, come on Jo-Jo. I didn't mean to make you cry." He picks up his helmet.

Shaking my head madly, I say, "Please don't go." He puts his helmet down on the stairs and waits.

I try to wipe my eyes with my stupid shirt but it's a crochet piece and the holey rag is useless. I glance back at

Will to ensure that he's not leaving and wipe my tears with the palms of my hands.

"I'm only crying because..." I stop to suck in a ragged breath. "Because I really, really missed you and I wasn't sure if I was ever going to see you again." I know I promised myself that if or when this moment happened I would play it cool, but that was a pipe dream of epic proportions.

Will gives a barely perceptible nod. I only see it because I'm staring at him so hard, trying to commit everything to memory.

"It's been too long," he says in a raspy voice. He looks away, blinks several times, and does this weird sliding of his jaw from side to side, before he looks back at me. "You're all grown up." His smile is soft, tentative, as he opens his arms and takes a step toward me.

I search for the boy I spent the first sixteen years of my life with. The brother who made me feel normal when everyone and everything else made me feel like an oddball. I search for the Will who walked me to every class my first year at junior high, knowing I was out of my league because I skipped a grade.

This man in front of me—whose recent years have shaped him into a person I don't recognize—was my first friend, sometimes my only friend, but most of all he was the big brother who always had my back.

And then one blustery early fall night changed every-thing. Will left the house to meet friends and a police officer showed up three hours later to tell us his car had hydroplaned off a bridge into the river below. Will spent eight weeks in the hospital and walked out of our lives the day he was discharged.

I rush into his arms, desperate to know that person again. Burying my face in his chest, I wrap my arms around him.

I dreamed about seeing Will again. Talking to him, maybe even hanging out. But I never imagined what it would be like the first moment I saw him. All my fantasies were after that moment, and I don't know where to go from here. My gut tells me he's skittish.

Unmistakably, he's no longer the boisterous boy I grew up with. There's hesitancy in everything he does, his movements, his words, and even his actions.

We step apart and our eyes meet, which makes us both laugh. The awkward tension that held us apart a moment ago is broken and evaporates, replaced by curiosity.

I take the metaphorical first step. "Want to get something to eat?"

He scrubs his hand over his face before smiling down at me. "I wish I could. I got this thing." He looks off toward town. "Trust me. I'd much rather catch up with you than do this dog and pony show."

I try to hide my disappointment by fixing my smile to my face. "OK—"

"But I have a few minutes." He motions to the step he was sitting on earlier. "Do you?"

"Of course." I move to sit on the step, leaving space for him. "Mom would totally flip if she knew you'd cut off all those beautiful curls." I nod to his head where large dark curls once resided, making girls swoon and desperate to run their hands through them.

He swings his jaw from side to side before answering. "It was useless to try and grow hair to cover this scar." He rubs his hand over the parting gift from his accident; a movement that appears so natural I'm certain he does it with little awareness. "She would also flip if she knew this thing I was going to was a book signing."

"A book signing?" Our mother was all about supporting the arts, especially the literary tomes that pontificated her beliefs. I gasp, covering my mouth with my fingertips. "You're a writer."

He ducks his head and grins.

"You're a writer of genre fiction. That's why mother wouldn't approve."

His laugh is quiet but deep. "Yeah. I am." He swings his jaw again and when he sees me notice he clamps his teeth together, popping the muscle in his cheek.

"Oh." I clap my hands together. "I have this great sci-fi book that you'd love. Every time I read it, I'm reminded of you. Hold on." I jump up and jog to my car, clutching my skirt in hand so I don't trip. In the car, I snatch up my purse and rummage through it until I find the book. I simultaneously pull it out and back away from the car before I jog back to Will.

"Here. It's fabulous." I toss the book in his lap and plop down next to him.

He holds it up and turns to face me. "You really liked it?"

"Yeah, crazy good. It's not worn because I bought it secondhand or anything." I lovingly caress the heavily creased spine and dog-eared pages. "It's worn because I read it that much."

His smile is open and wide when he says, "I wrote it, Jo. The second one comes out today. I don't really travel, so I concede to my publisher's request and do local signings."

My mind buzzes. My favorite book was written by my brother. More importantly, he referred to Daytona as local.

"You live nearby?"

He cups his chin in his hand. His fingers turn slightly white as he squeezes it before he lets go. Suddenly, he stands. "I live in Gainesville," he says in one breath.

"Oh, that's pretty close." About two hours away. What an incredible stroke of luck that I decided to start in Daytona. "Why Gainesville?"

I search my mind for the research I did on various Florida cities, trying to find one that might appeal to Will. Gainesville has a top-notch university, football, and is nowhere near the beach as it's closer to the center of the state. None of the things would have appealed to the brother I knew.

Pointing to his scar, he says, "They have an incredible brain institute. Since this thing is the product of a traumatic brain injury, I thought it made sense."

I nod in understanding. "I see."

I must be the dumbest person in the world, not thinking about his TBI. I searched artist communes, dude ranches, and ski resorts. I attended bike rallies in South Dakota. All of which were dead ends. But favorite places and hobbies of the boy I knew were all I had to go on. At least I was right about motorcycles, though I'd have guessed BMW before Harley.

"I never considered your head injury," I mumble to myself in contempt. I want to know if the injury affects him, or rather, how it affects him, but I'm afraid to ask, to push him into a place where he's not comfortable because this is a new Will I'm getting to know. This person is so much like the boy I grew up with but so different, and the water I'm treading might have a riptide.

He cocks his head to one side and looks at me. "What do you know about my accident?"

I look past his shoulder, letting the events flash through

my mind. Putting words to the vision makes my heart ache. "Just that you got stuck in the horrible storm, skidded on the bridge, and went over the side."

Will stares at me, searching my face for something, I'm not sure what. "That's it?"

"Yeah. Isn't that it?"

He shrugs at my question so I continue. "You've been in Gainesville for seven years?" I'm desperate to know more about him.

"No, but that's a story for another time." He moves to a saddlebag and undoes the latch, pulls out a book, and tosses it to me. It's his new release. I smile up at him and clutch it to my chest.

"Thanks. Now I'll be up reading all night."

A tinge of pink colors his cheek and I'm awed by this. As children, he was always the bold go-getter. Nothing stood in his way. He was purposeful and determined and certainly not the type to blush easily. Whereas, I was. Quiet, and in his shadow, I let Will lead the charge. Until the day he wasn't there any longer.

I pull the book away to look at the cover. "Hey, why Sam Frenick?" I ask, pointing to his pseudonym. His middle name is Samuel, so that makes sense, sorta.

He walks to my car and runs his hands over my tires. "Another time. You need to replace these as soon as possible, you know."

"I know. I had the car inspected. It's fine for now." My plan is to do the tires after my first paycheck from Alliance, which will be another two weeks.

"I'll pick you up in the morning and follow you to the tire shop. I'll take you to work." He walks back toward me and lifts up his helmet, tossing it in the air so it does one flip before catching it.

"You're staying in town? Want to crash here?"

Will buckles the chinstrap and gives a small shake. "Nah, my publisher put me up. I'll see you tomorrow. Seven-thirty work?" He straddles the bike, messes with a few switches, then stands it upright before using his heel to push back the kickstand.

"That's perfect."

"It's great seeing you again, Jo-Jo." He doesn't wait for a reply but fires up the loud machine. After a quick wave, he pushes the bike back a few feet then turns it around and slowly drives away.

For the first time in two years, I consider calling my mother. I have more questions now than ever, I'm certain she'll be able to fill in the void. But to call her will be mistaken as me waving a white flag, confusing my need for answers with my need for her, and I've no intention of that happening. I stare out toward where my brother once was and try to process everything that has happened in the last action packed eighteen hours.

Finally.

Finally, I found my brother.

Except I know nothing about this person I was just with, and I'm even less certain there's a place for me in his life. This Will is new and closed off, holding everything tightly to him.

Mosquitos and the need for food force me inside, where I take comfort with frozen lasagna, after which I lounge on my couch, wrapped in my green McRae blanket, and hold Will's book. Through searches on the internet, I find the bookstore where Will is doing his signing and consider popping in to see him in action, to further learn about this familiar stranger. But the vibe I got tells me I'm better off giving him some space. Instead, I investigate the book. There's no author bio or acknowledgment. Only a simple dedication: *To Daanya. Who not only gave me the courage to live again but also showed me how to do it.*

Why would Will need courage to live?

NINE

WHEN WILL CIRCLES the gravel lot outside the hangar, McRae and Zach are standing beside the large hangar opening, talking. McRae gives me a puzzled look and crosses his arms over his chest.

Will comes to a stop several feet away from the pair and leaves the bike idling. After sliding the helmet from my head, I strap it to the backrest.

"Thanks. We should get together soon." Though he showed up at seven-thirty sharp, he's made no attempt at further plans.

"I'll be in touch. It was good to see you."

Panicked that this might be my last time to see him again for another seven years, I take a chance and hug him. He pats my back and pulls away after the shortest moment time has ever created.

I wave and watch as he rides slowly away, a quick flip of his hand goodbye before he turns the corner out of sight.

I will not cry. I will not cry.

Instead, I swing my backpack over my shoulder and focus on the day before me.

"Morning, Josie." Zach says and favors me with a broad smile. "That bike is badass."

"Yes, Zach. It is bad ass." I meet his raised hand, slapping a high five, before switching my attention to tall and delicious. "Morning, McRae. How's your day going so far? Anything interesting planned?" I wink, follow it with a raised brow invitation, before I head toward my desk.

He follows me through the hangar and down the hallway.

"Are you staring at my ass?" I say over my shoulder.

"No."

When I turn to look his eyes are focused on the ceiling. I stop short and brace myself for the collision, but his reflexes are quick and he stops in the nick of time.

I laugh and start walking again.

"Uh, I'd like to review the day with you before I head out for my first lesson." He's repeatedly flipping his phone over in his hand.

"I bet that thing's been quiet," I say before dropping my backpack into the lower desk drawer, and I slide into the seat, booting up the computer. I swivel in my seat to face him.

"Eerily so." He briefly stares at the screen before sliding the phone in his vest breast pocket and meeting my gaze. "About today."

"I've got the day handled. I'm sure you're concerned about the mechanic coming in for an interview. I'll be here to greet him and will get it all set up for you. I'm also fielding three other prospects." Crossing my arms on top of my desk makes my cleavage more apparent. I'm not sure why I'm teasing him, other than because I can. If I were to dig deep into my feelings, my educated guess would be because I can't control anything with Will and that leaves me out of sorts.

"You're late."

"So I'll stay five minutes later."

"You're ten minutes late." He shows me his watch, the same one that left a dent in my back when he had me pressed against the filing cabinet yesterday.

"Your watch needs an adjustment because I'm only five minutes late." I show him mine, a diamond-faced one my parents gifted me when I graduated high school.

"Is this gonna be a habit with you? Coming and going as you please?" His eyes dart to the storage room and back, expressing his message.

"Don't be a douche. I didn't sleep with you so I can come in late or any other perk you may think I'm trying to angle my way into getting. If I'm late, I'll make up the time. I know our schedule, and if there's something super important for me to be here at the ass crack of dawn, I'll be here. Keep our extracurricular activities out of the job." I shift my focus to my computer instead of planting a heel strike to his solar plexus. "I knew you couldn't stick to the rules," I mumble.

I get it's hard for McRae to be outside his box of strict timeliness and no deviations, but I was kinda hoping to sample some more of him. But he's going to have chill the fuck out first if we're going to do it again.

Maybe I can help him do that. Show him how pleasant life can be without his sphincter being slammed shut all the time. It's adorable watching him struggle to find some control.

He shifts awkwardly and I continue to ignore him.

"Where's your car?"

"Getting new tires," I say then turn to him. "Is there something else, Mr. McRae?" I lift a brow.

"No, I think that's all. As long as we're on the same page."

"Mmm. That's doubtful, but the time to continue this discussion has passed. You need to scurry off to your lesson. If you don't hurry, you'll be five minutes late and we're both aware of what kind of message that'll send." I meet his gaze, daring him to a debate.

"Don't forget. I teach at the University today," he says and blinks once.

"It's right here on the calendar." I pull up the program. "The time is highlighted in orange." I return to my stare-down.

"I'll see you this afternoon." He stares back. Not blinking. When I turn away, he's out of the room faster than the speed of light.

I stare at the computer screen and force back the abundance of emotions within me trying to get out. But I'll be damned if I'm going to start blubbering through my days because my brother doesn't want to hang with me twenty-four seven and McRae is a tightly wound dick who did a remarkably good job getting back to business and not falling at my feet.

I don't know how I make it through the day, but I do, and without incident even though I feel shrouded in a weighted cloud that's pressing heavily against me and whispering for me to chuck it all and hit the road. Life is so much easier that way.

McRae's interview walks in ten minutes early.

Unfortunately, Mr. Brown possesses the qualifications this business needs and is willing to do it on a contracted basis. He ogles me without attempting to conceal it whatsoever. Like a buzzard, he circles around my desk, attempting small talk and making my defense radar ping madly.

I text McRae.

Hurry your ass up. I might 86 your interview.

He rushes into the hangar with two minutes to spare. I stand when I see him, breathe a sigh of relief, and move away from the creeper.

McRae rests his briefcase on my desk, having just come from his other job at the University. I can almost see him switching gears as he takes us in.

"Mr. Brown, this is Mr. McRae."

Compared to McRae's brawniness, Brown has the physique of a woman, an old, worn down woman with slumped shoulders and a shuffling gait. His premature balding and bad fake and bake tan only do more insult to his appearance.

"I appreciate your patience and timeliness, Mr. Brown," McRae says and subtly wipes his hand on his cargo pants when Brown turns his attention to me.

"Oh, no problem. I was just getting to know Josie a little better." He winks.

I reach out to grip McRae's briefcase. It's either that or snap the turd's neck.

McRae shoots me a puzzled look, which I return with an eye roll.

"Let's get started." He gestures to his office and waits for Brown to precede him.

"I need to grab a few things and I'll be right with you. Can I get you a drink?" McRae asks him.

I tuck McRae's briefcase under my desk and pull out my backpack.

"You OK?" he asks in a hushed voice and steps closer. "Did he do something?"

"Other than violate women with his presence alone, unfortunately not. Ugh, he's such a perv. If you hire him, there's a one hundred percent chance I'm going to end up kicking him in the junk. There's a seventy-five percent chance I'm going to lay him out on his back after I complete that kick."

"Did he say something to you?" McRae cups my elbow and pulls me closer. "He didn't touch you?"

I shake my head. "He gave me the same old shit guys like him always say. 'Oh, I bet you know how to have fun. I bet you have to beat guys back with a stick. You look friendly.'" I do my best impersonation and McRae chuckles, his thumb rubbing lightly against my elbow.

"I bet he took one look at you and lost the capacity for common sense. You have that affect."

I shake my head. Men are clueless when it comes to their own gender.

"You're going to have to make it work if I hire him."

"You'll be a fool if you do. He's a lazy prick. There has to be better mechanics out there. Every time you get in a plane he's worked on, you'll need to say a prayer." Mimicking, I cross myself like the Catholics do. "Know what I mean?"

I pick up my phone and show him the face. "I'm out of here at four-oh-five. If you're not done with that asshat, make sure the storage room is locked." I push him back because the sensation of his hand on my elbow is making me lose the capacity for common sense. I want to toss him down across my desk and have my wicked way with him.

"Smitty leave?"

"Yeah, he had a class."

He backs up. "Too bad we're not alone." He follows the words up with a look that makes my toes curl.

I wave him off. "Go do your interview."

I'm walking toward the restroom when he calls my name. "You need a ride home?'

"Nope, I'm running. But thanks for the offer."

"Running? To your place?"

"Yes, running. You know that thing you were doing last weekend," I tease.

"But it's far, almost eight miles."

"I'm only running to the garage where I have my car."

"Well, you might as well get a start on it now. That way when I get done here I can rescue you on my way out."

I laugh but it comes out a snort. "If you're that hard up to see me, McRae, you could always text me. Maybe we can find something to do together." I step out of the office space and hurry to change. If he does finish the interview before I leave, I'm not convinced I wouldn't take that ride and then some.

TEN

I'M HALFWAY to the tire shop and struggling with my run. My stride is off, likely because I have nothing to distract me from my thoughts, which go beyond the typical curiosity about people I'm getting to know. There's a neediness to develop something of quality with Will, my easy and trusty friendship with Jayne, and eagerness to see McRae again.

McRae. Mercy, that man.

He walks into a room and my nipples instantly harden, pushing against my clothes as if desperate for him to touch them again. Fuck all. He's good. Our collision of fun in the storage room was amazing and left me wanting a whole shit ton more. Soon, I'll need a distraction from him.

Now that I've found Will, or more, he's found me, I'm paralyzed with indecision. If I move on to another place, will my brother follow? But staying and fooling around with McRae could lead into that complacency I felt with Nick the Marine. I've never dumped someone and stuck around.

Awkward.

Not that McRae and I are dating. Technically, no dumping is required.

I groan with frustration at my erratic thoughts and pick up my pace. My phone, tucked in an armband, vibrates and the telltale chime of a text interrupts my music. I twist my arm and see it's a voice memo from Jayne. *"Total pisser of a day. Gagging for a drink. Want to join me?"*

I rip the phone from the band; continue to run and text my reply. *Hell to the yeah.*

She's quick to respond with another voice memo. *"Where are you? Can you go soon? The quicker I start drinking the better this day will get."*

Laughing at the odd way our conversation is occurring, I slow and come to the end of the sidewalk, where I jog in place and look around to get my bearings.

About four blocks from The Fox, I text, though not before debating whether I should simply call her and have this conversation.

Can you meet me there? she responds.

Now?

Another voice memo. *"Is there a problem with now? I believe I mentioned I wanted to start drinking sooner than later and if I start drinking at the pub my mum will be like, 'Oh love, what's the matter? You know Moira's son, Holland, is still single and a nice lad. He'd make a good husband, Janie-girl, and he's willing to move to America.' I bet he is."* Her voice drops low as if she doesn't want to be overheard. *"He's a DJ. A bloody awful one. I bet he'd like to come here and have me take care of him and his exceedingly large man boobs."* Man boobs?

Laughing, I picture a heavyset guy dressed as a really

bad rapper wannabe. A quick assessment of my status leaves me with clothes to change into but no makeup.

What's the purpose of going out if I can't wear war paint?

I'm running.

There's a long pause. I stop jogging at a crosswalk, watch a few cars go by and the street light change as I wait for Jayne to say something or text something more.

"Running errands or running running? I'm guessing the sort of running one does while wearing exercise shoes. Sod that. Run your arse here and I'll drive you home to change. If I don't get a drink soon I'm going to lose the plot," comes the memo.

I laugh and picture Jayne with her blond hair pulled back into a chignon, her designer clothes, and polished nails. She likes things structured, much like McRae, and the concept of running out in the open and not at a gym baffles her.

On my way. Give me 10, I text back

I tuck the phone back into the armband and take off, my thoughts and questions forgotten and my stride easy and quick.

Jayne is waiting outside her parents' bar by her little sports coupe. When she sees me, she shakes her head. "Why people run for sport is something I'll never understand."

"It feels good. Why people voice memo instead of text is something *I'll* never understand," I say and stretch out my legs before they stiffen up.

"Mmm. Other things feel good. Like sex, eating choco-late, and Jacuzzi. Any of those are perfectly good alternatives to running, and I voice memo because it's hard to text and capture my intonation and the loveliness of my accent."

We carry on two separate conversations with the ease of friends who've known each other years, when in fact the opposite is true.

"But none burn the calories like running does, and when I run I can eat as much chocolate as I like, guilt free. I'll be less judgy about your voice memos from now on. What's up?"

She doesn't look like her usual collected self. She looks distracted and a tad pissed off. Her lips are pulled back as if she's caught a whiff of something rotten and the odor has stuck.

"You remember that guy I was seeing? The one from Atlanta?"

Brad. The every other week shag. I remember her talking about him, so I nod.

"Turns out the wanker is married. With children."

Jayne is not a fan of children. Not that she dislikes them; she just doesn't want to be around them. She's quite proud of her lack of maternal instinct. But I know that's not what's really bothering her. She's not a homewrecker and to be placed in the position, even unknowingly, must have her experiencing fifty shades of rage.

"Seriously? How did you find out?" I stop stretching my calves and give her my full attention.

"His wife came to see me."

"Get the fuck out!"

"She came into the store and at first I thought she was a nutter, acting all dodgy, just walking around and looking at all the people in the shop. She never looked at the clothes. When I asked her if she needed some help, she looked me up and down and said 'I'm Brad's wife'. I'm such a slag. She showed me pictures of them with their kids."

"Did she want to fight or threaten you?" Jayne doesn't strike me as the type to fight back.

"Ha, no. Said he's done this before. Can you believe it? Fucking tosser. Men suck. I called the wankstain and gave him what for."

"Good for you." I can't resist teasing so I say, "I guess your radar for nut jobs only applies to women."

She laughs bitterly and pairs it with an eye roll. "Lucky me, right. Now I'd like to get pissed and toast my good fortune. Imagine being saddled with a bloke like that. We should have all men fully investigated prior to entering into any relationship." She unlocks the car and pulls open her door but doesn't get in.

"Unless your expectation with them is nothing but a good time." McRae's sixpack comes to mind.

She taps her chest. "Case in point. I wasn't looking for long term. I don't like being played or lied to."

"True. Good point. Can you run me by the tire shop to get my car? I had new tires put on."

"Ah, that explains the running." Jayne nods.

I pull the door open but stop when someone calls my name, followed by Jayne's. Over the hood of Jayne's car, our eyes meet.

"Bloody hell," she says then groans.

I look over my shoulder. Pippa runs toward us, waving. I'd met her a few days ago when I came into work and she was helping wait tables.

"Namaste, my lovelies. What are you two going on about?" She clasps her hands together in front of her and does a slight bow.

She's cute as a button, but an annoying one that won't stay fastened, and that's a clear sign she's an oddball. I'm also not sure if her brain has the capacity to power up fully or not. Her blond shoulder-length bob has light lavender streaks that match her cropped yoga pants and cream tunic, and she's always smiling and saying positive things. I want to throat punch her.

"I was just giving Josie a lift home," Jayne says.

"Might I come along?" Her face is smooth with ease; a slight smile plays on her lips. What would it be like to live in her bubble of happiness? Barf.

"Ah, well. We thought we might also get a drink." Jayne looks at me and I know that our party of two just grew. I shrug. After all, it's Jayne's night out. If she can stomach Positive Pippa then that's her call.

"Oh, fabulous. I've been baking with your mum all day. I could use a drink." She steps up to the car and I flip the seat forward to let her crawl in to the cramped backseat. After pulling on her seatbelt, she folds her legs, cross-legged, with one hand, palm up, on each knee. As if she's going to meditate on the way.

Jayne drops me off at the tire shop and follows me to my apartment. They wait while I do a quick shower and change. Jayne says we need loud music, booze, and the opportunity to turn men down, so she's taking me to some place called the Ocean Deck. Under Jayne's fashion wisdom, I wear cut-off jean shorts, a cream-colored, slouchy, loosely woven sweater that has more openings than fabric, and a coral tank underneath. I use my cork wedges to give me height and pull my hair back into a high ponytail. Jayne's in an aquamarine slip dress with beaded flats. Pippa has assumed eagle position and says she's OK with what she's wearing.

"Damn, we look good," I say, hoping to elicit a smile.

"Can you drive a manual?" Jayne asks as we're getting into her coupe.

"Is the Pope Catholic? You planning on getting that drunk?"

Her expression is serious as she backs out of the driveway. "Yes. Just make sure I get home in one piece and alone."

I nod to Pippa.

"Oh, I never learned to drive and I'm shite at saying no," Pippa calls from the back.

"She's right. Worse than shite."

"Wait. A few weeks ago you told me she was your designated driver."

Jayne throws back her head and laughs. "Too right I did. I wanted you to give me more wine and a lift home."

"Well played," I say. "OK. If you're sure you want to let it all hang out."

"I'm more than sure. I open late tomorrow and I need this." She peels out and speeds toward the beachside of the city.

The Ocean Deck is a loud, reggae music bar that opens out to the beach. I love it instantly. All sorts of people pack the place and the tension I felt during my run is gone as Jayne, Pippa, and I hit the bar and then the dance floor. But not before Pippa makes us take a picture of her doing a handstand next to the entrance of the Ocean Deck. I space out two cocktails and Jayne hammers hers back. Pippa drinks water.

The more alcohol that goes down Jayne's gullet, the louder she gets. The band takes a break and the piped-in music is great for dancing, so we don't stop, laughing and bumping hips as we move across the floor. Pippa is in the corner trying to incorporate yoga into her dance moves and that makes us laugh harder.

Still dancing, I lean in toward Jayne. "I'm dying of thirst. Ready for another?"

"Yes, and I think I may need some air." Her dancing has slowed to a floppy, half-assed swaying and there is a green hue to her flushed skin.

"Why don't you go outside and I'll grab you some water." Her chin-length hair has come out of its knot and hangs in waves around her face.

"And a beer."

With a shake of my head I say, "Yes, a beer too." I give her a push to the outside, signal for Pippa to follow, and then go to the bar to order drinks.

Once outside, I find Jayne leaning against a post and Pippa in tree pose. I hand Jayne and Pippa each a water and hold back the beer until Jayne finishes the water.

"That's really cool," the guy next to Pippa says.

"Oh, this? It's nothing. All about balance. But this...this is about strength." She stands, takes a step back, and does a handstand while leaning her butt against the post Jayne's leaning against. She lifts one arm.

"Strength," she repeats. Her top slides down and exposes her midriff.

"Wow, that's awesome." The dude bends down to fist bump her free hand before turning back to his friends.

"Thanks," Pippa says. She flips out of the position and points down the beach to a volleyball game. "Let's go do that."

"I think if I were to move suddenly I might cast up my accounts." Jayne leans her head back against the pole.

"Too much Downton Abbey," Pippa says sotto voce. "She wants to be Mary."

"Shush, Pips," Jayne says; her eyes flutter closed. "I am like Mary. Changing my small corner of the world one outfit at a time." Her lips curl into a slight smile.

"I'm all caught up on Downton," I say. "I've been mainlining Sherlock. Again. This wait for the next season is killing me." I lean against the railing and sip my water.

The phone in my back pocket vibrates and I whip it out.

It's McRae. *Thanks for this awesome online calendar. Used it twice this evening.*

I quickly respond. *UR welcome.*

Is that really why he texted? To thank me? I weigh the merits of waiting for the proposition or making one. "Are you getting a booty call?" Jayne asks.

"Nope, getting a compliment about my work."

"From super-hot pilot guy?"

"Maybe."

"Does he have any friends?" Jayne straightens up coming back to life. She tosses her empty water bottle in the garbage across from us. "Who might go for an arrangement like you have?"

"I don't think he has any friends, except his cell phone."

"And that girl at the bar," Jayne adds.

"Yes, her, but I don't even see how he has time for her. I put together his schedule and aside from the flight school he also teaches at the University, mostly evening classes. The man's a workaholic."

Another text from McRae. *What are you doing?*

"Look," I say and show the screen to Jayne. "He doesn't even use text abbreviations."

She gestures with her chin to the phone. "You're buggering off aren't you? To meet up with him?"

"What? No way. I'm all about this girls' night. Want to go back in and dance?" Miss this moment? Not a chance. This is what I should have done—even occasionally— while in college instead of trying to CLEP courses and outdo my already high marks.

Experiences such as this, well, maybe I should have tried to have them sooner, but I'll take this one right now and enjoy it for everything it's worth.

I text McRae. *Out with friends. U? Working, aren't ya?* This part of the night may be all about us girls, but the later part can be all about McRae in hopefully all his buff glory.

Jayne slides down the pole, coming to rest against her heels. "For future nights out like this I propose we do something either with less movement or alcohol. The combination of the two aren't working for me."

My phone zings in my hand. *Lots to do with Mark out of town.*

Oh brother. This guy needs a Josie intervention. *U+me=sex later?*

Yes.

It's funny how quick his response comes. *I'll text you,* I text back and refocus on Jayne.

"Have you had anything to eat? You're looking a weird shade of…"

"Puce. It doesn't work with your skin tone," chimes Pippa, who flips out of a handstand and stares down at Jayne. "I bet she's had a bag of crisps today and nothing else."

"You know me so well," Jayne says.

I stand and Pippa and I offer Jayne a hand. She takes ours and we haul her up.

"Any good restaurants around here?" I ask.

"I'd actually like to go home," Jayne says. Her hair is loose, sweat-formed strands clumped together, and her lips are devoid of the light pink gloss she favors.

"Home then," Pippa says and points down the beach toward stairs that I presume will lead up to the garage where we left Jayne's car.

It's slow going as Jayne stops to clutch her stomach every few steps.

"She's a baby," Pippa says. "Never could hold her drink. It's the only time she gets impulsive. Jayne lives to be deliberate."

By the time we climb the stairs and make our way to the parking garage Jayne is several feet behind us and moaning.

"Feeling that bad are you?" To give her a chance to catch her breath, I pull myself up to sit on the ledge of the short wall that was designed to keep people from trampling through the bushes.

"I wish I could toss it up already."

"Greasy food will soak it up."

"Ugh." She's still leaning forward; I suppose hoping gravity will assist. "Actually, that sounds good."

Pippa lines up, positioning herself to do another handstand against the wall.

"Fuck all, Pippa, just sit on the wall like a normal person," I say.

Jayne starts laughing and Pippa suppresses a grin. She doesn't sit on the wall but she doesn't do a handstand either.

"Come on," I say. "You can hang your head out the window if you think you might get sick. I know just the thing you need."

After driving through a local burger joint, the massacre

of three cheeseburgers and several orders of large fries, we arrive at Jayne's townhouse. She's caught somewhere between exhausted, too much booze, and a greasy food crash so we help her inside, out of her dress and into her bed. Pippa vanishes into the guest room after blowing me a kiss.

I place a large bowl on Jayne's night table along with a bottle of water and aspirin.

"Thanks, Josie," she mumbles.

"Of course."

"Take my car. I'll get my mum to come and get me tomorrow." Her voice is fading as if sleep is soon to claim her. I hear her breath even out and I click off the lights, leave her keys on the table, and pull out my phone.

Ready? I text McRae.

It's just after midnight on a work night. He's probably crashed out in some very serious pajamas that cover every inch of his body. But the dancing and pulse of the music still hums through me and I have energy that needs to be spent.

ELEVEN

I WAIT what seems like an extraordinarily long time before he replies.

Yeah.

Sleeping? I ask.

Nah. Still Working.

I glance at the time and am willing to bet he was out cold a few minutes ago. *I could use a ride. ;-)*

Seriously?

Yes. I send my location. *If you're hesitating, remember that you want me to be on time tmrw.*

I'll be there in 10.

I wait outside, leaning against the cool, dewy bricks of Jayne's townhouse. A beat-up old pickup rumbles into the parking lot and cruises slowly toward me. It's him, but I look in the passenger window just to make sure.

"Thanks," I say with a smile and slide in before pulling the door closed. "This truck new?" I tease. "Bench seat. Awesome."

McRae is all sleep-tousled and sexy with a simple green

T-shirt stretching across his divine body. He's pulled on worn jeans with a hole that gaps by his knee, so sexy I want to crawl across the seat and sit on his lap.

"This is mine; the other is Mark's company truck. Where's your biker friend's motorcycle?" He nods to the townhouse.

"What?"

"The biker. The guy that dropped you off this morning. This his place?" His hand rests on the shifter, as that's how old this truck is.

I give a short laugh and place my hand on his bicep. "How many guys you think I got on the hook?"

He shrugs.

"You know that bar I work at, the Fox and the Hound? This place belongs to the owners' daughter, Jayne. She and I went out tonight."

After a short pause, he shifts the truck into drive and slowly makes tracks toward our neighborhood. He's not looking at me and is not as excited to see me as I thought he might be.

As I am to see him.

"What's this about?" I flip off my seatbelt and scoot next to him in the space fondly known as riding bitch. "You jealous, McRae?"

"What? Hell no." He stares at the road.

"Mm-hmm. I see. This is about wondering if you're the backup hitter. Relief pitcher."

When he says nothing, I consider a new tactic, uncertain how to traverse these unfamiliar waters. But because my ponytail is too tight, I don't bother trying to use brainpower until I set my hair free, which causes the dull ache in my head to ease. I massage the spot and involuntarily moan. McRae shifts in his seat, adjusting his jeans.

"You want to tell me where we're going?"

I give a few short commands, steering him toward my place. He leaves the engine to idle and stares straight ahead.

I put my hand on his knee, the one exposed from the hole in his jeans.

"You're the only one I'm doing, McRae. Let's be honest, I should say you're the only one I've done because we currently aren't doing anything."

"So you and that biker guy... I mean, I just need to know because I'm not looking to get into a fight with some dude." Finally, he looks at me and I see something I recognize but can't label. Loneliness perhaps?

"There's nothing going on between Will and me. To do so would be punishable in a court of law, besides being completely disgusting. He's my brother."

"Oh. Right. I forgot you mentioned having a brother." He thumbs out a pattern on the steering wheel. "I just now realized I know hardly anything about you."

I turn the key and cut the engine. "Now is just as good a time as any to learn."

He glances around before leaning toward me. "What do you have in mind?"

Wrapping my arms around his neck, I kiss him lightly. He tastes of minty toothpaste, fresh. Nipping at his lower lip, I wrap my hands in his T-shirt and tug him closer.

"Let me show you. I'm an action kinda girl. Less talky-talky, if you know what I mean." I glue my body to his as I kiss my way up his throat and work my way to his mouth, where my initial light kiss gives way to something more fervent.

Eager to take this further, I fumble with the door handle, finally releasing the latch as we pull apart to catch our breath. We nearly tumble out through his door but Brinn's quick reflexes right us.

Taking his hand, I silently lead him up the stairs and into my apartment. The soft kitchen lamp I left on gives the living space a warm and inviting glow, but this is not my preferred destination. Instead, I continue through the laundry room and out the garage entrance, which dumps us in the backyard.

I lead him to the pool and push him into a deck chair. The dewy air around is a mix of salty beach water and the fresh droplets from the river.

"Sit."

Finding the matches on the table by touch alone, I light one hurricane lamp, then another, and finally a third before I come to stand in front of him.

"Jayne and I went to a place called the Ocean Deck and danced most of the night—"

"The Deck," he says.

"I beg your pardon?" I step closer.

"Locals call it the Deck. If you're gonna live here might as well blend in." He snakes out his hand to cup my calf, his thumb stroking the vines and flowers, causing my knees to wobble.

"Good to know. What I was saying is with all that dancing I worked up a good sweat and a refreshing swim would go a long way right now." I lift my sweater over my head and toss it to the ground.

"Right now? You want to swim right now?" he asks while staring at my breasts. "Lord, those are magnificent."

I step closer and stand in the space between his legs. "Can you help me with my bra?"

His gaze makes a leisurely journey from my chest to my face. Without breaking eye contact, he reaches behind me and deftly releases the clasp.

The smoothness of the move catches me off guard so I laugh. McRae's skilled. His lips twitch but go still when he returns his focus to my breasts.

The air is warm, as summer is in full force, yet my nipples gather as soon as his eyes drop to them.

"Jesus. I was going to tell you we shouldn't do this again," he says and bends to take one in his mouth.

"What a stupid idea that is." The quiver in my voice belies my boldness, as one touch from him and I'm pliable, bending to his demands.

"I agree." His head lowers, trailing kisses down my stomach before he dips his tongue in my belly button.

My shiver is joined by a moan as I make quick work unfastening the buttons on my shorts. I step back and he looks up at me with such longing and desire I feel like the center of the universe. After wiggling out of my shorts and underwear, I step back between his legs and straddle him. With our faces nearly touching, I flick out my tongue and lick his lower lip. He cups my rear with one hand and the back of my neck with the other and presses his lips to mine. Our tongues collide and I get lost in the haziness that is McRae and my sheer desire to be with him. To have him touch me. To exist.

It's a kiss that sets the bar and when we pull back, we're breathing heavily and my vision is blurry. I don't want to do it right here.

Correction, I want to do it but not in the small deck chair

when a larger one awaits us on the other side, so I gather what's left of my wits and slide off his lap.

"I'm the luckiest S.O.B in the entire world. Either that or someone has sent you here to torture me." He rakes a hand over his face.

"Come on, McRae." I run my hands down his arms, stopping at his elbows to tug him toward the pool.

"What about your landlord?" He nods to the house.

"You just now thought of that?" I'm not surprised he's having a hard time living in the moment. But it's a good sign it's taken him this long to ask the question.

He shrugs sheepishly. "You're a bit distracting. Chaos."

"I can be quiet if you can." I pull him to his feet.

"We can take this back upstairs. That's your place right?" He tugs me toward my apartment.

"Uh-huh. It's here and it's now." I lift the hem of his T-shirt and with his help pull it over his head in one swift movement.

"I don't know if this is a good idea."

Clearly, I need to amp up the distraction factor. Ironic how I get attracted to a guy who spends most of his time thinking with the wrong head.

"Stop, would you, and just live. Enjoy this moment." I step into the light and gesture for him to come on.

"Are they gun-toting people?"

I shrug.

"'Cause I don't want to be a ninety-year-old man with buckshot embedded in his ass," he says while looking over his shoulder at the house.

"At least you'll have a keepsake from this night."

"Come on, Josie."

"You come on." I'm standing at the edge of the pool and

beckon for him to follow. When he takes a step forward, a sign of his commitment toward tonight, I step back and drop into the water like an arrow plunging downward, smooth and sure. When I surface, I smile and notice he's come to the edge.

"Wait," I say.

"What?" He quickly turns and looks back at the house, positive someone is coming out.

I laugh. "You can't come in until you take your shorts off. Birthday suits only."

With his thumb on his jeans, he pauses, the internal struggle playing across his face.

"Come on, I'm waiting." My voice is throaty from the anticipation. In one swift movement, he strips from his jeans and plunges in the water. After he breaks the surface and shakes water from his eyes with a quick flick of the head, he pierces me with a look full of need and primal lust.

My insides quiver with eagerness as I flow into his arms. No words are required. The neediness in our touch says it all. We entwine ourselves; his large hands support me. I cup his face as we explore each other's mouths, and when we pause, reeling, I rub my thumb down his cheek and trace the path that is normally creased with worry or heavy thought but is now smooth and relaxed.

"You're so high strung," I whisper and wrap my arms around his neck.

"I'm driven," he says, skimming hot kisses up my neck.

I straddle him and nip at his earlobe, which elicits a moan from him so I do it again. His large hands cup my butt, pushing me hard against him. Slowly he walks us to the steps of the pool and rests me against them. When my breasts break the water, he bends his head to take one nipple in his mouth, sucking me in.

Forgotten are my family woes, doubts, and insecurities. The harshness of the world is lost and I wallow in the fuzzy softness we create.

He's pressed against my stomach, so I take him in my hand and begin a gentle stroke.

"Lord, Josie. You're going to undo me."

"Please," I say. "I won't make it much longer." I wrap my legs around his waist and line up all the important parts.

"There's a condom in my jean pocket," he whispers in my ear as I grind against him, kissing the space below his ear.

"Go. Hurry," I whisper with an immediacy I've never experienced. This man, this moment, is all I need but I need it now.

He carries me to the lounger, still pressed against him, and lays me down then snatches up his jeans and fumbles in the pocket for the foil square. It falls out of his hands onto my chest where I whip it up, open it, and with a small gesture ask if I can slip it on. He nods and I roll it down his length, caressing as I go. His eyes briefly drift closed as he moans.

Tightening my arms around his neck, I rub against him.

"Now," I whisper.

His hands hold my hips, bringing them forward, and in one swift movement he slides in me.

"Yes," I cry and arch toward him. "Yes, please."

His moan unravels me and we love each other hard and fast. I come apart in his hands and he wraps me in his arms, holding me together. When every possible surface of my body is touching his, he shift gears and strokes me with a slow ease. Just when I think I'm satiated, I become consumed with an incredible thirst for more.

With him, I'm lost and found.

I rise to meet him and push back. Where he once led, I now take over, whispering demands as our bodies move in unity, his hands doing my bidding. My sole purpose to give him what he's given me. When he draws close, I take him over the edge, hold on tightly, and we free-fall together.

TWELVE

MY LEFT LEG is entwined with McRae's right one as we lie on our backs struggling to catch our breaths.

"That wasn't much of a swim," he says.

"No, it wasn't. I got distracted." I turn to him. He's smiling. His face is soft with satisfaction and his eyes are closed. For a guy who is singularly focused on his goals and little else, when no demands are present other than achieving pleasure, he's quick to let his guard down. His ability to give unselfishly seems less about being an eager beaver desperate to please, and more about a hunger for closeness and the deep, soul-satisfying gratification he feels when that happens.

"Give me about ten minutes and I'll distract you some more." He strokes my leg, rolls toward me, and opens his eyes. My leg slides down his and I rest, half under him. He's incredible to look at, yet, with all the definition of his body, there's something soft in his touch and the way he presses his form to mine.

"If I could feel the bones in my body I'd go for a swim while you gather up your energy, but it appears I have the consistency of a noodle." I pick up my hand and let it flop on my stomach.

"I aim to please." He throws my words at me and we laugh.

He's beyond handsome with his straight nose and square chin. He keeps his hair short but it's grown since we met, long enough that I can tell it has a natural wave. His right incisor is turned slightly inward and I'm guessing he never had braces, not that he needs them. It lends character. I remember how crazy my mom was about our smiles, making us use whiteners. Her version of character was perfection. Next to McRae, I'd feel artificial—if I was the old Josie.

"You sounded pleased, I like it. It's a miracle we didn't wake your landlords," he says.

His five o'clock shadow's thick and it scratches my palm as I caress his cheek.

"She's out of town. There's no one home."

In a flash, he's up one elbow. "What? You coulda told me that in the beginning. I kept worrying that at any time someone was gonna come out."

"I think there might have been a moment when you were thinking of something else." I run my hand downward, tracing his outline from shoulder to waist. "That's why I didn't tell you. Adds to the excitement, don't you think?"

McRae's lips curl into a smirk. "I've enough excitement every day. I'm a pilot, remember? I get into the cockpit with teens who lack focus."

"True, but I bet you're so good at that you could handle an emergency with your eyes closed. This was taking a chance not knowing whether you're in control or not. I bet you don't do that often."

"I bet you do that all the time." Strands of my hair stick together in wet clumps and cling to my breast. He gathers them up and holds them in his palm.

"I used to not. That's why I move around a lot. My days used to be predictable and uneventful." My how they've changed.

"Where're you from originally? You never did tell me that."

"I didn't? Imagine that." I laugh. I generally don't like talking about my life before I split, but I can't get my brain to focus and opening up to McRae feels easy, natural. "Connecticut. My parents and younger brother are there."

"And the brother here is older or younger?"

"Older. He's in Gainesville actually. Where are you from?" Knowing I can answer the question about Will makes me smile.

"Good old Daytona Beach. I've lived in some part of Volusia County my entire life and have only ventured out for work. I used to think about joining the Navy or Air Force but that was never really possible." He says this while weaving my hair through his fingers, a gesture thick with intimacy and familiarity and I find myself leaning closer to him.

"Why not?" There's a faraway look in his eyes, as if the ghosts of his past still cling. I wonder if I look the same when I talk about home.

"That's a story for another day. From Connecticut, but I met you in South Carolina and your hotel badge said Washington. You're now in Florida. You get around. And with very little baggage." He lifts a brow.

"I've been trying to find my brother." I slide my hand through the opening between his head and arms and cup the back of his head, stroking it gently with my thumb.

"The one here?"

"Yeah. It's a long story too. Maybe better for another time." Our shoulders are touching.

"Summarize it for me." He picks up another strand of hair, adding it the bundle he has and continues to twist.

"Only if you summarize yours for me. You go first," I volley.

He goes still and looks down at the strands of hair in his hand. "My mom was an addict and drugs got the best of her when I was thirteen. Vann was eight. After some time in foster care, we landed at our grandmother's house, her mother, and she did most of her parenting with a belt."

I try not to flinch or do the typical girl coo of pity. It would be insulting to him. Instead I burrow between his side and the mat, pressing my length to his, using touch to express that he's wanted. I now understand why letting go and trusting others is so difficult. How often has that worked out for him?

"So you stayed because of your brother."

"Yeah, our grandmother passed when I was twenty, and I petitioned the courts for custody and won."

"Impressive."

His eyes meet mine and hold. The brief glimpse of his deep pain leaves me aching. At twenty, I was given a brand spanking new BMW Coupe and keys to my own apartment because I'd finished my first year of law school top of my class.

"I'm sure it had more to do with too many kids already in

the system and, unintentional, I'm sure, the gift of inheriting my grandma's house."

He's partly right with his assessment. I'd seen the stats of cases similar to this in law school. The odds were in his favor because of the overtaxed system, but he still had to prove he was capable and reliable. Obviously he succeeded.

"Your turn," he says and begins to twist my hair again.

"Will and I were always really close." I shake my head, belying my words. "That's an understatement, we were inseparable. My grandfather used to caution us about it. Encourage us to have different interests. But that never made any sense to me. He was my brother. What could be wrong with having so much in common with my sibling? Then a few weeks after he started..." If I say law school, it will create a series of further questions I'm not ready to answer. "His graduate studies, he had a car accident that changed every-thing. A day after he was discharged from the hospital, he was gone. Disappeared off the face of the earth."

"Just like that." His hand stops twisting.

"Overnight." When he looks at me there's only curiosity, and the lack of pity makes me feel comfortable enough to continue. "I tried calling and sending texts. About six months after he walked out, I get an email saying he's OK but to leave him alone. Nothing else for another year and half."

"And you've been searching for him ever since?"

I shake my head. "No, only the last two years."

He stares at me, surprised. "My brother is my only family. If he were to just disappear I don't think I could ever stop looking."

A spark of anger flares inside me and I swat him on the back of the head and come up on one elbow.

"Hey," he cries.

"You would if he'd sent you emails telling you to leave him alone. You would if he said he needed space, if you thought he didn't want anything to do with you anymore. I was seventeen when he left. Grieving for a loss so sudden it left me reeling. It may have taken me a while but I finally got it together." I pour my secrets out in one breath, wishing I could suck them back in with a deep inhalation.

I'm so ashamed I waited and went through the motions of life, stuck in the world's longest pity party. But I can't undo that. I have to keep trying to find a way to live with it. Unfortunately, finding Will didn't provide instant healing.

Brinn bends and places a light kiss on my forehead. "You've found him now. Yet, don't you plan on leaving?"

I shrug. "I don't know what to do," I whisper.

"Maybe you shouldn't fight it. Overanalyze it."

"Who says I am?" I'm unsuccessful keeping the defensiveness out of my tone.

"OK, maybe you're not." He smiles that adorable crooked grin and caresses my cheek with his thumb. "But if you were, maybe letting things happen naturally would get you the results you're wanting."

"Says the over-planner."

"I didn't plan this," he says and moves his thumb to stroke the side of my breast, bring my body into a humming state. Although I'm not sure it ever stopped humming. I've heard people talk about amazing sex, about climbing to a high place and losing themselves, and I've never felt that before. Until now, yet it's different. I don't lose myself when Brinn touches me, when our bodies come together. Instead, I find myself. As if all the edges line up and I become seamless.

"Does it hurt to have this done?" He places the strands of hair across my breast and moves his hand to caress the art on my hip. He traces it across my stomach, below my navel, and stretches his fingers to stroke downward.

"No, not at all. It can be a pain waiting for it to dry." I suck in a breath when his hand slips between my legs.

"Inking it must take hours." His voice lowers. Even at a whisper it's rough and deep and turns me on.

"Mmm. I've been lucky and found women who are deft and have been doing it a long time. They do the bigger pieces. I do the smaller ones." Warmth builds within me, starting from my center, and spreads outward. I wouldn't have described myself as insatiable. Willing, yes. But insatiable? Not until now. Lust is a motherfucker. If I don't watch it, I'll certainly become addicted to this guy and the feelings he gives me.

"You do it?" His gaze travels the length of my artwork.

"You do know it's henna, right? They aren't tattoos." His eyes come back to mine, and clearly he's surprised. "That's why this one is fading." I turn my leg slightly inward to show him the ones on my calf. The glow of the hurricane lamp doesn't cast enough light to show that the dark stain has faded to a lighter brown.

"Henna? I never even considered that." He moves his hand from between my thighs, runs it down my calf and then up again. He slides his hand up to my hip and turns me so I lay on my stomach. I cross my arms over each other, resting my cheek on them.

"It's beautiful work. Why the vines and leaves?" His fingers touch my calves and ankles and I tremble beneath them.

"They mean perseverance. A reminder for me to stay on my journey until I have achieved all that I can."

"And the flower on your lower abdomen?"

"That's for the light within. Once I started this journey, I really started to figure out what it is I want from life and who I am. It's still a process though." I give a small laugh.

"I think you're... Damn. I can't imagine you getting any better."

I come off my stomach and angle so my body is facing his. He moves his hand to rest on my hip. "That's sweet of you to say, but you're only looking at the outside."

"Yeah, the outside is spectacular. But I'm talking about what I know so far. Watching you stand up for yourself and flipping that guy in the bar, how you can walk into any room and own it. You just pack up and move. Some days, I hate this town because I'm stuck here and my plane is just a bungee cord that lets me go only so far. Other days I don't know if I'd live anywhere else."

I bite my lip, turning his words over in my head, "I think everyone feels like that. I know I did. That's part of why I'm here, right now."

"I keep telling myself that whatever it is I want to achieve can be done anywhere, so why not here? That this is where I'm supposed to be."

"Running an aviation school?"

"Owning it one day."

"With a jackass mechanic at your side," I tease.

"Nah, I didn't hire him. You called it right. He's an asshat. That's not a problem I want in a business I plan to buy. You keep sprucing up the place and Mark might never sell it to me. His kid might see it as easy money; you've done such an incredible job." His eyes meet mine and we pause, searching.

I have a million questions but there's a guarded look in his eyes, one that speaks of sadness, and I know the time isn't right to probe. I'm guessing he'll probably regret what he's shared with me already once the sun comes up. But the sun isn't up and his finger is making lazy circles on my hip. I reach behind me to find my shorts.

"What are you doing?" he asks. I've flipped onto my back and am patting the ground while I smile at him. I find what I'm seeking, and I tuck it into my palm and then come back onto my side, facing him.

"I'm doing this." I kiss him, slowly at first, enjoying the softness of his lips against mine. But the pull of him hooks me and I struggle to pace myself.

He pushes against my hip, forcing me to lie back, his fingers teasing the lotus flower henna on my lower stomach. "I don't have another condom." He slips his fingers between my legs to gently rub my sweet spot.

"OK, we can just do this," I say between pants.

I reach for him, pulling his head to me, and kiss him with all the heat inside me. It's amazing and terrifying how quickly his touch lights me up and there's no way I'll be fulfilled with this level of play. When it comes to McRae, I want to go all the way, every time.

"Wait," I say, as I lay in his arm, quivering, ready to lose myself in his touch. "If this isn't enough, we can always use this." I show him the condom I've palmed. The one I stuck in my pocket right after I called him.

"Thank God." He rests his forehead against mine. "It was going to be torture."

"Torture, hmm. I may know a few things to ease that." I wrap my arms around him, pressing myself into his hand.

We explore each other's body, learning more with each touch. We taste, nip, and suck without reservations. When he eases into me, our eyes meet and hold until our pleasure explodes in cascades of satisfaction. It takes me to a place I've never been before and I'm humbled.

THIRTEEN

IT'S a slow night at the bar. To keep myself from perseverating on the lack of contact with Will, I troll the web. My job at Alliance Aviation will be ending soon, as is my lease, but before I can decide on what direction to take I need to know all the options.

"You going on a cruise?" Jayne asks from over my shoulder.

I turn to face her, placing my phone on the counter. "Looking at jobs. They're hiring for their Mediterranean line. I was thinking of applying. I'm fluent in French so the other Latin-based languages should be a piece of cake."

"Calling it quits so soon?"

I shake my head. "Just figuring out a contingency plan."

"Because staying isn't an option." She's without her standard bar accessories, her ledgers. "Pour me a Riesling, please."

"Why stay if Will doesn't want me to?" I do as she requests and lean against the bar to continue the conversation.

"Because you like it here. You have friends here."

"I'm too young to settle. There's so much life out there to live." I fill a glass with ice and water for myself, wishing I'd ended this conversation.

Jayne snorts. "Is that what you think the rest of us are doing?"

"If I wanted to have a nine to five career, a steady, and whatever else it is everyone wants I could have stayed home."

"You could be anything you wanted at home?"

I shake my head. "No, at home I was expected to be a lawyer. Family business and all that."

"But you can have everything you want here. Or the last place you stayed. Yet, you keep moving on." She sits back in her chair and sips her wine with an annoyingly know-it-all expression.

"Because I was looking for Will." I place my hand on my hip.

"You've found him, but you're still planning your escape. Why?" She crosses her legs and if possible reclines even further in the chair, leveling me with a stare.

"Why not?" I grab a wet bar rag and begin wiping down the counter, avoiding her gaze.

"You say you want to know your brother again, but how can that be done when you're in some foreign port? Through emails? Texts? How'd that work for you before?"

"Where are you going with all this?" Frustrated, I slap the rag against the sink. "Do you know how hard it will be for me to live close to Will knowing he wants nothing to do with me?" If I could drink on the job, I think I would.

"Is it going to be easier in some place like Spain? At least here you'd be close enough should he change his mind."

I consider her words while running my sweaty palms down my jean skirt. "It would be really hard," I whisper.

"Some of the most rewarding experiences we have follow a really difficult journey. Pippa would say you have to be open to them, worthy of them."

Worthy? If I wasn't worthy enough for Will to allow me to help after his accident, why would I be now?

"Just think about it. For me. I'd really like you to stay. And I'd really like this topped off," she says, tipping her glass toward me.

"I'll need distraction," I say while reaching for the wine bottle. "Keeping busy is keeping me sane."

She laughs and does such a severe eye roll I'm surprised they don't pop out. "Yes, darling. Tell me about it. Good thing there's lots to distract around here. In the spring, we can hit up towns that host your American baseball players. Maybe run some of those bases." She wags her brows.

I laugh. "And there's the beach."

"Manatees to swim with, Bike Week, short trips to the Panhandle for getaways. Wild horses on—"

"You sound like an advert for Florida." The tension eases from my body.

She shrugs. "I could have opened my shop back in the UK. I've plenty of family there, but I like it here. My important family is here. The people I want to see all the time."

Of all my family members, Will is the only one I'd like to see all the time. Even this new, strange-to-me Will.

"Speaking of distractions, here comes a lovely one. Enjoy it." She winks and slips off the bar chair. "I think I'll go give mum a hug."

McRae is coming toward me. His dark jeans are low slung and show off his narrow waist and powerful thighs nicely. It takes a lot for me not to drool. My mood instantly lightens when he slides into the chair Jayne just vacated.

"What brings you in, McRae?" I don't bother to contain my smile.

"I wanted to bring you this." He reaches into his back pocket and produces a folded square that he hands to me.

It's my paycheck. "You know most companies are automated. It's easy to do. I can look into it for Mark."

He sighs and sits angled in the chair, one hand on his upper thigh. "Tell me about it. I've been trying to get Mark to automate for over a year. It'll be one of the first things I change when I buy in."

"If," I gently poke.

The waiting and dancing Mark's had him do drives McRae nuts. He tries to hide it but I'm getting to know him well enough to pick out the signs. Like a clenched jaw and loaded sighs. I get why he stays out of the office. If I had to go to the place where my goals weren't being actualized every day, I wouldn't be nearly as nice as he is. The man's resolve is steely.

"When," he says with determination. "It's only a matter of time." Who's he trying to convince, him or me?

"You staying?" I take the receipt and cash from the guy sitting next to him and throw the change into an oversized tip jar.

"I thought I'd have a drink."

"Giving this whole 'relaxing' thing a try?" I tease and hand him a menu.

"If this doesn't work, I hear there are other 'ways.'" He does air quotes and smiles.

"Hmm, I may know something about those 'other methods' but will they be enough to help you forget about all those papers on your desk? Or that PhD program you need to apply for?"

"If what I'm told is true, I should just skip right to that." His mouth lifts in that adorable crooked smile of his and he tries to hand back the menu. "I don't need this. I'll just have a Guinness. On tap."

I push it back. "I'm guessing you haven't had anything to eat since you had lunch at eleven. Am I wrong?" I place the Guinness before him. He laughs, shakes his head, and opens the menu.

A scrawny, pasty white kid with a rash of bad acne takes the seat next to Brinn. Not a chance he's anywhere near the legal drinking age.

"And what can I get for you, sir?" I know what's coming.

The kid clears his voice and gestures to McRae's beer. "I'll have what he's having."

"All right. Let's see your ID." Out of the side of my mouth, I say to McRae, "This oughta be good."

"You didn't ask him for his ID," the kid says, gesturing to Brinn.

"OK, that's fair." I hold out my hand. "Let's see it, McRae. Hand over your ID."

McRae puts the menu down, turns to face the kid, and while pulling out his wallet says, "I think I recognize you. We graduate together?" His expression is deadpan.

The kid sputters. "I may have been a few years behind you."

I stifle a laugh and indicate with my head a group of boys who appear to be the same age intently watching their friend.

I show McRae's license to the teen. "You see that? That's the year, and when I do basic math it tells me this guy here is twenty-seven. Oh, but lookie here." A bubble of an idea pops in my head. "It seems McRae here will be twenty-eight tomorrow. Happy birthday, drinks on me."

He ducks his head.

"Now, let's see yours," I say to the kid.

He sighs heavily, pulls out a license, and slowly hands it over. I scan it before turning back to him.

"Listen, I can appreciate a fake ID like the rest of them but this one is poorly done. It says you're Hispanic and thirty. If you're going to invest in an ID, at least try to make it as authentic as possible." I hope to ease my words with a gentle smile. "You should also know that if I serve you and the police catch me it's a second degree misdemeanor. Not only could I go to jail for a year, but I'd have to pay a fee that I don't have. You willing to loan me a couple grand? That doesn't include what the owners of this place will incur. So I suggest if you want to drink you fly to Europe where the drinking age is much lower. Now, I get that your friends are watching and I'm sorry, but high five for trying." I hold up a hand and slowly he reaches out and slaps his to mine.

"Here's what I'm gonna do for you. I'm gonna bring your table some appetizers, on me, and a few virgin drinks. How does that ease the pain?"

The kid shrugs before he smiles and nods. "That sounds OK."

"Great, but don't you tell anyone I did this for you or I'll have kids from everywhere coming in trying to mooch off me. Now scram. Get out of the bar area and get back into the restaurant part." I shoo him off the stool. "Wait," I call when he takes a step away. "Tell McRae here happy birthday."

"Happy birthday," he mumbles before slinking off. He

gives his friends a shrug, but I suppose the mention of free food is what has them high fiving.

"That was nice of you," McRae says.

"Ha. Poor kid. He's got balls for trying." I cut the ID into tiny confetti pieces.

"Remind you of your teenage days?"

I snort. "No, I was too focused on school and college."

"College? At sixteen?" McRae pauses with his mug halfway to his mouth.

I lean across the bar and come in close. "You may know where my sweet spots are, McRae, but there're other things you don't know about me. Like how I finished high school with two years of college already complete."

"Impressive, and yet I'm not surprised. You try to come off as nearly homeless with your four bags of luggage, yet you can create a spreadsheet in five minutes flat. You act like nothing bothers you, yet your voice breaks every time you talk about your brother. You face off men bigger and stronger than you without blinking and always come out on top."

What's with everyone analyzing me tonight? I turn to clear a spot and hide my embarrassment. I hadn't realized he was paying that close of attention. When I turn back, he's staring at me, the menu on the counter.

"So have you decided what it is you want?"

"Besides you?"

"I meant to eat."

"So did I."

The heat around us shoots up a thousand degrees.

"I get off really late."

"It'll be my birthday then."

I move closer with only the wood counter between us.

"What about vanilla scoop over there? She's been eyeing you since you sat down." I look over his shoulder and lift a brow.

He turns in the direction, gives her a wave, and then faces me. "That's Laura. We aren't dating."

"I didn't ask." I pour him a new draft to help feign my nonchalance.

"Yes, you did." He leans one arm on the counter and smirks.

"It's none of my business what you do outside of our time. That's part of the deal."

He's wrapped his large hand around the mug and is rubbing his thumb over the rim. I can't stop staring.

"I agree. It's none of your business. But if you wanted to know I'd tell you."

"What you want with Ms. Uptight Sweater I'll never understand. She's not your type."

"Given this some thought, have you?" He levels me with a stare.

"No, of course not. I made that assessment just now."

"Because she's wearing a sweater, she's not my type?"

"Because her nails are perfect, her clothes high end, and her friends look just like her. She's high maintenance, and you do not do high maintenance. There's no time in your life for it."

"Right now. Once I get into an ownership position, everything changes. I'd like to settle down one day. Maybe have some kids. You don't think Laura looks like the type to do that?" He shakes his head in confusion. "Point out a girl who does and I'll go intro myself right now."

The glimmer in his eye is a first and it dawns on me that he's teasing.

I respond by throwing a bar towel at his face. "Fine, she's

perfect for you. You can do the missionary position the rest of your life and only kiss with tongue when either of you've had too much to drink. Are you ordering food or not?"

"I'll get the fish and chips." He throws the towel back and laughs. "Is that why you called her vanilla scoop?"

I catch it with one hand and flip it over my shoulder. "Among other reasons."

Brinn laughs and sits back in his chair, rubbing his hands together. "But think of all the ways vanilla can be spiced up. It's the most versatile. Unlike flavors like rocky road. What can you do with rocky road? It's pretty limited."

"You're a pig." I swipe his half-empty mug and dump the contents in the sink to emphasize my disgust.

McRae tosses his head back and produces a deep, hearty laugh. "But you don't care or anything."

He's right, and I can't decide whom I'm more disgusted by, him or me. What do I care if he sees forever with country club type girl? Now I can't seem to abide by the rules I put in place.

He reaches across the counter and snakes my arm as I'm trying to walk away.

"Her brother is a college buddy of mine serving overseas. I told him I'd keep an eye on her and keep my brother away from her."

I stop and face him. "Vann's into her?"

He lets go, nods, and sits back down. "And she's into him. You're hot when you're jealous. Like hotter than normal hot."

"I'm taking my break right now. Sometimes I like to step outside and take in the fresh air."

He sits up straighter. "What about my food."

"Seriously?" I cross my arms.

"Yeah, now you got me all worked up to eat. Food is all I can think about."

If his lips hadn't twitched, I'd have had a hard time sussing out the truth. He has a clever mind. "It'll hold."

I walk from behind the bar and beeline straight for the back exit. I don't have to look behind me because the current radiating through my sensory system tells me he's a few steps behind.

As soon as I step outside, I'm pushed against the wall, McRae's body suddenly flush against mine. The exit door bangs closed but neither of us jumps. He lowers his head.

"What flavor am I?" I tilt my head to the side, exposing the area of my neck he's kissing, and lift my legs to wrap them around his waist. Thank heavens I'm wearing frayed jean shorts and not some confining skirt.

"You're every flavor. You smell like fresh oranges and sweet mint, and I can't go by an orange grove without getting a hard-on."

I wrap my arms around his neck and grind against him. "Happy early birthday."

"Best birthday ever," he says, pressing his lips at the top of the valley of my breasts.

What kinds of birthdays did he have? Did his mom remember or had she been too high to care?

"What's your best birthday memory?" I ask.

He stops blazing a trail of kisses across my chest and lifts his head. He looks at a spot over my shoulder and I try to quiet my lingering pants.

"No one's ever asked that before." He swings his gaze to mine.

"I'm guessing you don't have many stories of themed parties or get away birthday trips?"

"Birthdays were never a big deal in our house. There was this one year, we were just kids, but Vann and I spent it at the beach. I'd earned enough from mowing yards that I treated us to a day out. When we came home our mom was out for the rest of the night, so we watched movies until the late hours and ate junk food all night."

"And tomorrow?"

"Vann's working and I'll probably get caught up on a few things. But I got this going for me right now. How long's your break?"

"Only long enough to leave us both unsatisfied." I arch my hips to grind again.

"I'll take what I can get." He slips his hand up my thigh between my shorts and presses me to him as he crushes his mouth against mine.

WITH JAYNE'S HELP, I devise a plan.

My alarm goes off at seven and I want to throat punch it. Then I remember what I intend to accomplish today, so I drag my lazy ass from bed and stretch with some of my favorite yoga moves before I shower. I leave my hair loose and add a few curls before I pull the sides up. I dress in long white board shorts, a gray peasant shirt with aquamarine embroidery, and accessorize with aquamarine mules and a bracelet, all items Jayne's talked me into on a shopping spree. At this rate, I'll need another suitcase when it's time for me to bail.

The drive to McRae's is quick and I'm walking to the door when his brother comes out, sees me, and does a double take.

"Your brother in?" I ask.

Vann's wearing the uniform for the local electronics store and the moment for me to back out is gone. What I've planned for McRae negates the premise of booty calls and no-strings, but I want to do it for him more than I want to make sure we don't cross some self-imposed line. I want to leave him with a good memory of me, one that's more than us having sex.

"Uh, yeah. He's still asleep," he says, nodding to the house. "I'll just—"

"No, I got it." I flash him a smile and walk in.

It's exactly like I thought it would be. A large-screen TV hangs from the center wall, flanked by older furniture that's worn but clean. Wood floors appear to run throughout the house and floral curtains hang from the windows, clearly placed there by a woman who gave a shit. The place is small so it doesn't take me but a second to find his room.

He's sprawled on his back. The sheet barely covers his legs and I want to eat him up. His chest is toned and broad and though I've run my hands over his body before, it's an entirely new sensation to see him like this. The desire I have for him is palpable and insane. I've never experienced a wave of this magnitude every single stinking time I've looked at someone like I do when I look at McRae.

I must be losing my mind.

I ease onto the bed and he doesn't wake. The steady rise and fall of his chest speaks to how deep his sleep is. His mouth's slightly open but he's not snoring. What is it about this guy who works crazy hours, eats fish and chips with his fingers, and has no plans for his birthday? This guy whose lips are soft even when he's out of control, whose touch makes me see the light, and who no one ever made a big deal about the day he entered the world?

Until now.

I straddle him and plop down. He comes awake with an *oomph* and grabs my hips.

"Holy shit. You trying to kill me?"

"Wakey wakey. Time to start your birthday celebration." I run my hands across his shoulders, enjoying the feel of the dips and curves of his muscles.

He stretches beneath me, his pelvis rubbing against my girly parts, and I nearly come undone. He tucks his hands behind his head and his bemused, sleepy expression is adorable.

"Please tell me you came here to get naked. Because you keep that up, I'm pretty sure shouting out each other's names will be in our future."

"Ooh, predicting the future. That must be a sign." I tickle my fingers down his pecs and bite my lip. Maybe I should go stand outside the door and yell across the space to get him moving because scrapping my idea and staying in bed with him is starting to sound like the best idea of all.

"What are you talking about?" He circles my waist with his hands, his thumbs at my ribs.

"I'm talking about what I have planned for your birthday. You need to get up and get dressed."

"Isn't this crossing some line we aren't supposed to cross? Aren't we supposed to just have sex?" His face is serious even though he's trying to convince me by his tone that's he's teasing.

It's heartening to know that's he's got some unanswered questions like I do. Saying we were just going to have sex to burn up this chemistry was fine, in theory, but it's unavoidable that we'd experience overflow. Like a potential friendship.

And the chemistry?

Holy shit. It's just gotten hotter.

"It's natural, us becoming friends. Honestly, who could

just have sex and have nothing further evolve? Don't answer that," I say and point to him.

"Friends, huh?" His lips twitch. "So maybe we're more friends with benefits than having no strings attached?"

"Does it matter what we call it? We're having sex. We're trying to burn off this chemistry between us so that we can co-exist without the distraction—"

"Yeah, look how that's working out."

Our eyes meet and we laugh. "Let's not make it anything more than what it is today. I don't expect you to call me or take me to dinner or to only see me. I hope you feel the same way."

"But do you want me to take you to dinner?" he asks, seeking further confirmation.

"I don't expect you to date me. If we end up having dinner, great. For now, what I do want is for you to get your ass moving so we can celebrate your birthday." I swat at his shoulder.

"Yes, ma'am," he says and does the fastest gator roll I've ever experienced. One moment I'm straddling him and the next he's above me, the sheets tangled between us, his body pressing down on mine. I want to chuck all plans out the window and strip him naked. I want to feel his hands on me, his gentle yet eager caress.

I take in a shaky breath. "You better go soon or we might never leave this room," I whisper.

"That's every man's favorite gift." He dips his head and nuzzles my neck before placing a soft, moist kiss under my jawline next to my ear.

"Well, you'll just have to wait for that part of the birthday present. But have no fear, it's part of the plan."

"Score," he whispers and kisses my neck again.

"Go," I say, bundling up my energy and attempting to channel it into staying the course. "Go shower or we'll be late. Go." I push him off and it takes more resolve than I thought I'd ever need. With him, I'm more in my skin than I have been since I left Connecticut.

He grumbles as he shuffles out of his room and down the hall. I lie in the warm spot he vacated and listen to him going through the motions of getting ready. The shower goes on and I laugh when he begins to whistle, pausing, I presume, when he puts his face under the stream.

Resting my head on one arm, I go over my agenda for the day. It makes me feel like a giddy teen, but I drink in the smell of his simple light blue sheets. Brinn—funny, when did I stop thinking of him as the hulky, hot, good-for-a-one-off McRae?—smells like clean air—fresh and free with a hint of starched linen—and his room is just as crisp. His large bed is centered in the space with one dresser on the wall across from his bed. One night table to the right of his bed and a simple wood desk with three side drawers that looks like it's long past its prime is tucked in the corner. There are no extras. No books stacked along the wall, falling over. No half-full cups left on the tables. His coins are in a bowl, his keys next to that. His diplomas, undergraduate and graduate, hang over his desk and only one picture stands in a frame on the night table.

I roll over, stretch, and reach it. It's Brinn and his brother when they were kids. He couldn't have been more than fourteen and Vann even younger. They aren't smiling but sitting close on old worn suitcases, Brinn's arm around Vann. Their clothes are faded and well used, their pants too short, their tennis shoes coming apart at the seams. They look unkempt and I want to cry. I want to brush back this boy's long hair, pushing it from his eyes. I want to wrap my arms around him in a hug and never let go. This boy, this man who thinks birthdays are no big deal. This peek into his childhood changes me instantly. There's something in his eyes I recognize, and I'm willing to bet it's loneliness we share.

I no longer only want to jump his bones every other minute, but now I want to make him laugh and show him how to live life a little differently. It's not pity because there's nothing pitiful about him. But when you've grown up having everything, you've clearly got enough to share. And boy do I want to share with him.

I place the picture back on the nightstand and quickly jump from the bed. From the hallway I can look into the bathroom and Brinn is standing there, towel around his waist, shaving. His skin is tan and I flash back to when I watched him swim in the ocean.

The memory causes my stomach to flutter and my toes curl.

He bangs the razor against the sink, turns toward me, and our eyes meet. Brinn winks, drops the razor in the sink before resting one hand on the overhead doorjamb.

"Are you sure you don't want to keep the party here? Vann's out for the day." His other hand goes to his towel, gripping the fold, fingers teasing their readiness to let it go and drop.

I cover my eyes with one hand and reach out to feel the wall with the other. "Stop it. I'll not look therefore I'll not be tempted. Get dressed so we can leave already."

I feel my way along the wall, but before I can skirt around the corner he steps up next to me. I know he's there because my body tightens with need. It's as if we're on a pulley system that reels me in once we get within a certain distance from each other. I smell his shave cream, sandalwood, and it reminds me of how he tastes. I moan, push away from him, and run out of the hallway into the living room all while he laughs behind me.

"Keep laughing and I'll take the after party off the table," I call over my shoulder.

"You're a cruel woman, Josie Woodmere," he says and I hear drawers opening and banging closed. Hearing my name from his mouth gives me a warm fuzzy. That's how stinking hard up I am for this guy.

In the living room, I busy myself with looking at the other two photos of him and Vann. They look current. One is of Brinn graduating college.

Brinn comes around the corner dressed in tan cargo shorts, a solid navy button-down shirt. He's tucking his wallet into his back pocket when I push him out of the house. It's either that or strip him naked in his living room. Something as simple as watching him be all manly makes me lose my mind for him.

"Hurry or I might change my mind." I wait impatiently for him to lock the door.

"Hmm, such a dilemma." He smiles and turns the key slowly. A sporadic hum comes from his back pocket.

"Is that your phone?" I reach in and whisk it out before he can stop me. A glance at the screen confirms my suspicion. "I can't believe you forwarded the calls from the shop. I thought we'd kicked that habit." He reaches for the phone but I tuck it behind my back and step away.

"It's in case—"

"Of nothing. The only people calling are to cancel or schedule and they can do that during business hours or leave a message. That's how this works. Being at the beck and call of the shop is not going to make Mark sell it to you any sooner. Why would he? You do everything already and he takes the largest cut." I hadn't meant to bring up work frustrations on his birthday but it's hard watching him bust his hump so much—and for what?

"Hey, Mark gave me my first chance. Mark's the one who taught a young boy to dream and look at where I am now." He tucks his key into his pocket while holding out his palm, assuming I'll give the phone back.

"Ok, I'm sorry about trashing Mark. But it's your birthday and I want you to forget about the everyday stuff and just enjoy today, this moment." I play with a button on his shirt, ignoring his extended hand. "Let me keep the phone. I promise you won't miss anything."

"OK," he says without hesitation.

"Wow." I search his face, not moving an inch.

"What are we waiting for? Let's go." He nudges me to move.

"I'm waiting for some sign that you're really having a stroke or something. A tic maybe. You gave up that phone awfully easy."

Briefly, he looks over my head, lost in his thoughts, and following a light snort looks back at me and says, "I'm trying here."

I grab a fistful of his shirt and pull him toward me as I lift up. With my lips a breath from his I say, "That's good enough for me." I press a quick kiss to his soft mouth. "Let's do this." I let go of his shirt to grab his hand then pull him behind me to the car. Our first stop is breakfast then I drive him south toward Cassadaga.

"Seriously?" He motions to the sign that welcomes us to

a community of psychics, tarot card readers, and spiritual healers and guides.

"Cool, right?" My hair blows around me and he reaches out to snag a strand. I drive through the small downtown and pull into a spot outside a large farmhouse with a neon light flashing from the front window

"I don't know about cool." He tugs. "I hope we aren't stopping here."

I kill the ignition and tuck my keys in my purse before I face him. "I know you don't want to be here. I know this is something you would *never* do. *Ever.* But that's the point. Today is all about trying new things and stepping out of our comfort zone. A day of firsts. Besides, it's not like pilots don't have their own superstitions, so just think of this as a little more to the right of that." I lean forward and gently kiss him, hoping he'll grasp the moment and live in it.

There's surprise in his eyes as we cross into new territory —a place where we hang out, kiss, and spend this much time in each other's company without it leading to sex.

"Come on. Don't be so unexciting. It's not like I'm asking you to get a tattoo or do karaoke or sky dive into a volcano. It's harmless fun. I've never done this either and thought, if anything, it would provide for a good laugh." I elbow him.

He catches my elbow, cupping it in his hand. "You've never been to a psychic? Really?" His thumb strokes me.

I pull my arm back, shoving my hands into my hair, forcing them to untangle my curls. I'll not fall for his diversion tactic no matter how acute my need to touch him is.

"Nope. I've spent a lot of time trying to figure myself out by looking inward. The last thing I was open to was someone else telling me what they saw."

The hesitation from him is too long, and an ember of

anger pops up inside me. It's good we're keeping things casual, because I could see us trying to be more and his disinclination always being an issue between us, sparking fights. I shove his shoulder in hopes of pushing him out of zone.

"Okay," he says with a curt shake of his head. "What the hell am I thinking?"

"Yay." I clap my hands with both delight and sarcasm. "I promise this is going to be fun."

"I doubt you can promise that." He follows it with a heavy sigh.

"I promise you'll have fun. Even if it only lasts a small, teensy tiny moment." After a quick squeeze to his knee, I exit the car and let free the laughter bubbling within me. I wait for him on the sidewalk. His slow shuffle toward me is deliberate but I won't be baited. When he's within range, I grab his arm and tug him toward the big farmhouse.

"I hear this woman is the best."

"Oh yeah? Who's the reliable source? The internet?"

"Jayne." I reach for the front door, but he beats me to it and opens it, gesturing for me to precede him.

The house has not been renovated to become an office but instead still holds the original layout. The door opens into a large foyer with stairs and a large desk that sits across the hallway, blocking anyone from trespassing into the back space. Two rooms sit parallel from each other, one is open with seating, and the other is closed off by sliding wood doors.

A hipster-looking guy sits at the front desk. He puts the paperback he's reading aside and beams at me through his thick-lensed, black-rimmed glasses. Well, at my chest.

"Can I help you?" he asks my breasts.

"Yes, we both want a reading. Can you schedule that?"

"Yes," he says without looking away. "Madame Monica will be available in a few moments. Let me get some information from you. Like your name and phone number." He pulls a pen from the desk drawer, his smile never wavering.

"I'm Josie and this is Brinn—"

"And why do you need our number?" Brinn steps up behind me and places a territorial hand around my waist.

"Oh...ah...I...well, in case you wanted to step out and get a coffee, I'd then be able to call you when Madame Monica is free." His eyes go large behind his lenses as he looks between us.

"We'll wait here. You said it would only be a few minutes anyway, right?" Suddenly, Brinn's in charge.

He nods.

"Might as well not take the chance by leaving and maybe missing our opportunity with *Madame Monica*." He steers me from the front desk with an arm still around my waist and pulls me down onto the love seat, forgoing the large couch and individual chairs.

I bump him with my shoulder and arch a brow. "Something bother you, McRae?"

"I have no idea what you're talking about," he says while continuing to stare down the hipster.

Across the hall, the double sliding doors come open with a bang and a woman with crazy curly hair stands in the opening. I assume she's Madame Monica. She's not dressed as I imagined a psychic would be; I suppose I expected flowy clothes and several bracelets clanging together with her every movement. Instead, she wears jeans so tight they accentuate her front butt, a leopard print tank top, and sneakers. She's older and overly tanned.

One might think she'd have known to avoid the sun, as a

psychic, but then maybe she knows something the rest of us don't. The skin around her lips wrinkles in a perpetual pucker, already anticipating the next draw from a cigarette. As if reading my mind, she lifts an electronic cigarette, inhales long and slow before she blows out a puff of vapor smoke that smells like peach Schnapps.

"You two, in here." With the flick of her long, fleshy index finger, she commands us into action.

My heart leaps into my throat. I really didn't think this through. What if she sees something I have no business knowing? For the first time in a long while, I'm glad I'm not alone.

Blindly, I reach for Brinn's hand. Only when mine's cradled in his do I stand.

"What's the matter, Ms. Fearless?" he whispers in my ear. "Afraid to know what tomorrow holds?"

"Who wouldn't be?" I suck it up and tug him toward the room.

After closing the sliding doors with another resounding boom, Madame Monica gestures for us to sit at the cushioned dining chairs, which flank the only other piece of furniture in the room. Cigarette burns scar the large round table and I wonder which the table has seen more of, dinner or the future. The lighting is low and has a yellowish glow.

"So we can do a tarot card reading, I can look at your palm, or I can try to get a spiritual reading. You can also have all three if you want. Who wants to go first?" Madame Monica lights an incense cone and waves the smoke around with her hand. She sits across the table and waits for us to answer.

"Him." I point.

"Made you come, did she?" Madame Monica's voice is

rough from years of smoking. "I'll make this as painless as possible for ya." She grabs Brinn's right hand and holds it in both of hers.

"For you, we'll just try and get a simple reading. Just some basic questions, nothing more, and we'll stay within the limits you're comfortable. What's your name?" She closes her eyes and massages her thumbs into his palm.

"Brinn." He clears his throat.

"Brinn. Yes." She takes a deep breath and slowly lets it out. She does this two more times. "Brinn," she says. "It's not been easy for you but you should be proud of yourself. Damn proud." She opens her eyes and looks at him.

He shifts in his seat.

She continues, "There'll be little you'll not be able to overcome. But life will get much easier with the right partner." She closes her eyes and takes in more deep breaths in the series of three.

Brinn gives me a sideways glance followed by a short-lived smirk.

"Brinn," she says again as if we wouldn't know who she is talking to if she doesn't say his name. "You're at a fork in the road. Both paths look appealing and rewarding. I see that you're hoping to be able to do both and use one as a safety net." She shakes her head. "But what you don't see is that there is a third path, and if you can find your way to that path, you'll find all of your dreams will come true. You've paid the price with your childhood and the rewards wait for you now. If you choose correctly."

"Young Jedi." I finish for her.

She opens her eyes and levels a stare at me. "I beg your pardon?"

"If you choose correctly, young Jedi." I make my smile megawatt. "I'm sorry. I couldn't resist."

Following the smallest of glares, she returns her attention to Brinn and his hand. "I see an office and on the wall are pictures. Pictures of lots of planes. I see your name on the door and no one else's." She gives him a twisted little smile, drops his hand and then pulls out her cigarette, takes a puff, and blows the smoke over her shoulder.

She leans toward him, squints, and says, "It's OK to show the world what's written on your heart. Oh, and happy birthday, son." She squints, her way of smiling I suppose, and pats his hand three times.

I toss back my head and laugh. I couldn't have scripted a better reading. Unable to resist, I grab his forearm, lean across, and kiss his cheek.

"That was wonderful. I swear I didn't mention it to anyone that it's your birthday. My turn, please. My name's Josie." I offer up my hand.

Madame Monica stares at me, clearly still displeased with my Jedi comment. Finally she picks up my hand and does the three-breath ritual, her thumbs digging into my palm.

She sits back. "Wow. So much. I'm not quite sure where to start with you because the question isn't as obvious as it was for your friend." Again with the breaths before she continues. "Time is irrelevant. You should not put off what is your heart's truest desire because you think the timing isn't right." Madame Monica tilts her head and closes her eyes tighter. There is no sound but our breathing then the psychic sighs heavily and shakes her head.

"I'm sorry. I can't pick one thing. There's too much. It's beautiful and heartbreaking. Don't get me wrong, there's nothing to be worried about, but I'm unable to pinpoint down one specific area to get a good read." She opens her eyes and stares at me. Inadvertently, I sit up straighter and think of my brother.

"Ah, there it is." Madame Monica smiles. "This is your path. But know that things are not as they seem. Don't be like...like a...." Madame Monica tilts her head. "Like a...bunny." She pats my hand three times and lets go.

"A bunny?" Is she fucking kidding with this shit?

"Yes, a bunny. Rabbit."

Brinn and I exchange a look. I'm about to ask Madame Monica for further explanation when she takes three long drags from her electric cigarette and blows them out in a puff of rings.

"That is, I think, about all you two can handle. Enjoy your birthday." She gestures for us to get out.

We say our thanks and are at the door when she says, "And Josie, call your momma. All your questions could be answered. She's no longer mad."

"As if," I say. "If that were true then she can call me." I pivot and exit the room. After paying hipster doofus at the desk, I grab Brinn's hand and we walk out.

FIFTEEN

OUR HANDS fit together like meant-to-be-coupled puzzle pieces. Everything about being with this guy is easy. For the first time I wonder what staying in Daytona would look like.

"Want to walk the strip before we leave?" I gesture to the surrounding stores.

"Sure." He shrugs.

With my other hand, I take a puff from my imaginary cigarette and raise one brow. "But which way? There's a fork in the road but there are three paths." He steers me toward the stores closest to us.

"Do you see anything in my future about bunnies?" He waves his hands in front of his face, pretending to whisk away the imaginary smoke.

I drop the act. "What the hell does that mean? Stop being a bunny? What a crock of shit."

"Were you thinking of posing for Playboy?"

"No." I let go of his hand to swat his arm. "Maybe it means I should stop having sex." I purse my lips, trying to hold back the laughter.

"That's just wrong." He shakes his head emphatically. "She's stupid. No one should ever stop having sex and certainly not you. Ever. And never stop having sex with me."

"Maybe I'm going to use up all of my sex drive and ten years from now when I'll really need it, I'll be flat broke. Washed up. Dried up." I try to sound panicky for added emphasis.

"I think she didn't know what to say there at the end. She made that up."

"Maybe she's crazy? What was that business about showing the world what's written on your heart?" I throw the fake cigarette to the ground and grind it with my toe. Brinn laughs and wraps an arm around my shoulder as we cross the street.

"I have no idea. What about calling your mom?" he asks as we peer into the window of a bookstore.

I slide my arm around his waist. "I haven't spoken to my mom in about a year." Why bother pussyfooting around it? Bring on the questions.

"Really? Why not?"

I move to stand in front of him. "You see...I ...." How do I say it? "Twice now I was headed for the altar and bailed. The second guy she didn't like or, should I say, approve of. You think she'd just be relieved that I didn't go through with it, but not my mom. My mom is angry that I left Max at the altar. She's upset that I got engaged to this artist, she's angry that she found out because my brother saw it on Facebook, and really fucking pissed off that I made a spectacle of our family name, once again, by dumping him on the way to Vegas a few days before the event." I watch the questions cross Brinn's face.

His eyebrows shoot up higher with each incident until

they nearly reach his hairline. "You'd actually get married in Vegas?" He smiles.

I laugh. "I like you. You're all right." I know he wants to ask more but he doesn't and I appreciate that. It's not a story for the sidewalk in a tourist town.

"Thanks. You're not so bad yourself." He leans forward, gently swiping his lips across mine. It's spontaneous and sweet and makes me want him more.

"Even though I have a potty mouth?" I say, using my sassiest two-snaps-girlfriend tone and bobbing my head for emphasis.

"It's shocking sometimes. But hell, watching you take a guy out is too, so there's that." He shrugs.

"So guys are the only ones who are supposed to cuss? Like there's language for women and language for men? Language discrimination."

We walk along the sidewalk, purposefully bumping each other every few steps.

"I know it's a gender bias. I get that. But sometimes men like to have some things to themselves."

"So you want curse words? You have a penis. We don't have penises. That's not enough?" I drag him into a shop of stones and crystals.

"Dammit, I dunno, and I've a feeling this conversation is gonna get me in trouble with the bunny in you."

I laugh. "Seriously, what is it though?"

"Maybe the Neanderthal in me doesn't like it. It can be unattractive."

"So because I have a potty mouth, the attraction you feel for me is somehow diminished?"

"I wouldn't say that." He rubs his brow with the palm of his hand and shakes his head.

"What?" I ask as I step into his space.

He leans closer to me, his face mere inches from mine. His breath on my lips.

"Can you imagine? What if my attraction *is* diminished somewhat? What would our sex be like if that wasn't the case?" He's wearing a shit-eating grin. "Just think of all the things I could make happen for you. Like multiple orgasms. Oh, wait. I've already done that."

We stare into each other's eyes. I'm reliving every single touch and in those seconds they cumulate into a rush of sweet and unlocked desire. My knees threaten to buckle as I watch his eyes turn a darker green and his pupils dilate. I know he's thinking of us together. When I place my hand on his chest, his body vibrates beneath my palm.

"I suppose in the interest of science I should consider giving up naughty words for a few weeks. See what happens," I whisper.

"Science would be appreciative, though I bet there're some 'naughty' words that would be OK."

His lips brush against mine, lightly at first and then again with more urgency. I grab his shirt and kiss him hard and fast, our tongues entwined. I push him away with the same force and step out of his space. Throwing him down in a store is not on my list of planned events.

"Mm." I lick my lips then scan the counter for a lifeline. My gaze settles on onyx colored stones. "I should also grab some of these." I scoop up a handful of loose hematite stones because they're supposed to stimulate sexual energy. "In case this flame fades. Maybe they'll help preserve some of my sexual energy for the future, just in case I bunny it all out now." I want to crawl into this man's skin and stay there until I've had my fill.

"Jesus," he whispers. "Let's get out of here."

"Oh no, you don't. I've got plans for us."

"I do too, and I bet mine would make us both feel real good. Nice and relaxed." He steps toward me but I step back.

"No, we're sticking to the plan. It's not every day you have a birthday."

He shakes his head and scrubs his palms down his face. "I'll meet you outside." Before turning to leave, he tugs at his shorts. I quickly pay and find him leaning against my car.

We drive back to Daytona and spend the afternoon on the boardwalk playing arcade games like skeet ball, trying to squelch our current of sexual desire. Instead, we channel it into the competitive streak we discover we each have, get roped into a few games of beach volleyball outside the Deck, and walk along the beach enjoying the warm ocean water. We avoid talking about the psychic and spend the energy on more enlightening conversation such as our favorite foods and movies. To my relief, I find he doesn't have a shellfish allergy and, with what I hope is a covert text to Jayne, move forward with my plans for the evening.

I drive him to my place where, thanks to Jayne, a picnic awaits us, including a birthday cake. The hurricane lamps glow, and the kaleidoscope colors of the setting sun are our backdrop.

Jayne's placed a beautiful linen cloth and the tableware from my kitchen on the table. Two candles, a bucket of chilling champagne, and two covered dishes are out. She's pulled it off better than I imagined. I probably owe her my kidney or something, but it's a nice way to cap off his birthday. We've done something silly that he would never do, a fun day playing games—the dream of any kid—and the adult nice dinner out.

Brinn looks down at a side table that holds the cake. "You got me an airplane shaped cake?" Amazement and joy cover his face.

"Mmm. I wasn't sure if you like chocolate or vanilla, so it's strawberry. I'm told a Publix buttercream cake can't be beat." Apparently the grocery chain is famous for their frosting.

"It can't. Wait until you try it." His eyes are alight with pleasure as he looks from me to the cake.

"Well then, by all means, let's eat so we can get down to the cake." I gesture to the table with our food.

I light the candles before I lift the covers from the dishes. The full yet subtle aroma of creamy sauce and lobster greets us.

"That smells good. Lobster, right? Is that what all the shellfish questions were about?" He helps me into my chair and as he pushes my chair in, his hand grazes mine, leaving my skin tingling from the touch.

"Mainly yes, but it was nice getting to know you better. Like yesterday at the bar, I wasn't sure what you would want to drink. You ordered a pilsner the first time I saw you and a Guinness last night, but that might have been a one-time thing. I like learning about you."

"What were you going to serve if I had a shellfish allergy?" He's done with his lobster and already eyeballing mine.

"I don't know, peanut butter and jelly sandwiches? I was leaving that part to Jayne. She's the one that helped me set this up."

A quiet moment passes between us. He lightly places the utensils across his plate before clearing his throat.

He asks softly, "Is it hard?"

I'm caught off guard and I look around, wondering what he's referring to.

"I'm sorry?"

"Leaving. Making friends with people and purposefully leaving. Is it hard?"

Unsure of my answer, I take a sip of my wine instead and roll the question over, revisiting the memories of the last two years.

Gently, I swirl the liquid in my glass and focus on the motion and say, "Honestly, I don't think I stayed long enough to make those sort of friendships. It works out that I leave when things are on a good note and with social media, I can keep in touch with pretty much anyone. Trying to reconnect with Will is far harder." I look at him.

"You've seemed to make a good friend with Jayne," he says.

I nod and set my glass on the table. "Yeah, that happened quickly. It's never happened before." It'll be hard leaving here. That realization renders me breathless and now I understand why I struggled so with my run. Even then, almost two weeks ago, I was feeling more comfortable here than anywhere I've been yet. The connections here are greater, not better, but stronger, and knocking me off my stride.

"But what about home? People you've known for a long time."

I wonder why he's asking these questions. This guy who dreamed of leaving but never did. His history is here and nowhere else, whereas I have left a piece of me, no matter how small or insignificant, in different places.

"Funny enough, I don't miss anyone from home with the exception of some older relatives and my parents. I didn't have a lot of friends there." I roll my eyes. "But Lord, my mother. Why I miss her, I'll never know. She drives me nuts. But by being away from them I have Will again and I *really* missed him."

He leans forward, takes my fork, and finishes off my lobster.

"When he left I felt like a part of me was gone too. I felt so alone." I'm lost in the images of my past. It's like hearing an old song on the radio and being transported back in time. "What about you and Vann? Aren't you close?"

"Yeah, but it's different. I've been Vann's brother and his parent. I knew when he was born that it would be up to me to protect him. Pretty serious business for a five-year old."

"Was it terrible? Your childhood?" Will he meet me half way? "Are we going to eat that cake or talk about shit that's depressing as hell? Because if I had a vote, and I think I should since it's my birthday and all, I'd vote on the cake."

"Nice deflection." I stand and bring the cake to the table, place a two and eight candle in the cake, and light it.

"How'd you know how old I was?"

"Just like I knew where you lived. I memorized your driver's license, Brinn No-Middle Name McRae. Make a wish." I step aside and present the cake with a flourish. He turns his chair, and grabs me, fitting me between his legs.

Our eyes meet and a current of energy crackles and sparks between us.

"A wish, huh?" His voice is low and sexy.

"Make it a good one."

With a quick puff, he blows out the candles. He slides his hands up my legs, beneath my shorts and a primal moan escapes me. "I really hope it comes true." I wrap my arms around his neck.

He stands and lifts me to straddle him. "There's a good chance it will," he says before kissing my piercing.

"I hope you didn't waste your wish on me." I arch as he travels kisses across my jaw and down my neck.

He lays me down on the platform chair and I tremble with anticipation. "Nothing about you is a waste."

SIXTEEN

TODAY, for lack of a better expression, has sucked major balls. But even saying that doesn't sound bad enough. Today, more than any day so far since living in Daytona, I want to pack my shit and hit the road. Turning my back on everything in this stupid state would be a wise move.

All because Will stood me up.

I knew it was too good to be true when he texted and asked if I wanted to hang out. All the previous offers I'd made to do the same were met with a quick and decisive no. But today he reached out. Today we were going to hang at the beach and I was going to work up the courage to ask him all the questions that'd been with me since he left.

Why did you leave?

Why wouldn't you let me help?

Why am I so easy to forget?

But with my picnic basket loaded full of gourmet sandwiches and snacks, I sat on my blanket and waited over an hour past our rendezvous time. I'd even taken the day off from work.

Nothing.

I text him one simple question.

Will?

Sorry is all I get.

I dump the food in the garbage by the boardwalk and ride my bike home so fast and furiously that I don't feel the tears on my cheek until I pull into the driveway.

I don't understand.

I thought I was done grieving for him, but every time he pulls away, it's as if the wound is flayed open again.

I lose my shit in the shower. Sitting in the corner with the hot spray beating down I let it all out. Sob until I am deplete of tears or energy. I'm not sure which.

The only way to cope with this is to make a plan, so after my shower I boot up my laptop, and after a brief search, I find a cruise line job that I apply for. The timing is perfect as I have my lease until the beginning of September, which is when Mark's daughter is scheduled to take over. In case I need further proof that Karma exists, the cruise line training is scheduled to start (if I get the job) that same week.

Planning doesn't get more perfect than that.

The likely truth of this whole situation is that there is no place for me in Will's life. The sooner I accept that the sooner I can get about the business of making my own life. Wherever that may be. I no longer need to seek him out and pick my destinations accordingly.

So for now, work will be a distraction I'll take. Not willing to linger over my broken heart and somewhat energized by having a plan in place, I dress and set out to enjoy these last few weeks I have here. Starting with Brinn.

I'm pulling in the office parking lot as Brinn is walking out. I cut the wheel to make a sharp turn and park, my steering belt emitting a high pitch squeal. I do a thumbs up and smile at Brinn through the windshield, laughing as he shakes his head at me.

"Hey," I say, climbing out of the car.

He looks me up and down before he asks, "You got any spare clothes in that car of yours?"

I look down at my outfit. I'd kept my hair casual, capturing it in a long fat braid.

My long jean skirt and white T-shirt are so simple they're almost uninspiring. "What's wrong with what I'm wearing? Holy shit, this is conservative. I refuse to—"

He walks to me and puts his lips to mine, effectively shutting me up. Who is this handsome stranger who is at such ease with his public displays of affection? His phone rests beneath my palm, silent in his vest pocket. A little light of happiness charges through me, dissipating the aches. A little. "You look fine," he says before nibbling on my lip.

"Fine?" Is that a veiled insult? Fine sounds boring.

"I like the skirts with the slits in them better." He rubs his hand down my thigh.

"Is that why you wanted to know if I have clothes? You planning on making this dirty?" I fist his shirt in my hands and pull him against me.

"Man, I love where your mind goes. But no, I wanted to know if you had clothes because I'm going to Fort Lauderdale and I thought you'd like to come with me. It's an overnighter for business. You ever been down there?"

"Once, to catch a cruise with my parents, but I was just a kid. I can't go. What about work?"

"You're not even supposed to be here. Why are you here?"

My smile wavers and try as I might I can't keep the stupid ass tears from springing to my eyes.

"Hey." He strokes his thumb down my cheek. "What happened?"

I drop my head forward, my forehead resting on his shoulder. "I was supposed to meet my brother. We were going to hang out this weekend. But he stood me up."

"Why?"

"I dunno. All he said was sorry. I even took the weekend off from the bar." Which will cost me handsomely in tips.

"Not knowing your brother, I can only guess, but maybe he needs more time?" He wraps his long arms around me and snuggles me against him.

"Time for what?" I say in his throat. "What did I ever do to him? He's the one who left and didn't look back. I'm really trying here and one moment he gives a little and the next he takes it back."

"A trip to Ft. Lauderdale is just what you need. You can practice letting it go. Tell yourself you're giving him the space he needs if that's what it takes. But don't stay getting all worked up over something you can't control. Tomorrow's the weekend and the expense is on Mark." He strokes my back.

I step away with a shake of my head, crossing my arms over my chest. "You can't fix this, Brinn. Don't even try. No stupid-ass trip is going to make this better."

He tucks his hands into the front pocket of his jeans. They ride even lower with the weight of his hands pulling them down and see the top of his tighty-whiteys. I strain to ignore the stirring of my girly parts. It'd be easier to ignore a gorilla tossing hundred dollar bills at me. He's the perfect remedy for my disappointment.

"I'm not trying to fix it. That has to happen with Will, but I am trying to make you smile." He leans toward me. "I'm trying to distract you, even just a tiny bit." His smile is small and crooked, and I want to lick him from head to toe he's so freaking adorable.

"Why are you going to Fort Lauderdale?" Moving back into his space so I can touch him, I play with the zipper on his flight vest, my shoulders relaxing while I visualize the schedule. This trip isn't on it.

"Because of Mark's new 'business partner,' Erik." He rips his hands from his jeans to do the air quotes.

"That's the dude that was in last week when Mark came back. The real estate investor?" I remember him as being harmless and wardrobe challenged.

Brinn rolls his eyes. "He's convinced Mark there's some land down there that would be a good spot for a school. I'm to check it out and decide if it's a go or not. I really think it's because he couldn't get a charter out. Gave me some sob story about how terrible it is he can't find a charter when he needs one and how he refuses to take a commercial flight because of their little bags of nuts and minuscule bottles of booze."

I pause my zipping, one hand still on his vest. His entire body tenses under my fingers as he talks. There's no need to mention how this shafts Brinn, who is desperate to be Mark's business partner. He's good enough to have the final say in this deal, yet he's not good enough to sell part of the business to. Today has shit on both Brinn and me, and in his defense, I want to go inside and stomp on Mark's white-sock-and-Croc wearing foot before I deliver a knee to the belly.

"This Erik dude—"

"Is an annoying piece of work. When he laughs I want to

peel my ears from my head." Brinn's hands are on his waist and the anger he's experiencing is barely tethered. It pulses off him.

"Isn't it a crazy long drive?" "Yeah, that's why we're flying." My fingers still.

"I love this piercing in your mouth," he whispers and bends to kiss it, his tongue teasing the area, his hands going to my waist.

But it doesn't help. I shake my head, drop my hand from his flight vest, and step away. "Uh, flying? No, thanks."

He searches my face before snaking his arms around my waist, pulling me against him. "You're awfully pale under that sun-kissed skin. Wait. Are you telling me you're afraid of flying?"

"I'm telling you I don't want to go." I try to push out of his arms.

He lets me go but keeps me from walking, maybe running, back to my car by holding me at the elbow. "Seriously? You made me go to a psychic. You called me...what was the word—"

"Unexciting," I whisper and look at the small coffin that he calls a plane sitting in the hangar. I shake my head.

"Yeah, unexciting. You gave me this whole speech on adventure and you won't get into a plane with me. You're a hypocrite."

That does it. I laser focus my attention back on him and point my finger toward his face. "I'm *not* a hypocrite. You weren't going to die if I took you to see a psychic."

"I might have. You don't know." He crosses his arms over his chest and lifts a brow.

"What? She was gonna read your palm too hard? Cut

you with the tarot card?" I hope he recognizes my you're-an-idiot face.

"Maybe she was gonna tell me something so devastating I would take my own life."

"Oh for fuck's sake." I roll my eyes and turn to leave.

"No you don't." He jumps in front of me. "You can't call me boring and chicken and not have your helping of crow."

"There's nothing you can say to make me get into a tiny tube of steel and go hurtling over the earth. Nothing."

"First, it's not hurtling. It's flying. We aren't taking a rocket. And second, I never figured you for a scaredy-cat. So much for all that talk about adventure and experiencing life. Guess everyone has their scaredy-cat limits."

I gasp, not caring my mouth hangs open. "I'm not scared."

"Yeah, I believe that." He laughs in my face. Right up in there, taunting me like a playground bully. "Scaredy-cat. Scaredy-cat," he sings.

"Shut up." I narrow my eyes.

"Bauk, bauk, bauk," he adds.

"That's a chicken." I cross my arms and stick out my hip, smug.

"That's you," he says. "A scaredy-cat chicken."

"That's the stupidest thing I've ever heard."

He continues making noises. But it's his laughing that gets me. "Look who's not so tough."

"Oh, all right. I'll go. Shut up already." I bite my lower lip and bend over at the waist. "I think I might be sick." I hate being a coward.

"Hey." He takes me in his arms. "It's gonna be OK. Trust me. I'm a pretty good pilot."

"You better be fucking awesome." I bury my head in his shirt, my breath on his chest.

"I'm the guy who showed awesome how to be better." He kisses my forehead.

"Now go home, pack, and be back here in forty-five minutes."

"We're leaving that soon?"

"Yup."

"But Mark." I motion to the hangar as if it'll throw me a lifeline.

"You're not even supposed to be here. Go." He spins me around, swats me on the ass, and gives me a gentle shove toward my car.

"I just won't come back," I mumble.

He stops me with a hand on my arm. "You're right. You won't come back. We'll just pick you up some things down there. We can expense it or something. Why don't you go wait in the office? I'll come get you when the pre-flight checklist is done."

I flip him a bird over my shoulder as I hustle into the hangar. I'd seen Zach's scooter alongside the building, and I figure I can slip out the other door and zoom away before Brinn clues in. I can hide at the mall or something.

I hate flying that much.

I find Zach by the water cooler filling a bottle.

"Give me the keys to your scooter," I say and look over my shoulder.

With one hand he digs in his pocket, pulls out a silver skull keychain, and drops it onto my palm.

"I promise to bring it back. I'll take good care of it," I whisper and scan the space for Brinn. He's likely almost done with his checklist.

"I have no idea what you're talking about, but that scooter's not going anywhere."

I roll my eyes. Boys and their toys. "If I crash it I'll replace it."

He flips off the cooler's tab and replaces the lid on the bottle. "It won't start. The engine's flooded. I'm about to work on it now."

"Then why did you give me your keys?" My fear has been replaced with frustration.

"Because you asked for them." He shrugs as if to say 'duh.'

I roll my shoulders back and force a deep, hopefully calming breath before I say, "I need a way outta here, Zach. Fast."

"I'm giving you a way out. My plane," Brinn says from behind me, his hand coming to rest on the small of my back. "Trying to escape, were you?" he whispers in my ear.

I should tell him that I'm not going. He can't make me and even though he'll see me for the coward I really am, at least I'll be alive. Never mind all those times he's been out in the plane and come back unscathed.

"I can't do it," I say. Then bite my lower lip.

With his free hand, Brinn pries open mine and removes Zach's keys, tossing them to the kid.

With his other hand, he gently rubs my back. "Babe, it's gonna be OK. I'm gonna be right there and you're gonna love it."

I shake my head.

"Don't let fear get you, Josie. You can beat this."

"Not if I'm dead." It's sound reasoning. Who can argue with that?

"Come on," he says and takes my hand, leading me to the plane.

"Tell the world my story, Zach," I yell over my shoulder while reaching one hand toward him in a last ditch effort to cease this madness.

Brinn traps me between the fuselage and his body. "Here, start chewing this." He hands me cinnamon gum and I take two pieces.

After he practically carries me to my seat in the cockpit and straps me in, he hands me headphones, which I can't get on as my hands are trembling too much. Brinn takes them, lowers them on with ease, then kisses my nose.

"Wowza. Hello sweet Josie," Erik says, standing outside my door. His hands are in his pockets and he continually pulls them up, forcing the pant material to bunch up at his crotch. If that's not bad enough, I see he's wearing dress shoes with no socks.

I ignore him, focusing on the steady chewing of my gum, smacking it loudly with the occasional popping of bubbles.

Hey," Brinn says to Erik while pointing his finger at me. "She's off limits to you. You understand?"

Erik puts up his hands. "Territorial much? Hey, where are my headphones?" He looks around.

"Broken." Brinn climbs in and goes through the checklist before we taxi to the runway.

I stare out the window; my gum smacking comes to a halt as we're cleared for takeoff. I pop another piece into my mouth.

"Trust me," Brinn says and pulls back on the throttle. I nod but as the plane increases in speed so does my chewing. When we lift off I involuntarily slam my eyes shut and reach out to grip Brinn's forearm.

We clear the airport air space. I know this because I can hear the communication over the headset speaker.

"Josie," Brinn says over the speaker. "Babe, look out to your right. There's a pod of dolphins."

I peek out from under my lids. Brinn nods with his head to look out my window.

I make slow work of turning to the window. Erik's face is pressed against his and he glances at me before maniacally gesturing to the beach below us. Peering over the edge of the sill, I catch sight of the jumping mammals and lean closer.

"There's a baby." I bang my head against the glass, hoping for a better view.

OK, so the scenery *is* fascinating from this height. In one direction, there's a vast blue canvas with puffy white clouds. From another I can pick out landmarks and stores. I see people swimming in their pools. It's a mesmerizing perspective. The lack of turbulence goes a long way toward easing my angst. Twenty minutes into the flight, Erik tips back a flask and follows it up by slumping into his seat, drool sliding from the corner of his mouth.

Following a grimace and an eye roll, I nudge Brinn to look at Erik. In turn, he leans toward me and even draws my attention to my right.

"Kennedy Space Center," he says in a husky-makes-me-horny voice. "Want to try?" he asks, indicating the yoke.

"OK." I tuck my gum into my cheek, which makes it protrude like I'm storing a wad of tobacco.

"Jeez, you're adorable," Brinn says and launches into the dynamics of aviation.

SEVENTEEN

THIS FOOL, Erik, is sticking to us like unwanted body odor. First, he manipulated us into driving him around, starting with the supposed site of the new school, which Brinn pointed out would not function because of the non-existent access to a runway. Sort of a necessity for the business.

"I should have scoped it out with Google Earth first," Brinn mumbles before he explains to Erik that, yes, a school in helicopter instruction would be good but not as profitable as one that offered a variety of aircraft instruction. Therefore, his backup plan of helicopters only wasn't the most fiscally smart.

"You should stop drinking," I say and take Erik's double scotch on the rocks the waitress just delivered.

"Hey, fun police, give that back." He gives a half-hearted lurch toward the drink but I have the advantage seeing as how I'm sober and he's not.

The hotel we managed to find is definitely high-end. The city, hosting a Brazilian jiu-jitsu national conference, is overrun with tourists, limiting our choices, but since Brinn is expensing the trip, he set no limits for the hotel. Funny enough, I stayed here when I was a kid and we'd all flown down to catch the cruise. I'd taken a muscle relaxer for that trip. Funny, how I'm staying here again. If memory serves, they have a pool that's beautifully landscaped and a swim might be a prelude to events planned for later tonight.

I hold Erik's glass and slap at his hand as he tries to take it again. Though we managed to score two rooms, we haven't managed to shake Erik for dinner, and if a higher power exists, I pray with every fiber in my body that we'll be able to eighty-six him at the end of the meal.

I order a black coffee for Erik and work on his scotch.

"Here's a fine offer, Brinn. If you're willing, I'd like to put you on retainer," Erik says, his words starting to run together.

"Retainer?" Brinn takes the scotch from me and swallows a large gulp. "Why would I want that?"

Erik laughs and I now know why it makes Brinn crazy. The poor guy's laugh is one of those monosyllabic sounds that's high pitched and repeats, much like a braying jackass.

"You and I are alike. For guys like us it's about making money. You want that as much as I do. I can tell. I'm intuitive like that." Slapping Brinn on the back, he says, "If I buy a plane you can be my on-call pilot." Erik sits back and glares at the coffee.

"That's a huge expense." Brinn holds up his hand as Erik begins to bluster. "I'm not saying you can't afford it, but the administration commitment is as big as the financial one."

"Just where does your money come from?" I ask.

"Real estate mostly." He gestures to himself and inadvertently pokes his own eye. "I've a good eye for land."

"Just not what to use it for," I say and Brinn chuckles.

"Tell the truth, you inherited some of it, right?" Brinn asks.

Erik shakes his head and reaches out, pulling his coffee toward him. He leans forward to meet this cup, lips pursed, head bobbing every so often. After an audible slurp he says, "Nah, my mom passed when I was in college. Left me a tiny life insurance policy." He holds his thumb and fingers up to show us what his version of tiny looks like. "I bought and renovated my first apartment building and built it from there. About my offer. Interested in working for me? Being my on-call pilot?" he asks with the one eye closed.

"I have a pretty tight schedule with the school and teaching, so it's unlikely that arrangement would work. And the chances of me purposefully nose-diving out of the sky to put us both out of our misery is pretty high."

"Well, there is that." I laugh.

"I'm not miserable," Erik counters and slurps his coffee.

Brinn and I catch each other's eyes and laugh again. Poor suck.

Erik leans over his coffee, tucking his head in the palms of his hands, and sighs heavily. "There's got to be a better way to fly. A different option. Not all charters work within my time constraints and there's nothing out there that fills the void."

For a drunken guy, he's pretty coherent even if he is slurring. Makes me wonder how he spent his college days, probably at one of those fraternities that spent more time with bongs, hazing, and tossing back shots during beer pong competitions than on academics.

"You need a company similar to charters but with a fleet large enough that it supports last-minute flights. Like fractional ownership, there are several companies that offer it." Brinn pushes away his plate.

"Yeah but I've looked into them, for me that's not smart money. The taxes alone turn me off. I've figured it out." He taps his head. "You're smart, start up something that does what I need and I'm in. I'd invest in that like this." He tries to snap but his fingers slide more than they collide. Erik's chin drops onto his chest, and he looks moments from checking out.

"I imagine you want something more along the lines of a turbo prop or business jet, not a single engine, with the expediency of online scheduling and flexibility."

Erik points a weaving hand toward Brinn. "Precisely," he says following it up with a hiccup.

"Can't have it. There'll always be a compromise. You need to decide which you want more, the convenience of short notification scheduling or a luxurious plane. You can't have both all the time."

Erik nods, presumably digesting the information. "I think I'd give up the type of 'craft. As long as it's relatively comfortable." He slides toward me and I push him back upright.

"To tell you the truth, I like the idea of a hybrid like that. But man are they risky. Sure, it sounds good on paper, but it's impossible to get good estimates on profit because the market is unknown," Brinn says mostly to himself.

Typical Brinn. He prefers low risk or none at all. What will it take to free him from the unyielding belief that Mark's business is the end all? Other companies call for him constantly, the University wants him on staff, and Erik is all but offering Brinn his wallet.

"I can name ten guys willing to take that risk and invest,"

Erik says with fluttery eyes. "I had a college roomie that's a math genius and I can get him to run the numbers. His ability for predict—" Erik's head slumps forward and jerks back up, and he sways in his seat. "—shon, predishing is bar none."

"Prediction," I say.

"Yes, that." He stares down the length of the single finger he's pointing at me. "Predishing."

"Come on, big guy. Time to go home." Brinn hands me the business credit card. "Pay the check and meet me in the lobby, please." He pulls Erik up under his arms and steadies him on his feet.

"What are you gonna do with him?"

"He lives in town and he has a driver with a car waiting outside. I'm gonna toss him in it and slam the door."

"Good luck with that," I say and flag down our waitress.

"These shoes hurt my feet," I hear Erik say as Brinn nearly carries him out of the restaurant.

"You should try them with socks," Brinn says and I laugh out loud.

I pay the check and wander into the lobby. It's overrun with people in various degrees of martial arts uniforms and it makes me think of my short time in Dallas. Which, funny enough, seems like a lifetime ago even though it was only two years. The person I was when I arrived there, scared yet excited to reinvent myself, has morphed into what I hope is a more steady, balanced person who's trying to grab life by the balls.

If I think about where I am with Will, I'll cry.

I search the lobby for Brinn and catch his eye as he walks toward me. He winks and his smile opens up, pulling me toward him.

"How'd it go?" I ask, stepping into his space.

"He kept offering me a job. Raising the wage every few minutes. As if it were that easy or I'd work for him." He rubs a hand down my arm and slides it around my waist.

"He's certainly annoying but he's okay. There are worse guys to invest with. Erik is still trying to figure out who he is. I should let Jayne get her hands on him; she'd burn his clothes and love every minute of it. In fact, I'll do that. Are we seeing him again tomorrow?"

"Unfortunately. You'd do business with him?" He pulls me closer and tucks a strand of hair behind my ear.

"Yeah, you wouldn't? He's proven he's skilled with making money. That thing you said about the online scheduling sounds amazing. It's not like things with Mark are going anywhere." I remember the days my father would storm around grousing about the ineptness of charters. Enough so that he eventually bought a company jet. Erik's frustrations are not isolated to him.

"But they will be. Soon, I hope."

"There are just as many risks with that plan as there are with Erik's."

Brinn shrugs, but I can tell he's rolling the idea around in his head by the few irritated sighs he's making.

"It would take a lot of capital for that startup. I just don't know if I could tolerate him. He pretty much says what he's thinking so there'd be no mystery." He shakes his head. "It's a wonder he's ever made a dime."

"It's something to consider."

"Nah, between trying to buy into Mark's and putting together my application for my PhD, there's really not much to consider. I've got all the options I need and they are sure things."

"Do you really want your PhD? Was it something you were thinking of getting before the school made the offer?"

"No but that's because I was single-focused on Mark."

"The psychic said you had three paths. Maybe this one is the third."

Brinn laughs. "Doubtful. Speaking of which, the university has this big charity shindig thing next weekend. I usually don't do these sort of things but I've been told it would behoove me to go. Care to come with me?"

"Casual or formal?"

"Formal. I have to dig up a tux."

"Tuxes cannot be 'dug up'. They have to fit. They should"—I sweep my hands over his shoulders and down to his waist—"show this off. Jayne can help you."

He groans. "Let's forget about all this. I saw a movie theatre across the street."

"We're alone in a hotel and you want to go to a movie?" I wrap my arms around his waist.

He laughs. "Yeah, actually. I'd like to do something with you other than sex and food. It's not a date or anything, because we don't do that sort of thing."

"Not a date?" The noise of the hotel is a whisper compared to the hum of our bodies.

"Nah, not a date. I mean, you know, even though it looks like what all other normal people do on dates. Dinner, movie, hold hands."

"Entertain a drunk man."

"See. Not a date. Just friends or maybe even co-workers, that's how un-date like this evening is, and because it's not a date I don't have to acquiesce and agree to some chick flick just to try and impress you with my soft manly side."

"You already scoped out the selection, didn't you?"

"Yeah. Liberation, the new alien sci-fi movie, is out and I'd love to see it. Come on. You like sci-fi. It's been ages since I went to a movie."

I shrug. "Are you sure you don't want to stay here, have another drink, and take it upstairs?"

"I can't believe I'm saying this, but there's more to life than sex."

I purse my lips as if I'm considering the plausibility.

Brinn laughs. "Yeah, it sounded stupid in my head but I said it anyway. I'm tempted, you know I am, but I'd really like to see a movie with you. Besides, these BJJ's are all bad ass looking in their gis and I'm thinking I need to get you away from all this testosterone."

"You know I learned self-defense from a BJJ. In Texas."

"You lived in Texas?"

I nod and tell Brinn how I met the owner of a Brazilian jiu-jitsu school at the bar where I'd taken a job when I escaped to Dallas following my runaway bride act. How upon arriving, I realized my options were limited as far as jobs were, so I scored one in a bookstore and the other in a bar. Using the experience I gained during my short stint as a barmaid for one of my mother's gambling themed charity events. Being of a studious nature, more so back then versus now, I'd read several books on the art of cocktail making. Instant job skill.

"Then Utah?"

"Yes, I worked as a ski instructor. After Utah was Washington State—that's where I met the artist I was engaged too. But I found out he was marrying me because he thought I had connections in the art world. And here I thought it was about an evolved relationship with an open concept. No real strings."

"You could do that? Share your spouse?"

I shake my head. "I realized I couldn't on the drive to Vegas. Right before I figured out I was being played. I think I was just lonely. That's when I got this." I touch the piercing he likes to kiss.

"From there?"

"South Carolina and now here."

"Any chance you dated this Brazilian jiu-jitsu instructor?"

"Maybe." I shrug.

"What if he's here right now?" Brinn scans the crowd, his eyes coming back to me, the corners crinkled with repressed laughter.

"Holy shit, you're right. I don't think he'd be too happy to see me. I dumped him over a text message. We should get out of here. Fast. To the movies," I say. I try to make light of it, only now thinking back on it all, I don't feel adventurous, but more like a shit bag.

"Yes!" He plants a fast kiss on my lips and lets go of my waist to grab my hand. He drags me through the lobby, weaving between the sea of uniforms, and we quickly make our way outside but are forced to stop at the crosswalk, waiting for the flashing white man to give us the approval to cross. Thunder booms overhead.

"Come on," he says when it gives us the cue, tucking my hand into his. We run across the street as fat, unexpected raindrops splash down on and around us.

"It's cold." I'm surprised.

"Enjoy it. It's a rare thing." We jog through the crowd as others scatter in all directions hoping to find cover before the deluge begins. Brinn leads me toward the theatre doors.

"Don't we need to buy tickets?" I tug him toward the

booth but he tugs back, bringing me in front of him, and pushes me gently through the door.

"I bought tickets earlier from the concierge. Popcorn?" He points to the concessions counter.

I snatch the tickets from his hand and read them. "You're a lucky son of a bitch. If these tickets were for a specific movie and not a voucher, I'd be giving you hell for playing me like that. What if I'd said no to a movie?" I hand him back the vouchers.

"Ha, no way."

"Maybe I would've fought hard for a romantic comedy."

"Nope. You got all the romance you can handle right here." He pats his chest a couple of beats, puffing it out. I roll my eyes and turn away but he snags me by the arm and pulls me into his embrace, wrapping me tight.

"Just two co-workers, huh?" I say.

"Yep, after the movie I'll show you how to fix the copy machine." "Is that office talk for playing doctor?"

He laughs and brushes a kiss along my lower lip. "When it's time for you to go, don't end it with a text, please."

"Are you ready for me to go?" I find that asking the question makes my breath freeze in my chest.

"Nope, I just don't want to always be worried that's it's a good-bye every time I get a text from you." The darkening of his eyes speaks to the depth of his worry even if his voice feigns indifference. I see the Brinn who was always let down by people he let in, people he trusted. I see a little...reticence I now recognize is a part of him in everything he does, as if he's bracing himself for the inevitable abandonment. Except for when we're having sex; that's when he opens up. That's when he's the most exposed. I'd rather rip my own heart from my chest than be one of those people that put shadows in his eyes.

"Never." I take his face between my hands.

Our eyes search each other's and I let out a slow, shaky breath. "I hope this is a short movie."

"Maybe we should skip it." He wags his brows slightly.

"Oh no. You really wanted to be here, so we're staying. Now go get me the biggest bucket of popcorn they have *with* butter." I slide my hands around his waist so I can slap his ass.

He laughs and hands me the voucher. "Go turn these into tickets and you better not choose a different movie. On second thought." He snatches the vouchers from me and hands me some twenties. "I'll go get the tickets and you go get the popcorn."

It's been years since I've gone to the movies, as I use Netflix for my instant gratification fixes. But sharing popcorn, our hands brushing as we reach in to grab the snack, is the sexiest turn on yet. The movie is a perfect distraction, enough action that I find myself grabbing Brinn's arm occasionally. We leave holding hands, talking about some of the better scenes. In the elevator, alone, Brinn presses me against the sidewall and kisses me soundly, rendering me a brainless nitwit.

"Since we're co-workers and all, here on business, I should probably let you off on your floor and go up to my room," he says, his lips close to my ear.

"That's such a bad idea," I whisper. My hands tremble. I want to strip him of his clothes. I want him to take me here and now, quick and hard.

"The path between what's right and what's wrong is before me," he says.

"It would be wrong to leave me alone in my room where something could happen to me. It would be right to make me feel comfortable. I really need you to make me feel comfortable."

The elevator chimes my floor. We're frozen, staring into each other's eyes. Something's passing between us that I don't entirely understand, but I recognize losing this moment will change our lives and not for the better. Perhaps it's the moment we'll remember long after I'm gone. Yet I know this is the memory that will always leave me with the what-if questions. What if I stayed? What if we wanted the same things? What if he was the one for me?

The doors slide open.

Regardless of the consequences, I want this memory, this moment. I want to be that person who has a past rich with experience even if saying goodbye hurts.

I slide away from him, taking his hand in mine, and lead him to my room.

There're no words, just the heavily charged air between us and the burning need to be with him. I want to round out the night in his arms, feeling a part of something bigger than I have ever felt before, something I've only felt with him. He closes the door and latches the security bolt. I unzip the sundress I bought earlier and let it fall to the floor, wearing only my bra and panties. He sweeps me into his arms and carries me to the bed.

"I'd do just about anything for you," he whispers before he removes my bra and takes one of my breasts into his mouth.

The satisfaction of his touch makes my soul bend with pleasure, my body arc. It's not until he kisses me, his lips pressed tenderly to mine, that I ease his shirt off. With

Brinn, I become centered and balanced. Yes, our sex is frenzied and needy but it's more than that. It connects us in a way I've never experienced with another person. I kiss the spot over his left pec; his heart thumps steadily beneath my lips.

"You're one of the best things about moving here," I say, helping him slide his jeans off. My words are clearly an understatement. With all the feelings of failure regarding my brother, it's my time with Brinn that gives me light.

"I want this to last. This moment." He cups my face and kisses me across my jawline.

With his light touches and scattered kisses, the heat from his body pressed to mine. I'm desperate for more of him. To be joined together, entwined. The three seconds he uses to put on the condom feel endless, an infinite moment.

"Please," I beg. "Please, Brinn, I need you to fill me."

"I love it when you say my name."

"Brinn," I whisper and moan as the tip of his penis presses against me.

I lift my hips, hoping to coax him in, but he holds me back, his hands on my hips.

"Josie." His voice is deep and raw. "I—"

"I know," I say. "Together."

He enters me as I slide my legs around his waist, tilting to let him bury himself deep inside me. He slides all the way in slowly and I break and shudder, crying out his name.

He moans my name.

"Closer." I press hard against him, and we rock together, finding a rhythm that is ours, driven by our want for each other, our need, and powered by our feelings.

Together we ride the energy, climbing higher and higher until we climax again, this time as one, spreading wide and soaring into a state of bliss I never imagined existed only to collapse in exhaustion.

I wake up pressed to him, his arm over my shoulder, his face buried in my neck, and I bask in the warmth and security that comes with being wrapped in his arms.

The clock tells me that it's the new day and we'll be leaving soon. I ease away from him, planning a shower, but his hand snakes out and pulls me back into his arms.

"You know what would be good?" His voice is raspy with sleep and he yawns against my shoulder.

"I know a lot of things that are good. I showed you a few last night."

"No, those are amazing. Awesome. Fan-fucking-tastic. Very bunny of you." We laugh and I rub my rear into his crotch.

"Babe," he says and follows it with a groan. "We have to fly out in a few hours, and if you keep doing that I don't think we'll leave this bed today. At all."

"Sounds heavenly."

"Doesn't it though."

"Just a quickie?" I flip over and straddle him.

"Where do you get the energy?" He palms my boobs, thumbs teasing my nipples into hard points

"I suck it from your soul." I drop my head back, letting myself get lost in the sensation.

"You make me breathless," he says and slides his hand down my side, bringing it to rest between my legs, teasing me with soft strokes. I unravel, opening at the seams, letting myself free and bring him inside. We make it quick as I take the lead and ride him hard, hoping to satiate at least some part of me. We take our fill and collapse on the bed.

"I need food," he says, his hand entwined with mine.

"Room service."

"Why not? It's on Mark's ticket."

I look at Brinn across the pillow, sun-kissed skin dark against the white linen of the sheets.

"What?" His eyes are amazing, green and clear, and I warm, knowing I've had a part in making him relaxed and happy.

"Will you think of me when I'm gone?"

Briefly, his thumb stops stroking my hand. "I'll try not to because every time I do I get a boner and that's awkward."

I nudge him with my foot and he laughs.

"Of course I will."

"So I should look you up whenever I'm back in town?" Suddenly the thought of never seeing him again makes me sad. I resist the urge to hide my face in the pillow.

He slides his hand from mine and rolls onto his back. "What do you want from life, Josie?"

I shrug one shoulder. "To experience it before I settle down. If I settle down."

"Before. If. It's not in your immediate future, settling down."

It's not really a question but I shake my head anyway. Words lost in my throat.

"But it's in mine. I'd like to come home to someone. I'd like a family. Sooner rather than later. So if you come back into town six months from now, a year maybe, I don't think it would be a good idea to look me up. It's likely we'll have different lives then—"

"And we can't just pick up where we left off." I finish for him.

He stares at the ceiling. "Do you think you're still going?"

"Yeah," I whisper before I slide from the bed.

Without looking back, I close myself off in the bathroom and prepare the shower. When I go, there'll be two bits of my heart I'll leave behind, one for Will and the other for Brinn. Once under the shower stream, I convince myself that none of the water on my face is from tears.

EIGHTEEN

I HAVE every intention of escaping into a good book, letting go of my reality for a different one. With my legs over the rattan loveseat on my balcony and an iced tea at my ready, I no sooner slide my finger between the cover and first page when my phone chimes a text message.

I am totally giving Brinn a hard time if he is texting me already considering we just got back a few hours ago.

But it's from Will.

In town. Want to meet up?

My heart clenches. I respond as fast as my fingers can press the screen. I have to.

It's why I'm still here. Mostly.

Love to! Without car. Come here?

When Brinn and I got back to town, we discovered my car wouldn't start. So he dropped me off with promises to fix it tomorrow.

How about Chinese restaurant around the corner from your house?

Again, another pang of rejection. He continues to keep

me at arm's length. I try not to take it personally that he seems unwilling to come to my house, other than the first visit. I push it aside and text my answer.

I can be there in 15 minutes.

Great! Us too. CU there.

Us?

I hop off the loveseat and kick my tea over in the process. Righting the glass, I leave the mess for later. A quick glance in the mirror answers my question about being sufficiently presentable, my hair being my only obstacle. Forgoing a braid, I pull it into a high ponytail then check my makeup. I want him to know I'm not the complete train wreck he might think I am. Why else would he keep his distance?

I'm good to go.

After locking up the place, I borrow my landlord's bike and set out for the restaurant. I arrive in exactly fifteen minutes and Will's motorcycle is parked out front. A deep breath does nothing to steady my racing heart as I try not to set expectations for this visit, the brother whose counsel, even at my early age of ten, had been a guiding force. He was my Obi-Wan and there is no denying that after he left I succumbed to the dark side. A life designed by my parents, for my parents.

I lean against the stucco wall of the strip mall and give myself a stern lecture.

If Will has no interest in developing a new sibling relationship, I'll be OK. I'm getting pretty good at going at life alone. Maybe I'll stay here and build a community of my own. I already have Jayne. And Brinn, maybe.

Once inside, the first person I see is Will. He's sitting in a booth with a dark-haired girl. She's petite and beautiful with a heart-shaped face and angled eyes. Her light brown skin is flawless. She wears her hair long like mine, bangle bracelets cover her arms, and Mehandi art decorates her hands. It explains why Will asked so many questions about my henna when we first reconnected.

She leans into my brother and his smile is quick and easy. I watch him say something in her ear then kiss a spot beside it. We're all grown up, Will and I, and perhaps I expected our new, rebuilt relationship to be similar to our childhood one, which consisted of crazy face making contest and fart jokes. Huge error on my part.

Hesitantly, I move to the booth, not wanting to interrupt a beautiful moment between two people so clearly in love. It's tiring being the outsider, especially with the one person who gets why I am the way I am because he grew up in the same house as me.

"Hi," I say, hoping my expression's light and friendly. It's not that I'm feeling unfriendly, just unwanted, and I hate myself for being so damn needy.

"Jo." Will slides out of the booth, a large smile on his face. "Thanks for meeting us on such short notice. This is Daanya. Babe, this is my sister, Josie." He offers Daanya a hand, helping her from the booth. She takes my extended hand between both of hers, pressing lightly.

"It is wonderful to meet you. Will speaks of you often, and now I finally get to see you in person." She kisses one cheek and then the other.

"It's nice to meet you too." I look at my brother, whose jaw is swinging back and forth. "He mentioned me?"

"So much that I am at an unfair advantage. I know far more about you than you me, I'm sure." She squeezes my hand again before letting go. Effortlessly, she glides back into the booth. Will gestures for me to sit and I do, letting my shoulders relax a little.

I've spent years searching for the Will of my youth, the brother who might give me the answers to all my questions like he did when we were children. But that boy, and frankly, that girl, are gone and before me sits a new opportunity for not one but two new connections.

"I love your henna." Her hands are covered in a beautiful design of vines and leaves.

"Thanks, I do it myself. I like yours as well." She gestures to my arms.

"Didn't I say you'd have a lot in common?" Will asks her as he places an arm around her shoulder.

She laughs softly and reaches behind her to squeeze his arm. "Yes, you did."

"What brings you to town?" I slide a menu from behind the napkin dispenser and play with the edge.

"Daanya has three days off. She needs a break. Works too hard. We're spending the night here and going to St. Augustine tomorrow." Will rests his chin against her head and the swinging motion he does ceases.

"I'm a surgical resident at Shands." Shands is the large hospital in Gainesville.

I blink in effort to mask my surprise. "Is that how you met?"

Daanya shakes her head slightly and glances at Will. "I'm from Jaipur. That's where we met. I was home on vacation and he was living there." She takes my brother's hand, the one resting on her shoulder, and entwines it with hers.

I craft the pieces together. "That's the first place you went, Jaipur? When you left?" The breathless fear I'd experienced when Will told me he was leaving to find himself a new life just hours after he was discharged from the hospital revisits me. Back then, I wasn't sure what was wrong with the old one.

"Yeah, I went to the airport with all the money I could pull together and told the lady at the reservation desk to put me on the first international flight out for under twenty-five hundred dollars. Delhi was the winner. From there I migrated to Jaipur."

"It's funny that you should go there. I find myself drawn to that region, the Mehandi art, yoga, and other eastern philosophies." I grab the tiny thread that could connect us and hold on.

Will nods. "There's lots to recommend. I learned how to deal with the panic attacks I was having and how to face my fears. But it was hard. I avoided it at first. I went to Istanbul, Sri Lanka, Burma, and Laos before I went back to Jaipur."

"Panic attacks?" I lean toward him. "When did you start having panic attacks?" Daanya and Will share a look and once again I'm odd man out.

Frustration gets the best of me and I slap my hand on the table. "Someone please fill me in."

"How do you not know?" Daanya asks softly.

"Know what?" I look at Will, my shoulder lifted in a shrug. "What?"

Will's inhalation is sharp and he looks upward. "All this time and you've had no idea. I didn't know that. I thought you were avoiding it," he says the last part when he looks at me. "What did mom and dad tell you when I left?"

There's a vise grip of fear around my heart and tears press against my eyes. What's coming carries a weight so heavy I expect the clouds to darken and the lights to flicker.

The way Will has tensed up and Daanya rubs his arm in a soothing manner only adds credit to my worries.

"Nothing. They acted like you never existed. No one was allowed to say your name for fear mother would flip out. They seemed angry. I kept to myself and studied more, which seemed to make them happy. When I got into law school, they let me move into the apartment they'd bought for you. But not until after the first semester."

"Nothing?" He nods and turns back to Daanya. "They told her nothing."

"I thought it was pretty stupid. It was unreasonable for them to expect all of us to get law degrees. And why can't you do what you want to do? Be who you want to be? I get why you did it, why you left. Either you're exactly what they want or you're not welcome." *But why did you leave me?* I want to add. But I'm too afraid of the answer.

"No, Jo. That's not how it is." Will scrubs his hands down his face and turns to Daanya. "This is not the place."

"Yes, but this is the time. You can't not tell her. We can't have dinner with this out there." She turns to me and extends her hand across the table, palm open to me. She nudges Will and he does the same. I take each of their hands into one of my own and hold on for dear life, trying not to tremble.

"I didn't go off to be my own person. I went off because if I stayed then I knew the chances of killing myself were one hundred percent."

"What?" If I lean any further across the table, I'll be lying on it.

"I have schizophrenia, Jo Jo." He looks right at me and slides his jaw from side to side.

I jerk my hands free to cover my mouth and my eyes

slam shut, hoping to keep the words from being true. There's too much swirling through my head to make sense of anything. I search for clues, a hint that Will was sick. Anything to make sense of what he just said. I open my eyes to find my brother staring at me, his hand clasping his chin.

"How can that be true?" I whisper from behind my fingers. "How did I miss it?"

Will takes my hand and clasps it between his. "Think, Jo. Because you didn't miss it. You didn't know what you were seeing. Remember my closet?"

"Oh my God, your closet." I clutch his hands.

Will had come home for a long weekend, work-release I'd termed it, because we had to spend the entire time working in Dad's firm learning the ropes. One night, I found Will shuttered behind his closet door, drawing madly, and pinning pictures to his closet wall. I thought he'd been hiding out. I'd thought it was a prank. That maybe he was really looking at porn or something.

"Shh," he'd whispered and put a finger covered with dark ink up to his lips, his eyes darting quickly between me and the door I was holding open. "Don't tell mom and dad. That's all kinds of wrong. All kinds. Go. You must go. Hurry before you're seen."

It all becomes clear. The odd late night wanderings and rants he'd started having, the angry moments that were unexpected and nonsensical. I pull my hand from his and hurriedly brush away the tears coursing down my face.

"Yeah," he says and slides into the booth next to me, his arm coming to rest across my shoulders. "Mom and Dad found the stuff in my closet." He pauses a beat. "And my apartment. But not until after the car accident."

"The accident," I say on a sob. "That's what started it all?"

"That's what solved it all. From what I understand, the cops asked mom if I was taking drugs. I suppose they searched everything and that's when they found the stuff in my closet. The pictures and words." His Adam's apple bobs from the heavy gulp. "I'm surprised they put it together as quickly as they did. It's because they did that I didn't go into psychosis."

"I didn't know, Will. I swear it. I would have—" I search his face while looking for my answer. I would have done what? Something more than the actual nothing I really did.

"I know that now."

I look into his eyes and see a person who used to be as familiar to me as I am to myself. But I see more. I see a death in his eyes, a loss of that boy who used to quote Star Trek and the teenager who found his passion as the editor for the school paper. I also see a weary survivor that will persevere.

All this time I thought my brother was out living a full life, a grand adventure, and I'm not sure how to process these new facts. I'm not sure what to make of it all because what once was...is now something entirely new.

Another tear slips out and slides down my face. "After your accident, you left so quickly. I couldn't help but think that it was all of us you didn't want to be around. Then I started to look at us. To *really* look at us and I could see why. But now, knowing this, I feel as if I failed you. You needed us and it was our job to help you." I brush away more tears.

Will shakes his head and hands me a napkin. "It wasn't your job to help me. Besides, even if you could've, I don't know if I was open to it. That night I drove my car off the bridge I was hallucinating. When I came to and actually got in my right mind, the one thing I couldn't argue was that as Mom and Dad's demands became greater, my grip on reality slid further away. My shrinks talked about triggers and in my mind, I couldn't afford to stay home any longer. All I could think about was getting away so it would never happen again."

"Has it? Happened again?" I reach up, grab his hand, and give it a squeeze.

He shakes his head. "I've been vigilant about my meds and have some incredibly good doctors. They manage my TBI and the schizophrenia. In fact, I was selected for this new trial of meds that won't have this stupid side effect." He points to his jaw. The repetitive sliding motion he does has become a part of who he is as much as the scar that runs across his head.

He searches my face. "I'll admit that I thought you were totally avoiding my diagnosis. Trying to pretend it wasn't real, but then Daanya pointed out that maybe you didn't know—"

I shake my head wildly. "I didn't! I emailed you all the time. I tried to call too. You answered with short replies and I thought that meant that I was bothering you."

In a flash, everything is clear and the wall between us is suddenly gone. I have scaled the obstacle without realizing it. Or perhaps, Will scaled his side and met me half way.

Will shrugs. "I was scared you were a trigger for me. That's why I didn't show up the other day. "

The last thing I want is to make my brother sicker.

"Am I?"

He shrugs again. "I dunno. We'll see. But I'd like to have you in my life. I missed you. So until we know we'll just take it slow. OK?"

We're interrupted by the waitress and place our orders. I suspect we all just order the first thing we see on the menu.

When she's out of range I reach across to touch my brother, who's moved back to sit next to Daanya. "I'm here if you need anything."

"Are you? You travel around a lot."

I don't get the vibe that he's pushing back, questioning my dedication to him, but that he's feeling me out for my plans.

"I was looking for you. Partly. I was also looking for me." Such declarations are hard for me. They leave me feeling raw and exposed.

"You found one, how about the other?" He leans back against the booth, his arm across the back.

I shrug one shoulder. "Bits maybe. It's coming together slowly. What counts is having you back in my life, but any time that I'm..." It's hard to say, knowing I could be a cause to his mental illness. "...a problem, you let me know."

"If you are a trigger then you need to be prepared for me to shut you out again. At least until I can get a handle on things." He meets my gaze, but I can't hold it and look away.

I nod my head, blinking to keep back the rain of tears.

"You can't take it personally," Daanya adds softly.

But how can I not? "Sure," I say, amazed I'm able to force out the words. I can barely get air in and out.

"Jo, I live every day on the edge. Fighting chaos and risk with one foot in reality and the other in a world full of hallucinations. Every day I choose to wake up is a risk for both me and the people I love." He looks at Daanya and strokes a hand down her cheek. "I've learned that my journey is found in staying and seeing things out. It's about living the life that's been dealt me and making it everything I imagine or more." He leans over and kisses Daanya gently on the lips.

I try not to be jealous of what they have together, honestly. But it's hard not to want a connection like that to a person who feels for you what you do for them. Sure, Brinn and I have a connection but it's sex-based. When it comes down to the person he wants to take a risk on, it won't be me. As much as he's too straight-laced for me, I'm too outside the lines for him. Maybe we've moved a little further away from having no strings but they certainly haven't turned into heartstrings.

"So you'll understand if things between us progress slowly?" Will asks as the waitress delivers our food.

I nod. The truth is a part of me does understand.

But, part of me doesn't.

NINETEEN

I RUN my hands down the smooth curves of Zach's beat-to-shit scooter while trying to tune him out. Zach's lamenting the woes of the machine while casting furtive glances back at the hangar. It's clear this is more about what Brinn will say than the flaws of the vehicle.

Brinn comes out of the hangar, aviator shades already covering his eyes, but I can tell he's looking at us. I feel it in all my important parts. Zach tries to take the keys but I snatch my hand away and grip them in my fist.

"He'll kill me," he pleads.

"Don't be ridiculous." Gesturing for him to step back, I straddle the cracked faux leather seat and let my skirt fall open at the part, revealing most of my thigh and the new henna I created from the pattern Daanya drew out for me.

After lunch, we spent the remainder of the day together at the beach and later cooking out at my house. It seemed so natural and normal that I almost forgot our relationship was held together with years-old duct tape.

But it's hard to forget you might send your brother into a psychotic state.

"I can't imagine why you want to sell this. I love it," I tell Zach as I watch Brinn stride purposefully toward us. I can almost hear his teeth gnash from here.

"Because it's a money pit, because it looks better than it runs, because it's the smart thing to do," Brinn says and tucks his hands in his pant pockets. "Get off that thing, Josie."

"I want it," I tell him.

He shakes his head. "You're not getting it. You'd be—"

"I already told her everything that's wrong with it and that I couldn't sell it to her in good faith," Zach says.

"Good man, Smitty." Brinn nods at him.

"Hold up, you two. I'm glad you both have it worked out, but you've forgotten one important element. What I want. And what I want is to buy this." I toss my hair over my shoulder, dismissing them both as I slide the key into the ignition.

"Josie," Brinn says and takes a step toward me.

"Shut it." I put a hand out to stop him. "I already know that the throttle can stick or the brakes may be unreliable. I know there's a problem with the fuses and sometimes the lights don't turn on. I still want it. I have an interview with the cruise company and if I get it I'm gonna need something to get around different ports. This is perfect." I turn the engine over. It roars to life.

"Amazing," Brinn mumbles.

"What?" I call out as I rev the throttle.

"I said you're lucky it started on the first try. How's that gonna work for you when you're stuck in some port and it won't start?"

I adjust myself in the seat and push the scooter forward, releasing the stand. With my gentle turn of the throttle, the scooter eases forward at a lazy crawl. I pull my feet up to rest on the running board.

They watch me ride around the large parking lot, navigating between the cars, over the dirt patches, and looping through again. With trepidation, I slowly increase my speed and revel in the sensation that comes from having my hair whip behind me like a flag.

"Hey, make sure the brakes work before you accelerate more," Brinn yells.

"Yes, Dad." I test the brakes by jerking the scooter forward for twenty yards. "I think the brakes are OK." I do another series of stop-starts, making the tires squeak each time. When I pass Brinn, I laugh. His hands are on his hips, his lips a thin line.

"Did you say there were brake problems?" I jerk by him, smiling and watching the muscle in his jaw tick.

He shakes his head and folds his arms across his chest.

I twist the handle and accelerate, pushing the scooter to the limit.

"Oh, oh no, Look at me. Living on the edge." I weave around them, shaking the scooter from side to side.

"Slow down," he says.

"No."

"I don't have the time to take you to the ER." He whips off his shades.

I weave through the cars and try to get the speed up by crossing the parking lot in a straight line. I hunch low and hear Zach laughing. When I look over, Brinn shoves him in the shoulder. I lean into the curve and catch some gravel that causes the scooter to wobble. When I come out of the curve, I sit up straight and meet Brinn's glare.

"Guess what, Dad, the brakes aren't working." There's a patch of gravel ahead of me.

"Seriously?" He hands his shades to Zach.

"Seriously. Get ready to catch." I weave around the patch of gravel and make a large arc, turning back toward Brinn.

"Catch what?" he calls while walking toward me.

Goofball doesn't think I'm serious.

"Catch me, dumbass."

Timing is everything. I flip both legs to one side and force my skirt part open wider, knowing I've ripped it a few inches. I'd take it off if I could because I'm going to need mobility. I stand on the small running board, one foot in front of the other, distributing my weight so the scooter is balanced, before I bend over the dash, testing the brakes one last time with no success.

"Get ready, McRae."

He steps closer, widens his stance, and opens his arms.

Fifteen miles per hour doesn't seem all that fast until you're speeding toward someone and planning to leap into their arms.

"I'm coming in hot," I yell and can't help but laugh at the ridiculousness of it all. I'm within a breath of him, certain I've run his toes over, when I let go of the handles and spring from the footrest, arms wide.

Our bodies collide with a thud. He rocks back slightly while pulling me in tight, absorbing the impact. We stare at each other.

"I knew you'd catch me."

He tosses back his head, laughing, but the sound of the scooter colliding with the hanger and the echo bouncing around the parking lot cuts the laughter short.

Somber, we look at each other.

I say to Zach, "I'm totally buying that scooter."

And Brinn drops me on my ass and walks back to the office.

∽

The voice memo from Jayne cracks me up.

"Fuck all, Josie, I nearly want to gouge my eyes out. Please, please, please meet me for food. My life is in your hands. If I continue with this inventory another moment, I can make no promises as to what will happen. I'm holding matches."

I text her with the name of a restaurant and a plan to meet there in thirty minutes, then walk to Brinn's office. "I'm headed out. Meeting Jayne for dinner." I stand in the doorway of his office. He hasn't looked at me all day, not after shouting some heated words about me buying Zach's scooter.

"How you getting there?" His face is impassive as our eyes meet. My car, still in the shop, won't be ready until tomorrow and he picked me up and brought me to work this morning. Jayne's food invitation comes at a perfect time. Avoiding him is the right move. It's time to start laying the foundation for my exit. His anger at today's events is a clear indication that we're getting too attached. My one simple goal is to exit from all this on a high note, leaving warm memories in my wake.

"I'm walking. It's just down the street."

"I'll give you a lift." He closes a file and straightens the folders on his desk.

"I can walk. You stay here and get caught up." Because

of being short staffed and our unexpected trip south, he's even further behind on recruiting for a mechanic and a pilot, his Ph.D. application, and the books.

"I need a break from these books." He stands then comes toward me.

I step away from the door, out of reach. He flicks off the light and gestures for me to lead the way.

"Avoiding the books seems to be going around." I think of Jayne. "I can take on some of that for you." I hope he sees it as the peace offering it is.

"I might do that actually. I seem to have lost the drive for some of this." He gestures to the building, looks at me, and snaps his mouth closed. As if he forgot he's mad at me.

I want to touch him, run my hand down his arm, and give him comfort of any sort. Lately, he's become more disenchanted with the business and particularly in the runaround he's been getting from Mark. But I also want to punch some sense into him and knock his bad mood right out of him. He has so much going for him yet only sees one thing.

Because I'm torn on which one he deserves the most, I do neither.

We walk out of the office in silence. Perhaps it's the stress of the heavy quiet but I find my patience is thin. I'm not the sort to tiptoe around stuff. Not anymore. To do so rubs me, leaving me raw as if I'm covered in hives.

"Thanks for the ride," I say.

He won't look at me. His jaw is set. I imagine if I move closer I'll hear his teeth grinding.

I'm the one who should be mad. Telling me what I can and can't buy. "Did you hear me? I said, 'thank you.'"

"I heard." He sounds as if he's pushing out the words between his teeth.

"Well you don't have to be rude," I mumble and reconsider kicking him in the shin.

I wait for Brinn to lock the hangar and to check and double check to make sure all the doors are secure. The evening is cool and behind the building, the fading sun waits to dip into the waters of the Atlantic. I stretch my arms over my head and entertain the idea of riding my bike to the beach for some exercise, once dinner is over. Brinn finishes his checking routine and gestures for me to lead the way to his truck.

An idea takes root.

He opens the passenger door of his truck and offers his hand to help me in. So sweet. Chivalry at its finest in this one. I make use of his hand because the lift helps and I know touching me makes him horny, even something this simple. He slams my door as I reach across the space to pull up the lock and push open the door for him.

He gets in with heavy movements and sighs. "Why do you even need the scooter?"

"I told you about the ports, and the scooter will be fun."

"Until you're dead on the road and then the fun will be over." He puts a hand on the steering wheel and turns to me.

His worry is sweet, and looking at his face, with his concerned eyes, makes me hot for him. I scan the parking lot and buildings. The security lights are off and the area is void of cars except for his.

"Remember what I said about having some fun? Spontaneity and all that?"

"Yeah, but buying a scooter is not being spontaneous."

"I'm not talking about the scooter." I climb up on the seat, pull my skirt up to my thighs, the part opening to reveal my hip, and I step across, straddling his lap. I ease down, facing him, and tuck my skirt around us but have it raised high enough so that my panties are pressed against his jeans.

"Oh," he says and wraps his hands around my waist.

"We have thirty minutes before Jayne will get to the restaurant. Knowing her, we really have forty-five."

I work the buttons down his shirt while I press a soft kiss to his mouth. I flick my tongue out and lick his top lip before deepening the kiss and bringing my tongue to meet his.

He pulls me close; his hands come to rest cupping my rear, pushing me harder against his crotch.

"Have you ever had sex in a truck?" I ask when we break the kiss. Our faces are close so I whisper.

"Uh, yeah. Isn't that where every high school kid has sex?" He laughs and I pull back to look at him.

"Is it? Feel like having sex in a truck again? I can take you back to your high school days."

"No, thanks." He leans forward and kisses me briefly. "Wait. Are you saying you want to have sex, here? Right now?"

I shrug, press my chest to his, and kiss his neck.

"Come on, Josie. You really don't want to do that."

I sit back; widening the space between us, making it larger than it's been since I straddled him moments ago. "What did you think I was hinting at here?"

He shrugs. "I thought a little slap and tickle, maybe."

"You don't want to have sex? Are you that mad at me?"

"I'm not mad at you and yes, I want to have sex with you, all the time. Of all the places we could do it, my truck never crossed my mind."

"You're not mad at me?" I raise a brow to emphasize my skepticism.

"No, I'm worried about you. I can see you gettin' hurt on that scooter and it makes me feel—"

"Helpless?"

He shrugs.

"Sex in your truck would make you feel better. Let's do it." I unsnap his jeans and ease the zipper down as I wag my eyebrows at him.

"Don't you remember what it was like? It was all elbows and assholes in high school. It can't be much prettier now."

"I've never had sex in a car or a truck."

"What? You?"

"What's that supposed to mean? Just because I propositioned you with this whole no-strings deal means I've had sex everywhere?"

"No, I mean... I just assumed—"

"You know what they say about assuming." I lean back against the steering wheel and cross my arms over my chest.

"It's just that you're so adventurous and I figured your Texas boyfriend at least. He sounded like the type to...never mind." He reaches for me but I slap his hand away.

"Beau always wanted to do it in his dojo; you know, all those mirrors and all. The artist I dated always wanted to use media like edible paints and food, and this other guy—"

"You're killing the mood here." His hands are on either side of me, gripping the steering wheel, and he shifts in his seat.

"You killed the mood when you called me a slut."

"I did not call you a slut—" He stares at me.

"Oh, I'm sorry. When you *assumed* I was a slut." I emphasize assumed because of the whole equating him to being an asshole and level my gaze right back at him.

Brinn leans in, trapping me between his arms and body.

"It only takes one person to have all those experiences with, Josie, not a dozen. Just you and *one* guy. I figured that since you were so adventurous with me you surely were this way with someone else. It's who you are. I pretty much figured I wasn't going to bring anything new to the table." He finishes with a kiss to my chin before slowly working his way across my jawline.

"But you are. I'm stretching my boundaries. Trying new things with you." I shift to expose my throat and when he kisses the hollow between my neck and collarbone, I shiver.

"Well then, by all means, let's do it in my truck." He lifts up and I help him pull his jeans and tighty-whiteys off his hips. When he settles back, he pulls my T-shirt over my head and sucks in a breath as he stares at my breasts. I have new henna art that peeks between my breasts and reaches up and over each one. It's a delicate vine of filigree that leads a path down past my belly button.

"Jesus, you're amazing," he whispers and kisses a flower that rests on my right boob.

"Do you want to know?" I run my hands up his back and into his hair.

"What?" he mumbles.

"How many guys I've been with?"

Brinn looks at me, his eyes cloudy with passion. "The number is irrelevant. The memory is the key." He moves his hand to my inner thigh and pulls my panties to the side.

We press together with need and desire for each other, craving one another's touch. In the spirit of adventure, we ignore the elbows that collide with the driver side window and a knee that knocks the shifter. When he enters me, it's with an immediacy I've felt since I first set eyes on him and I arch back and cry out his name, pressing into the horn.

But the honking is just a sound, background noise that doesn't interrupt our purpose. Being together is chirping birds and butterflies, volcanic eruptions and hurricanes. When he touches me, the world goes soft and all I know is him. Where he is, his breathing, the gruff sounds of pleasures he makes, and the taste of him on my lips is imprinted on my soul. Between us there are no rules or expectations. He wants me as I want him and I want him in ways I never understood possible. I want this. I want right now, and when this is over, I will be looking forward to tomorrow when I'll want him again. Being with him is easy.

I collapse against him, our timing in sync, and my body pulses with satisfaction as little goose bumps consume me.

"Are you cold?" He wraps his arms around me, enveloping me into his warmth.

"No, I'm perfect."

"Yes, you are."

"I won't buy the scooter," I whisper.

He rests his forehead against mine. "Thank you." He kisses the tip of my nose before moving to nuzzle my neck.

I giggle and rub against him knowing it will make him crazy.

"Are you hungry?" I ask, leaving the interpretation up to him.

TWENTY

JAYNE IS MY GO-TO GIRL. She opens at noon on Wednesdays but is coming in an hour early so we can have the place uninterrupted and I can search for just the right dress to wow Brinn.

I tap on the lightly frosted glass door of her shop, the Daily Mirror, while eating a bean burrito. The plaza where Jayne's shop is located also houses an organic grocery store and cafe with outdoor seating and as I scarf down my non-organic, not wheat, made with lard lunch, I make sure to slurp the oversized soft drink that accompanied it, extra loud. Brinn is out of the office until this afternoon, but I don't want to take the chance that he or Mark will come in earlier than expected and give me shit about my time out of the office. So I multitask.

Jayne opens the door, lets me in, and closes it behind me. The closed sign, decorated to look like a cute ETSY-style price tag, swings and thumps against the glass. Her shop is a clever mix of posh and artsy. It isn't overly crowded with racks, but clothes are arranged so that their colors play a part in the decor. This is where she shines. Half the store is consignment pieces from the fashion elite of Florida that Jayne caters to and does custom shopping for. The other half of the store is designed for off-the-rack fashion that Jayne travels overseas to purchase. Not fashion that comes from a French runway, though there is some of that, but beautifully ornate yet simple saris that she displays as evening gowns, plaids from Scotland, kimonos from Asia, and leather from Italy. Unique pieces and fabric that make me want to run my hands over them and revel in their satiny touch or gossamer lightness.

"Hallo, lovely," Jayne says and kisses each of my cheeks once. "Thanks for seeing me home safely the other night." We'd spent another Wednesday night enjoying two-for-one drinks for ladies only at the Deck. Pippa included.

"Of course. Thanks for doing this." I hand her a pastry box from her favorite bakery. She flips open the lid, moans, and rewards me with a large smile.

"Éclairs. Nom. Nom. My favorite." She sniffs the desserts and closes her eyes.

"I know. I wish I could do more for you, but I have a feeling I'm going to be spending a lot today." I pull my hair up, winding it into a loose bun.

"I've taken the liberty of pulling some dresses for you. I've one in particular that will be phenomenal on you, but I'm not going to sway you one bit. Because it's an evening affair and it's mid-August, the night may still be warm, but I've pulled shawls just in case."

She leads me to a dressing room and I see three dresses hanging off the hooks. One is minty green, the other a light, bright blue, and the last is a silvery gray. I'm instantly drawn to the gray. The bodice is ornate and dips into a sweetheart bust line but comes up into a halter. The dress is chiffon, the bodice made of intricate beading that weaves around much like the filigree henna I tend to favor. The skirt falls to the floor, flaring out slightly at the hips. "I love this one." I look at Jayne.

She laughs. "That one's perfect for you. Hurry, let's get it on you."

The dress almost fits me. It needs to be taken in slightly at the waist and the length is an inch too long, even if I wear crazy high heels.

Jayne wags her brows at me, her smile large and excited. "Damn, if I'm not brilliant with clothes." She steps back and signals for me to twirl. "You should keep your hair up. Show your back."

I look over my shoulder to the mirror and am pleased with the image. I try to imagine Brinn's expression when he sees me.

"What are you thinking? Your cheeks are red," Jayne asks as she pins the waist.

I give a slight shrug. "I was wondering what Brinn will think. You know, gotta represent."

Jayne's quiet; her eyes searching my face. "Methinks you're in love. This is more than shagging."

I snort. "*Methinks* you're crazy. It's good sex, I'll give you that, but there's nothing more to it."

She levels a look at me.

"OK, maybe we're friends. We have a friendship." I shrug and look away first.

"But I'm leaving soon. I got the job on that cruise ship."

Jayne doesn't cease her pinning. "Yes, because that ensures you can't be in love. Leaving."

"Why should I stay and be a reason my brother has to live in a mental ward?"

Jayne rolls her eyes with such severity I'm afraid they'll get stuck. "Is that really the case? Did he go check himself in after spending the day with you last week?"

"No.

"Then stop with all the drama. Life dishes out enough without having to create any more."

"But he needs his space."

"Which can only be given to him by getting on a cruise ship and sailing far, far away. Yes, I see your point." Her accent almost makes the sarcasm get lost. It's hard when she's so droll anyway.

"Even if I do stay, how do I end it with Brinn?"

She continues to stare, only this time somehow manages to look down her nose at me, from the floor. "Why would you end it? Most people date their crushes, not run from them."

"Even if it's a crush, it's a little one." I show an inch of space between my thumb and index finger. "We aren't what the other wants. He's so freaking tight-assed sometimes—"

"The lady doth protest too much." She finishes the last pin and stands.

"The lady is going to shop somewhere else. Someplace without all the lip."

"Because the truth hurts. Why does it matter if you love him? You won't enjoy being with him less. Why would you walk away from something that's working? At its very core, life is about falling in love and seeing if it might go somewhere. If it doesn't then you'll, hopefully, have sweet memories to take with you as you move on to the next one," she says matter of fact. "Will it be this one or do you want to try others?"

"We're talking about dresses, right?"

Jayne shrugs, a smile twitching on her lips.

"I'm going with this one." I smooth my hands down the bodice and across the skirt as I process what Jayne said.

I look up at her. "I'm leaving," I say it with determination as if the words will make it true. "I have to leave. It's what I do."

"If you say so. You could do something different and stay." She leans back against the wall of the dressing room, one arm across her chest, the other resting on it, her chin cradled in the palm of her hand and gives me a pointed look.

"I'll think about it." I ignore her smile and stare at the dress, afraid she'll see the truth in my eyes.

That I have been thinking about staying.

Leaving home with the intention of finding myself had no fixed rules or guidelines, only self-imposed ones that I created along the way. But I never thought about when I should end this journey. I never even imagined it. I suppose everything had a timestamp based on finding Will.

What if I did stay? I'm not sure I know how. What would that be like? When Brinn and I decide to call this quits, do I pretend indifference when our paths cross, as they inevitably will? Do I want to call it quits with him?

I can't deny that Jayne has become my first girlfriend with any real depth and the thought of leaving makes me want to weep. Or that I wake up every day excited to see these new people in my life. Or how I can't imagine snuggling up with anyone other than Brinn.

But the underlying fear of them walking away from me stops me from dwelling on the picture of what staying would look like.

TWENTY-ONE

I ARRIVE at Brinn's faculty charity event alone. He wanted to pick me up but I wanted a grand entrance.

I step into the ballroom and spot Brinn instantly. He's leaning against the bar, a beer in one hand, talking to a guy I've never seen before. When he sees me, he stands up tall, beer and guy forgotten.

As I walk across the room toward him, the beads on the bodice of my dress catch the chandelier's crystals and bounce off, surrounding me in a halo of color. The moment is magic. The kind you fantasize about but never experience. The kind where everything around you falls aside and there is only you, the guy you can't stop looking at, and this connection that can't be defined.

I press my hand to my belly but it does nothing to calm the butterflies within nor the tremble in my hand.

"You look amazing, Brinn." He does. Jayne fit him in a classic black tux with matching vest. A gray tie gives contrast to the suit and the white shirt, and his raw manliness and all over badassery leaves me feeling parched and only a cool glass of him will satisfy.

"You look unbelievable. People can't stop staring at you," he says, stepping forward to plant a light kiss on my lips.

"It's not me they're looking at. It's this." I turn and show him my back. On a whim I'd texted my brother and asked him if Daanya would be willing to apply silver body paint, henna-style, down my back to complement the severe cut of the dress.

They didn't invite me to their place, but coming to mine on short notice is huge. I call that a win. And to put a further exclamation point on the whole thing, they are staying over at my place. Granted, I told them I would be out for the night, but still!

He gives a slow whistle. "Wow. That's amazing." He traces the art, caressing my spine, and when he gets to where skin meets dress he splays his hand wide to rest on my lower back. He leans in to whisper, "Can I get you a drink?"

"If you are planning on trying to booze me up to get me out of this dress, don't worry. You don't need the booze. That tux does it for me." I turn back to face him and find I'm wrapped in his arms. "Jeez, how are we gonna get through the night?" He glances over my shoulder. "There's a guy heading toward us, he's the dean of my department, Dr. Hughes. He's the one pushing me toward the doctorate program."

"And so it begins. You better get me a white wine, please."

His boss arrives and on his heels is another guy who looks nothing like the academic sort. A lumberjack, maybe. A professor, no way.

"Dr. Hughes," Brinn says as they shake hands. "Allow me to introduce my date, Josie Woodmere."

"You, my dear, are quite lovely." The dean tells me as he shakes my hand, his firm and not the least bit sweaty.

"Thank you. It's nice to meet you. Brinn speaks highly of you."

Dr. Hughes is an average man who is best described as...ordinary. Difficult to pick out in a lineup. He gestures to the lumberjack. "This is Shawn Henderson, Shawn and I go way back to our days at Riddle," Dr. Hughes explains. "We're having a discussion—"

"An argument," Henderson says, then leans next to me and orders a double scotch, neat.

"Fine. An argument. About how the aviation industry is changing. Shawn believes it's changing more rapidly than I do. He thinks chartering is going to become more lucrative. Like people will be using apps and—" Dr. Hughes shakes his head.

"I said chartering is no longer something for the wealthy. That a co-op is the way to go. First-class passengers would prefer to spend their money on charters and if they could manage it all through an app the better." His drink is gone in two swallows and he orders another.

"I told Shawn here you have a keen business mind for aviation and we should get your take." Dr. Hughes waves at Brinn to chime in.

I smirk at Brinn. Seems I've heard this conversation before.

"Well, sir. I've thought long about this topic and I actually agree with Mr. Henderson here with the exception of co-oping. That becomes less cost effective for the traveler. The way to go is to marry the best of fractional ownerships with charters and create a hybrid with a limited fleet. They buy on with a certain amount of miles; get the quality they are looking for, with some variety. Each plan could be customized based on their needs." He turns to me. "I've been giving it some thought."

"That, son, is a brilliant idea." Henderson slaps him on the back. "I want to be in on the start-up." He pulls a business card from his pocket and hands it to Brinn. "I'm serious. I'm looking to invest in innovative, forward-thinking companies and that one is the best I've heard in a long time."

Brinn tucks the card inside his breast pocket. "I'll keep you in mind should I decide to go forward with it, but currently I'm wanting to buy into a flight school."

"Ah, you're wasted on that. Get out there. Change the scope of aviation. Shake it up," Henderson says.

"I agree," I say and tuck my hand in his. "Capital be damned."

"Atta girl." Henderson swats me on the back. "Capital can always be found for something worthy."

"By the way. Your application hasn't crossed my desk, Brinn. I hope you're still considering applying for the Ph.D. program. You've one week left."

"Well, sir," he says and shuffles next to me.

I hold my breath. Could it be?

"I hope you'll understand that I've decided not to submit my application. I enjoy working at the university. But I don't see myself building a career in academia. It is truly an honor that you believe I'm suited for that. I appreciate that." Brinn extends his hand and the dean shakes his head before taking it.

"Maybe next year," Dr. Hughes says. "You understand

that I'll likely have to give your adjunct job to one of the Ph.D. candidates?"

Brinn nods and I wrap my arms around his and squeeze.

"Seeing past the current play?" Henderson asks Brinn.

"Without a doubt."

Again, Henderson slaps him on the back. "Hall of Fame quarterbacks always do."

A tall redhead with creamy white skin and a ginormous diamond around her neck joins the group and links her arm through Henderson's.

"Pardon, darling, but I must steal you away if you're talking business or football. You have six other days to do that."

"Suzanna, this young man is the next big thing in aviation if we can convince him to run with his idea. This is Brinn McRae and his girlfriend..."

"Josie Woodmere," I say and extend my hand. I let the girlfriend remark go.

Suzanna Henderson leans in closer to me and stares. "You look so familiar to me. I just can't place it. What did you say your last name was?"

"Woodmere. I'm not from here. I grew up in New England."

Suzanna snaps her fingers. "Is your mother Cassandra Woodmere?"

I stiffen and feel Brinn's attention snap to me. I try to breathe. "Yes, she is."

Suzanna claps her hands in delight. "Oh, I love your mother. We went to Vassar together. We were in the same sorority and pledged at the same time." She lowers her voice. "Of course, I knew her when she was Cassie Williamson and used to... Well, those are stories I'm sure she'd rather you hear from her. Is your mother here?" Her head moves as if on a swivel searching for my mother.

"No. She's not." I have to consciously force myself to relax.

"Well you tell her that Suzanna Simmons Henderson says hello. You look just like her. She was just as beautiful as you are, and I'm sure she still is."

"Thank you. It was nice meeting you. I'm sorry but I must excuse myself. I have to catch up with someone before they leave." The urge to run out of the room and to the next town is crushing.

I hold it together long enough to execute a polite smile before I slip away. Brinn says his farewells and I sense him come up behind me before I feel his hand on my back. I continue walking to the exit.

"Hey, you OK?"

I huff out a heavy breath. "My parents don't know I'm here and I really didn't want them to. I'm sure Suzanna Henderson will let my mother know first chance she gets."

"Is it so bad that they know?" He propels me toward a small alcove that provides us some privacy.

"I don't know. After the incident with the artist in Washington, they really did a heavy campaign for me to come home. It's not me they wanted. Just another Woodmere to walk around my father's office. When I didn't, it made 'Cassie' even more furious."

"What's the worst that could happen? You're an adult."

"I know. I just like having my anonymity." I hold the lapels of his tux, rubbing my thumbs up and down, and my panicky, erratic pulse is replaced by a steady, excited one. "Did I say yet how incredibly hot you look in this?"

"You did. Did I say how totally stunning you look in

this?" He sweeps his hands down the bodice, resting them on my hips. "We should stay a little while longer and then we can get out of here. I have a surprise."

"A surprise?" I ask in my most sultry tone.

"Yeah, a surprise. You know, like the surprise of finding out that your mom went to Vassar. Where did you go to school?"

"Let's talk about you for a second."

"I really don't want to—"

"I really don't want to talk about me or my mother." I can't help my clipped tone. Talking about my mother does that to me.

"OK. We'll start with me. What do you mean you agree that I'm wasted on flight training?" He lightly traces his hand up my spine where the design covers my skin.

"I meant that you do a wonderful job there, but it will go nowhere other than being an instructor and owner. You can open more schools but where will that take you? You're bigger than that. The idea about the startup is crazy good."

He nods slowly. "I've wanted to buy into Mark's business since I was sixteen years old. It's been my sole plan. This idea, this timeshare thing is nuts. It's unheard of. Besides the crazy, *crazy* capital it would be really hard work—"

"Because you're no good at hard work."

"I don't know. It's just an idea."

I wrap my arms around his neck. "It's a fabulous idea. You're fabulous and..." I exhale slowly before I add, "I went to Yale."

"Yale?"

"It was close to my house."

"You don't say. What did you study at this little hometown college?"

I press my lips together, dreading this moment. For two years, I've never shared this with anyone other than Jayne. Will it change the way he sees me? And if it does, how will I feel about that?

"Law."

"You're a lawyer?" He steps back. Though I'm still between him and the wall, he blocks me from running by boxing me in by bracing his arms against the wall. "That makes complete sense."

"I'm not sure how to take that. I'd like to mention that Mark knew this about me and didn't tell you." It a juvenile effort to deflect the attention from me.

"That you're a lawyer?"

"That I went to Yale." I search his face and watch as he fights back the doubt.

He shakes his head. "He just forgot to tell me. He's been busy."

I cup his cheek. "Brinn, babe. You're trying to buy into his business and he doesn't disclose everything about a new employee. Temporary or not." It breaks my heart watching him struggle to hold fast to his teenage dream. But if there were ever a time to consider all the options, now would be it.

The struggle of emotions is still clearly expressed on his face. It's a lot of new information to hit a guy with.

He squints at me. "How is it even possible you're old enough to be a lawyer? I thought you were twenty-four?"

I shrug again and skim my finger down the edge of his lapel. "I skipped a grade and took college courses my last two years of high school. I mentioned that, right?"

"Yeah, that part you did." He looks over his shoulder, his

eyes darting around the crowd before turning back to me. "You belong in this world. Don't you?"

"Maybe once. Even then I'm not so sure because I was pretty lonely in that world." I bite my lip.

His eyes wander over my face and stall at my piercing.

"Tell me what you're thinking?" I venture.

"A lawyer? I'm wondering why I didn't see it."

"If it makes a difference, I've never sat the bar so technically I have a law degree but can't practice."

He nods slowly.

"Please don't be mad." I try not to beg but there's a hitch in my voice that gives me away.

He takes my face between his hands. "Babe, I'm not mad. Surprised. But not mad. I'm just seeing things differently and—"

"Nothing has changed. We're the same two people who met here tonight. Let's not complicate this." I step up on my toes and deliver a gentle kiss that ends with a little sucking of his bottom lip. "We still have this. And speaking of surprises..."

His laugh is soft and deep. "The surprise is that I got us a room here."

"Ooh, that's a good one." I lift up again and whisper naughty suggestions in his ear.

"I've lost the ability to think," he says before kissing me longer and harder than the one we started with. "Let's just hold on to this," I whisper and make it a fervent wish.

TWENTY-TWO

JAYNE SNAPS a pencil in two then flings the pieces on the ground. She jumps off her bar chair and stomps on the pieces, muttering words I'm sure would send the queen into an apoplectic fit. After she's spewed her anger, she slides back onto the chair, pats down her hair, then stares up at the ceiling.

"Please distract me with something. Anything. I know you said the ball was uneventful but you have to tell me something. Make it up." She looks at me and picks up a new pencil. "I beg you."

Jayne's working her books again as she does every two weeks. Forced torture, she calls it. When I asked her why she does it twice a month she said if she spread it out any further she'd never do it and that's simply irresponsible.

"You should hire someone. I've done what I can for you, but if you can't keep your shit organized, you're a lost cause."

I spent an entire Saturday setting Jayne up. Trying to make her life easier and streamlining her bookkeeping. It lasted an entire two weeks before it looked like a tree exploded in her home and store office. I take her books from her, close them up, and tuck them in her oversized bag she calls a briefcase—because it's more fashionable then a square attaché case, her words. Papers are crammed at the bottom of the bag, all wrinkled and twisted.

"I said distract me, not belittle me." She gives me the British two-finger version of up yours.

I laugh and give her a side hug. "OK, there was this one thing…"

"I knew you were holding out on me." She gestures for me to continue.

I fill a couple of drink orders before I lean across the bar and say, "Remember when I told you we got a room afterward?"

She nods.

"Turns out Brinn rented a donkey and a trapeze so we could—"

Jayne chucks her pencil at me and covers her ears. "Shut up. Shut up. I don't want to hear your lies or crazy sex-capades."

"You said make something up." I laugh then sip at my iced water.

"Honestly, that's it? You two are disgusting. You're so smitten." Her expression is hopeful and playful.

"I'm having a good time," I say and pour a Riesling for Samantha, a customer who comes in on Wednesdays looking as if she's taken on the world and the world kicked her ass. Twice. Her standard is to imbibe two glasses of Riesling, briefly participate in the conversation, maybe laugh, and then leave looking a little less worked over. Lately, she's been staying after the vapors from her second drink have long left the glass.

"Both of you need a good time. Especially Samantha here, who continues to torture herself every Wednesday," I say.

I've learned over the course of the last few weeks that Samantha is a lawyer and Wednesdays are her pro bono days. The stories she hears shatter her and, maybe it's because she seems so adrift that I confided in her that I, too, have a law degree. Since then she's been trying to coax me into coming to work for her and eventually sitting the bar and mentoring under her.

"I have a good time waiting for me at home. I should get there sooner rather than later." She places a few bills on the bar. "If you come work for me I wouldn't have to come in and drink on Wednesdays."

"If I came and worked for you, *I'd* need the drinks. Thanks, Samantha but no thanks."

"If something changes, the cruise line doesn't work out, you know where to find me." She waves on her way out and I clear her space, readying it for the next person.

"You just like what you can do at your job. With your boss," says Jayne.

"When you say it like that it sounds so dirty." I wag a brow at her.

We laugh as Pippa joins us. She moves Samantha's seat aside and lifts her leg, placing it on the bar, stretching it.

"Bloody hell, Pips. This is a bar not a yoga studio. Put your leg down." Jayne turns to me, rolls her eyes, then shrugs. "It's her mating call."

"You two will miss me when I've gone," she says and moves into tree pose.

"Shall I take you to the airport now?" Jayne teases.

"I might actually miss you, Pippa." There is some truth to my words. Both friends look at me, surprised.

"You're like a conversation piece. A coffee table book. Look at what my friend Pippa can do. You're a tool to help us pick up guys. They see how limber you are and they're all in." I lean across the bar to briefly squeeze her hand. It baffles me the speed in which these two have become important to me, having never experienced my own girlfriend clique before.

"As if you have ever picked up any guy when we've gone out," Jayne says.

"We do make a lovely trio," Pippa says and moves into the splits, balancing between two stools. "If you are ever in India, Josie, look me up."

I smile and nod my head toward incoming. Two guys, both college-aged, come to stand beside Pippa and strike up a conversation. Pippa waves at us and we laugh.

"She's brilliant," Jayne says and I agree. Pippa knows how to work a room.

"Meet my cousin," Pippa says and introduces Jayne to the friend that was working as the first guy's wingman. Unfortunately, he's not very tall and when Jayne stands, she towers over him. He backs away and stands behind his friend.

"He's wearing pleated pants," I whisper to her. "As if you could really be interested in a guy with pleated pants."

"This is true. He's more your size anyway," she says.

I shake my head. "I already have my good time."

We watch Pippa ease herself from the stools and walk to a table full of other guys, apparently the friends of the two that approached her.

"She's such an attention whore," I say.

"Well, here comes Mr. Good Time now." Jayne arches her brows and I look toward the door.

Brinn comes across the room and slides onto a stool. His smile gives me a warm fuzzy, essentially making my day.

"What'll it be, handsome?" I lean on the bar and present my best smile.

"How about a kiss?"

"Mmm. See, I'm at work and that's probably not going to fly since the bosses' daughter is right there." I jerk my head in Jayne's direction. "How about I get you a drink?" I tease though I'd like nothing more than to lean across the wood counter and plant my lips on his. "I can meet you by the restroom at my break and maybe our lips can accidentally collide."

"I can't wait. Until then I'll take a Guinness. What're you doing later?"

"This tall guy. Short hair. Has a thing for flying. I'm going to so totally do him. Really work him over." I pour his draft and place the dark stout in front of him.

"Lucky bastard," he says with a wink.

"Josie?" I hear my name from behind Brinn and look over his shoulder to find the source.

I can't believe my eyes.

"Max? What are you doing here?" Maxwell Gardner, my ex-fiancé, is staring at me.

He looks the same, maybe a tad tanner, which shows off his dark hair and eyes. His suit is not the Brooks Brother's type he used to favor but looks like Armani. I move from behind the bar but freeze mid-stride when I spot my mother walking toward me, tucking her phone into her purse.

"Hello, Josephine." She hasn't aged as well as I'd

expected. Though her mouth has always been a thin line expressing her perpetual irritation, it now has a slight downward curve. She looks tired. There are more lines around her eyes and a pallor that she's never had before.

"Mother?"

"Is she wearing Chanel?" Jayne asks in a hushed voice.

I nod. "Mother," I say again in a flatter, here-it-comes voice, which is hard to emulate as I am ticked off six ways to Sunday.

I glance at Max, who's giving me an apologetic shrug. Mother steps closer and scans me up and down, at least the parts of me she can see, and her lips disappear altogether. She lets out a sigh though her nose as she looks heavenward.

She steadies her stare on me. "Josephine. Might I have a word with you?" She tucks her bag under her arm and narrows her eyes at my piercing.

"All right." I wave for her to continue.

"Privately. Might I have a word with you privately?" She gestures away from the bar. Her bobbed dark hair still falls to her shoulders; nothing about her has changed.

Her limited wheelhouse of emotions are the same. Disappointment, frustration, and impatience have left their mark, creasing her face. I used to look so much like my mother, before I left but I hope, now that I've changed my path, that laugh lines are what will age my face. I don't know what she could possibly say to me, but I've no interest in hearing it considering what she kept from me about Will.

"I'm working, Mother. I can't just walk away."

"Oh, I see you finally learned something." She arches a brow.

"I walked right into that one," I say to Brinn.

He's looking from Max, to my mother, and to me, his beer forgotten.

"Mother. Max. Would you care to have a seat? I have a break coming up. We could talk then." I turn to fill a few orders and then turn back to Max. "Why are you here?"

"It was either me or Stuart," he says.

I shudder. My kid brother Stuart is my parent's sycophant, who went from sticking toads in my bed to hacking into my computer to steal my term papers in the course of one summer.

"Ah, I see. Thanks then, I suppose. What can I get you to drink? Mother, a vodka tonic?" I pull a tumbler from the shelf and make her drink. All my life all she's ever drank was vodka tonics or wine. The conversation is lacking as everyone is looking from one another and my mother is laser focused on me.

"Mother. Max, I want you to meet my friends Jayne and this is...this is Brinn." I gesture to them and give Brinn a smile.

Max gives Jayne a quick handshake but when he and Brinn clasp hands it appears to be a pissing contest of sorts determined by whose grip is stronger. Brinn wins.

"I'm assuming you found me through your old school chum Suzanna Henderson." I give Brinn an I-told-you-so look.

"Actually, we already knew where you were." Cassandra Woodmere sips her drink as if the glass might not be clean enough for her.

I run several probable ideas through my head before I realize the truth. "You hired a private investigator?"

I should have known. It was something they talked about doing when Will left.

"Of course we hired a private investigator. Had you been responsible and simply told us of your whereabouts, we would not have had to resort to such measures. Your father is running for a public office, after all. We needed to make sure the other candidate couldn't surprise us with anything. Like a husband or a child." Mother finishes her drink.

"Well you should fire that shit bag you hired because I have both." I roll my eyes and step away to fill more orders, ignoring my mother's gasp of surprise at my language. I've never cussed in front of her but my anger at my naiveté in thinking I might actually be away from the ever-watchful eyes of my parents has left me fuming.

After reining myself in, I step back to where my friends and family sit. I lean across the bar toward my mother. "Cut to the chase, Mom. Why are you here?" I stare at her, my eyes not wavering. I've come so far from the scared girl I was two years ago when I stood in front of them, holding my wedding dress in one hand, and told them I was leaving, my knees knocking.

"Enough is enough, Josie. It's time for you to come home. We need you. Do the right thing." She stares back.

Wow. That's a loaded sentence coming from someone who should've done a whole lot more regarding her family, a mental illness, and keeping us intact. Would things have gone differently if we'd all been a part of Will's illness and treatment? We will never know.

The tension is palpable and no one talks. "What brings you here?" Brinn asks Max, breaking the silence.

"Ah," he says before he finishes his drink and slides the tumbler toward me. "I thought I might be of some assistance." He gestures to my mother before he turns to Brinn. "And I'd wanted to see my girl, Josie, but I'm guessing she's no longer my girl. But then I guess she never really was."

I throw back my head and laugh. "Wow, you make it sound like you've been pining away. I've seen your Facebook page. Daphne, that's her name, right? She's the law clerk you were crushing on when we were engaged?"

Max has the good sense to look embarrassed. "I owe you an apology."

"You did me a favor," I say while looking at my mother.

"We're really here about the business. With your father no longer able to work in the practice due to his schedule there's a...concern that there isn't enough Woodmere presence at the office." Max says.

"Stuart's in the office. I'm pretty sure that's a lot of Woodmere presence."

My mother slaps her hand on the counter. "Your brother is a boob, and with William having not finished law school, it's now become your responsibility."

"William," I say, mocking her tone, "is an amazing writer, Mom. Have you read his book? And while we're on the subject of William. How dare you keep—"

"And let you and your brother worry if it was going to happen to you?" She grips her clutch, tucking it under her arm.

"But he needed—-"

She steps up to the bar, her eyes flashing. "You have no idea what it's like to watch your children turn their backs on you when they need you the most, and I hope you never do. Whatever you may think of your father and me, Josephine, it would behoove you to acknowledge there are two perspectives."

I struggle with my words, wondering if perhaps an apology might be warranted.

"Mother—"

She cuts me off with a wave of her hand. "It's time to come home."

Max leans against the bar. "It's a great position, Jo, a chance to make partner in a few short years. You just have to come with us. We have the private jet on standby."

"I didn't even take the bar, that's how uninterested I am in practicing law."

Brinn tosses a ten-dollar bill on the counter. "It was nice meeting you both. I have to get going, Josie. See you at work tomorrow." He nods to Jayne and rises to leave.

"Wait," I say but he ignores me.

I come from around the bar and catch up with him at the door. "Hey, what's wrong?"

"Nothing." He shrugs my hand off his arm, his eyes scanning the room.

"Oh really? Because you could've fooled me. I thought we were meeting by the restroom and later tonight.... Talk to me." I move to stand in front of him.

"Your family's in town. I'll just get out of the way—"

"That's stupid. You are not and will never be *in the way.*" I try not to roll my eyes but fail.

He shrugs his shoulders before he steps around me and leaves.

"Work tomorrow?" My mother asks when I return to the bar.

"Yes, Brinn and I work together. He's a pilot." I can tell that in my mother's eyes Brinn's value has risen. Slightly.

"Enough is enough, Josephine. Come home. You're

needed." She says needed like it gets caught in her throat and she has to cough it out.

"I'm sorry but I'm not coming home."

"Ever?" Max looks at me; his eyes wide with surprise because I'm shaking my head long before I even process his question.

"Not to live. I may for a visit every now and again. But..." I laugh and look at Jayne. "This place is more home to me than Connecticut."

"Hoorah," she exclaims and reaches across the bar to hug me.

"This is ridiculous. You belong with your family and your people," Mother says.

"Go home, Mother." I cross my arms and meet her stare. This time there is no nervousness, no trembling or uncertainty.

"You cannot mean to say you're staying here?" She gestures around the bar.

"Sure, I mean that." I don't correct her and mention my cruise line job.

"You will be disinherited, Josie. I'm not kidding. This has gone on long enough." My mother rises and tucks her purse under her arm. "I'm staying at the Four Seasons. Come tomorrow and we can make plans regarding your move home."

I come from behind the bar again and stand before her. "I don't care that you'll disinherit me. Frankly, I thought I already was. I still have my trust fund from Granddaddy." What's left of it. "But, Mother, I'm not coming home. I have no intention of ever working for Woodmere, Woodmere, and Gardner. I'm sorry. I know that I've disappointed you once again, but if I might make a suggestion—if you could stand to see me for who I really am, maybe you'd stop being disappointed." I want to hug her. I want to find some way across this invisible line that's been drawn in the sand but I have little faith it will happen.

"Woodmeres for four generations have been practicing law. It's what you're supposed to do."

"You have Stuart."

"Stuart failed the bar. Twice now." I might be wrong but I spot a tad bit of sadness in her eyes.

"I'm sorry, Mom. But that's not home for me anymore."

She squares her shoulders, straightens her spine, and her nostrils flare, "There are no words for what I'm feeling at this moment, Josephine."

"You should leave early tomorrow. I'm assuming you flew down on the company jet. We're expecting some bad weather and you don't want to get stuck here," I say.

She steps around me and storms out.

Max looks apologetic. "For what it's worth, this"—he gestures to me—"looks really good on you. I'm happy for you. But shit, we need help at the firm."

"I'm sorry." I give Max a quick hug and watch as he leaves, in no rush to catch up with my mother.

"That's too bad about him being an ex of yours," Jayne says.

"He's pretty good looking," I agree with her.

"And taller than me," she says with sadness.

I rub her arm and pull my phone out of my pocket. I text Brinn several messages, which he ignores and irritates the shit out of me.

If I didn't know he has a crazy schedule tomorrow and needs to get enough sleep to meet FAA guidelines, I'd drive myself over there and kick his door in.

But I don't. Instead I get off work and go straight home. No drive-bys or midnight stalking for this girl. I force myself to call it a night, believing a good night's sleep will make everything better in the morning. Only to spend most of the time tossing and turning, punching my pillow, and checking for text messages until I finally pass out from exhaustion.

TWENTY-THREE

IT MAKES the day easy when two people who work together and sleep together have a fight and then don't have to face each other the next day because one of them spends the day outside the office, communicating via email, because he's a coward. A big giant suck of a coward.

I've done all my work and part of Brinn's, hoping it would settle my frustration. But I finished early and now Zach and I stand at the door of the hangar and stare out at the field toward the runway and the International airport. I had Zach check the flight plans and confirmed that my mother and Max did indeed leave this morning.

The weather looks calm even though the sky is cloudy. I listen to the weatherman on the computer and stare across the horizon.

A hurricane?

"We need to get Brinn involved," Zach says behind me as he scrolls through various weather reports on his smartphone.

"I texted him and I've heard nothing." It's the part of

Thursday where he disappears, and I have no idea where he goes. Sometimes he shows up later at my place but the gap is there and I'm not unbalanced enough to follow him. I figure he'll eventually tell me. Maybe he goes to his mom's gravesite or is taking a foreign language. He has pretty sweet dance moves; maybe it's because he takes lessons.

"Yeah, he won't see the text because he's teaching," Zach answers.

I turn to look at him. "At the university?"

"Nah, at the Boys and Girls Club in Daytona."

"What's he doing there?" That, I never imagined.

Zach shuffles on his feet. "Ah, I wasn't supposed to say anything."

"How do you even know this?" I'm intrigued.

"That's how I met Brinn, through the club. My mom works a lot so... Anyway, you should go on down there and get him."

I hug Zach, another kid from the old neighborhood whom Brinn offered a way out. I can tell he's embarrassed but I do it anyway.

"I'll go get him. I've backed everything up. You unplug what you can and move computer stuff to the storage room. Put it high up in case of flooding and then go home." I grab my purse and nearly run to my car.

The drive is quick and only a few cars and Brinn's old truck are in the parking lot. A few parents are picking up their kids and an employee is standing at the steps looking up at the sky. More clouds are moving in as the bands of the storm race to come ashore.

"I'm looking for Brinn McRae," I tell the employee.

He sighs, continues to look at the sky, and says, "In the gym" before he puts a walkie-talkie to his mouth.

The Boys and Girls Club is a large building made of concrete blocks. The interior walls are painted with fun murals of kids swimming, playing soccer, taking karate, playing chess, and a large assortment of activities.

Down the hall kids shout out "Yes, Sensei" in unison. I follow the noise as they count in Japanese, and when I look through the doors, they're performing a series of blocks and kicks all led by Brinn. A black belt is tied around his waist, his uniform white and crisp, and his feet are bare.

"*Hajime,*" he says. "*Ichi. Ni, San, Shi.*" His voice carries across the gym, the kids moving with each count. They're all in white uniforms with a variety of belts. Some uniforms are dingier than the others but none are wrinkled. They do moves to the count of ten and drop to the mat, bow, and wait for Brinn to continue.

He gives them a pep talk about getting through the tough times, how to be smart in confrontational situations, and to know there's more than what they have today. When he dismisses them by giving them all high fives, I step from around the door.

He does a double take, and I hope my smile says nothing more than how amazing he is. The fight is not important. It's just a stupid fight. But this, this is amazing.

"What are you doing here?" he asks quietly and pulls me back into the hallway.

I have so many unanswered questions. "Why didn't you tell me about the karate and the Boys and Girls Club?"

I know we've kept secrets but this is an amazing thing to share. Something to be proud of.

He shrugs and folds his arms behind his back, as if he's standing at rest. "Why is it you think you need to know everything about me? Until yesterday, I didn't know everything about you. Like your other ex-fiancé is mega rich with his Rolex watch and sports car."

"You knew I went to Yale and you're a smart guy. I figured you'd make the leap that my family has money."

"I'm not talking about money. I'm talking about Max, the guy you almost married and his net worth. I'm nothing like him. I never will be."

"Almost married. *Almost* but didn't." This conversation is stupid. Doesn't he realize if I wanted that I'd have it?

"I didn't share everything with you because we're just having this, whatever it is." He gestures between us. "And you're going to move on and I'm going to still be here doing the same things. I wanted to leave something untouched by you."

"Really? This?" I mimic his gesture, ticked that he'd reduce what we've shared to something he can't even put to words. "Whatever this is? Is that what you said? Is that what you think? This is 'whatever?' Because at its very core it's a pretty good friendship. A genuine liking for each other."

We've shared an intimacy I've never experienced before and to do so requires a certain modicum of trust. Yet, he's defensive about me knowing this and I'm stunned into realizing there's a strong possibility Brinn doesn't see beyond the casualness I've been so adamant about keeping.

"Yeah, you're right. We should keep this about the work and sex." I sound like a bitchy girlfriend but I can't stop the words from coming out.

"You wouldn't understand." His tone is dismissive, making the words condescending.

I slug him in the upper arm. "I wouldn't understand how you like to foster the self-esteem of kids and give them a life skill and options to think outside of the life they know?" I slug him a second time for good measure. He doesn't move. Just stands there and takes it.

The wall between us is high and wide and it's as if every time I take a step closer he adds another layer. Now is the moment I could use to walk away, but I remember the look in his eye when he asked me not to end it via text message. I think of all the people that have let him down and I don't want to be on that list. When this ends, if this ends, I want him to only have fond memories of our time together.

"Help me understand," I say, nearly pleading. Not only because I want to be let in but because I want us to be more than this moment. I want what we've shared to have more depth.

Slowly, he lifts his hand to rub his arm and looks at the space over my head.

"Even if I tell you what it was like, you won't get it. You grew up with ready access to food, in a warm house, with more than enough. I grew up raising Vann, working so I could buy food to feed us because our mother spent every dime she could get on booze or worse. We slept in our car when we were between government housing. I washed in sinks at gas stations or at school, and I had to fight for every single thing I have."

He tells it like a veteran talks about a war, a statement of fact. There's no bend toward heroics or a ploy to make me feel sorry for him because pity is the last thing he wants. He doesn't tell it with anger but the weariness I've also seen in Will. The weariness that comes with extensive struggles. Struggles Brinn has certainly had, but for him it was just a way of life. For Will it was a loss of a way of life.

"What you do for them is wonderful." I step toward him, hoping to close the gap.

"I do it just as much for them as for me." He glances at me but doesn't come off the wall.

"Who doesn't? That's the whole purpose of doing something of this nature. By giving, you get—"

"No, I do it to remind me. To keep me in line. Sure, my main reason is to help these kids. To be a positive role model and show them that they have options other than what the street offers them. I want these kids to be able to protect themselves from not only other kids but adults too. But I also do it as a reminder of how far I've come and how much further I have to go." He remains rigid against the wall.

"I think you're amazing," I say softly. "You're right. I only understand as much as I can from this position, but just because I had more doesn't mean I don't recognize how lucky I am. Life must have been very—"

"Chaotic," he says, his gaze meeting mine.

"I suppose chaos is one word." Funny how Will had used that sometimes, too. "I was thinking uncertain or unpredictable. Living with constant uncertainty can be very frightening." I want to touch him but he continues to stand tall and stiff and my hesitation feeds into my doubt.

On a sigh his shoulders slump. "It got better when we moved in with my grandmother. At least there we knew we had a steady place to sleep and didn't have to move schools. Though, she used to try and hold food over our heads to get us to comply. It never worked though because I was working two jobs by then and would take Vann to the little mini mart down the street and get him a hot dog and a Yoo-hoo."

"How old were you then?" I move to the space next to him and lean against the wall sideways, my shoulder resting next to his.

"Fifteen." He looks down at me.

"You're a good brother." I place one hand on his bicep.

His lips twitch.

"It's okay to smile," I tease and squeeze his arm.

He drops his arms to his side and faces me. "This one time, when we were living in Deltona in this real dump of a place, my mom was gone—had been for a few days. It was raining, hard, and Vann's scared of thunderstorms so I didn't think I could leave him alone without him freaking out. There was nothing in the cabinets to eat except a box of Dream Whip. Why we had Dream Whip, I'm not sure. Maybe it was left over from Thanksgiving when my mom, in her completely manic way, got it in her head to make us a real Thanksgiving dinner, except she never did because she'd get too drunk or too high and the dates would slip past her. But we had this box of Dream Whip and food coloring. So I made it up and added the coloring to make it seem like we were getting the food groups. That's also why I come here. To see if these kids are getting fed. To bring them a balanced meal so that they may be getting at least one quality meal."

"And to give them strength." I lean toward him. I want to wrap him in a hug but I know he'll shrug me off. "You should teach a self-defense class for women. Like Jayne and Pippa—they could use it and I could use the additional practice."

His eyes search my face and I desperately want him to lean forward and kiss me. Kiss me good, too. The laughter of the kids in the gym behind us floats through the door. I smell the food, the welcoming aroma of the fried chicken.

"Where do you get the food?"

"From that diner down from my house." He smiles and picks up a lock of my hair.

"You have the diner make up a meal every week?"

"Yeah, I worked out a deal with them. They write off

half the expense, I pay the other half, and every week I bring a well-balanced meal to these kids. The club provides the milk, paper plates, and stuff."

"I'm a shitty person," I say and lower my head. "I've never done anything like this because I wanted to. Charities are always an *event* for my family. A chance to look like you mean well while you look good." I look up at him.

"There's always time to change." He drops my curl to stroke my arm, his lips lifting in a tease. "How did you find me here, anyway?"

"Zach," I say, followed by a gasp. "Oh, shit." I slap my forehead.

"What?" He grabs both my arms and pulls me upright.

"The hurricane has shifted. The projected path puts the eye right over us. Mark called and said he wants you to fly the Cessna south. The TV says that even if the path shifts it will only shift more north so Mark thinks the best route is to go south. He said if we take a direct hit, we can still function with one of the planes. He was real emphatic about getting the plane out." I roll my eyes. The urgency is lost on me as a gymnasium full of children is behind me, their value far greater than an airplane.

"It's because that's the one we use the most. Most of the flight training can be done in it."

"Oh." That makes total sense.

He lets go of my arms and takes a step back. "How much time before landfall?"

"About six hours from what they're predicting. It's increased in speed and winds."

"OK, get back to the hangar. Back up the computers and make sure you make two copies. One I'll keep with me when I fly down to Miami, and put the other in the safe."

"I've already done that." I pull the external hard drive from my purse and hold it out to him. "What are you going to do? What else can I do?"

"I have to make sure these kids get home. Most of their parents get off late, and I usually stay here with the staff until seven."

I look at my watch; seven is over two hours away.

"I'll stay here. You go to the hangar and start prepping to leave," I say but he's already shaking his head.

"Brinn?" A stocky guy, wearing a similar gi but his belt is a dark purple, steps through the door. '

"Charlie," Brinn says. "We need to get these kids home. The hurricane has shifted its trajectory."

"That's what I was coming to say. Kim," he says, pointing behind him, "is calling as many parents as she can to come now."

"The city will be shutting down soon," Brinn tells me. "They don't mess around with hurricanes, especially as Cat four."

"Cat five," I say. "They think it'll hit as a Cat five." I try not to tremble.

My experience with hurricanes is limited to what I've seen at the Jersey Shore, devastation nonetheless, but it wasn't a first-hand experience for me. I was also able to go back to an intact home, electricity, and everything where I left it.

"You need to go inland. Can you go to Will's? Don't stay in your apartment. It's likely that area will be evacuated anyway." He starts walking down the hall but turns back and takes two large strides back.

"Or come with me. Either way, go home, grab some clothes and anything of value to you. Text me and let me know if you're going to Will's." He slips an arm around my waist and pulls me close, planting a quick but meaningful kiss on my lips.

"Be careful driving, Josie. Once those rains start coming in the roads get covered quick." He rests his forehead on mine for a brief moment before he lets go and starts walking toward the gym.

"OK, you be careful too. Can I—" But he's gone into the gym and is starting to organize the delivery of thirty plus kids.

Where did he go as a child when the hurricanes came? Was he solely responsible for Vann during those scary times? To shelters? He's right, there's no way I would understand what he experienced other than to experience it first hand, and driving around the country trying to find myself while I have my grandfather's trust fund waiting for me in an account makes me wholly unable to comprehend even a smidge.

I do the fastest walk to my car that my heels will allow and dial Will's number as I slip into the driver's seat. I leave a voice mail when prompted and send a text, as if that might reach him.

Where R U? Can I come stay with u? Hurricane.

I wait but there's no response. It's not lost on me that the night Will's car caught air off the bridge was a night similar to this. Torrential rains and unpredictable weather patterns.

TWENTY-FOUR

ZACH'S SCOOTER is resting against the side of the
hangar. The air is muggy and heavy with moisture. There's
no sound of anything but twin engines and propellers spin-
ning. Occasionally a horn sounds through the air but the
leaves barely rustle, the birds have long flown away from the
impeding storm.

I stare at the long line of planes waiting to take off and
worry Brinn won't get out in time.

I glance at my phone, looking for some word from either
Will or Brinn. I press the link that will dial Will directly and
wait for it to ring through. Nothing happens so I try again. I
still can't get the call to connect and decide to try Brinn and
get the same response. Nothing.

After leaving Brinn, I dashed home for a quick change of
clothes, throwing my laptop, a change of clothes, and my
hematite stones in a bag. Don't ask me why I grabbed them.
They were sitting in a bowl on my counter and I snagged
them on the way out the door. I've changed into jeans and a
tank top and tied a hoodie around my waist. To keep the

wind from owning my hair I've pulled it back into a low ponytail.

Back at the hangar, Zach is trying to get Brinn's plane ready for takeoff.

"Is he here yet?" I ask Zach.

"No. He better hurry because he might miss his window out." He looks toward the runway.

I retreat back to the offices to make sure I've stored, backed up, and protected all the important stuff and anything else. Then I wander aimlessly around the room trying to call them both.

"You coming with me?" Brinn asks as he walks into the office.

A sigh of relief escapes me. One accounted for. One to go.

He's changed into jeans and a T-shirt with his flight vest. He does a quick scan and follows it with a brief nod before signaling me to follow him. I try Will again. Nothing.

"When are you leaving?" I walk behind him to the hangar doors.

"About forty minutes. Why, what's wrong?" He looks out toward the runway and then back at me.

"Nothing. I can't get a hold of my brother."

"Leave him a message and come with me."

"If I could just get a hold of him," I mumble and chew my lower lip.

"He's probably fine. He's far enough inland." Brinn glances at his watch and a fat drop of rain lands on its face.

I look up at the sky. The green is mixed with the fading yellow of the sun and clouds are rolling in, thick and heavy, holding back the weight of flooding rains.

"We've got to go," he says. "Smitty, how are you getting home?"

Zach is pulling his scooter into the hangar. "My mom is picking me up." He nods toward the entrance of the aviation park.

"Go now," Brinn says and takes the scooter from him. "Where are you going?"

Zach grabs a backpack that's lying against the hangar wall. "To the high school shelter."

"Here, take some cash." Brinn hands him a wad of bills. Watching the struggle on Zach's face makes me want to turn away. "You're going to need it."

"Take it from my pay," Zach says, taking the bills.

"Sure." Brinn clasps him on the back. "Now go."

Zach takes off at a run, and I start chewing my other thumbnail, having worked the first one down to nothing.

"You look worried," Brinn says. "Try calling him again. Call his girlfriend." He rubs my arm, sliding his hand to mine, taking the thumb from my mouth.

"Daanya! Why didn't I think of that?" Relief that Daanya had had the foresight to give me her numbers blows through me. Now if only the call will connect. As I wait for the ringing sound, I step closer to Brinn and lean against him.

"Daanya," I nearly cry into the phone. "It's Josie. I'm sorry to call you at work but I've been trying to get a hold of Will. The hurricane is headed for us and—"

"Will is in Daytona," she cries. "He wasn't feeling well this morning when I left for work. I asked him what he was going to do, and he said make sure you're leaving town because of the weather. I didn't think he would drive there."

"He came here?" I look at the sky and remember a night seven years ago similar to this.

"I pulled him up on the Find a Friend app and it stopped updating an hour ago. It says he's by the speedway. He's on his bike and he is very agitated today. Not himself."

"I'm still in Daytona. I'll start looking for him and get back with you as soon as I know anything." I disconnect and put my forehead on Brinn's chest, trying to steady my racing heart and erratic thoughts. I need a plan. I relay what Daanya told me. That Will is likely in town.

"What are you thinking?" He rubs my back.

"I have to go look for him."

"Where do you think he went?" He searches the sky. "You don't have much time."

I step back. "He hasn't gone to my place. He knows where I keep the hide-a-key and he would've called by now wondering where I am." I wrack my brain. When a horrific idea settles, I shake my head in denial, pressing the heels of my hands to my eyes to hold back the threatening tears.

"What?"

"He's probably gone to the beach or...the St. John's River Bridge." I drop my hands to look at Brinn.

He shakes his head. "Why would he go there? That's suicidal in this weather."

My voice breaks when I try to say the words. I blow out a slow breath. "Because my brother has schizophrenia."

"What? Why didn't you ever tell me that? Like today when we were talking about keeping secrets—"

"It's not my secret to share. It's his. I just found all this out myself. That 'accident' he had was caused by hallucinations."

"What's this have to do with the bridge?"

"He drove off a bridge. The hallucinations told him too. It was during a storm similar to this." Tears slide down my cheeks.

"Cops won't let him sit on the bridge. They'll make him move or forcefully move him. Start by calling the Volusia County Sheriff's office and I'll call State Patrol."

The rain has started to fall in steady drops, long past hinting at what is about to come.

"I'll call. You need to get out of here. Get in line and leave." I gesture to the runway that is still congested.

"I have time to call."

Our calls result in no information, even the one to the hospitals. The process to get information is painfully slow but the upswing of the time spent on the phone is the improvement in line for the runway.

"Come on, get in the plane. You can keep calling as we fly down." He pushes me toward the hangar. "We are out of time. If I don't get off soon, lightning will ground me."

For seven years I wondered why Will left me. For the few weeks since I've learned of his mental illness I wondered why he wouldn't let me help. Now I have this moment. This decision and the truth is there really is no decision to make. I know what I need to do.

"I can't go. I have to go look for him." I pull away and jog to my car.

Brinn follows me. "How do you think that's going to happen? Look around you."

"I'll start with the beaches and work my way inland."

"Josie, the beaches are closed. The cops will have it blocked off. The beach side will be evacuated or is in the process." He grabs me by the elbow and pulls me up short.

I take this moment.

Stepping into his space, I cup my hands around his face. "I have to look. I have to try." I kiss him gently. "Be careful, please. Have a good flight." I wrap an arm around his neck and press several more urgent kisses against his lips.

Pushing at his chest, I back away and give a small wave.

"Call me," I say. A heavy, foreboding cloud has come over me and I can't shake the feeling that after today nothing will be the same.

"Shit, Josie. You can't go looking by yourself, and not in that car. Once the rains start, your car will get stuck in the first puddle. This is crazy." He rakes a hand over his face.

"I can't leave him out there. He might be in his right mind or he might not. Give me your keys. If I wreck your truck, I'll buy you a new one. I promise." He's made a good point about my car.

"I don't care about my truck, I care about you." He steps toward me.

I move closer and start digging in his pockets. He catches my hand in his as I pull the keys out, stopping me from stepping away.

"I'm coming with you."

"No way. Are you fucking nuts? You've got to get that plane out of here or Mark will lose his shit." I push against his chest. "Go."

"Your brother is more important than this plane. It's insured right. Right?" he asks.

"Yes, the insurance came in a few days ago." I laugh more from hysteria than anything and throw my arms around him. "You really don't have to do this."

"I know I don't." He lets go of my wrist. "Move my truck over to the side and put your car where mine is. I've got to secure everything here and I'll meet you in the truck."

It takes fifteen minutes to get everything situated before we drive away. The rains have increased and his wipers work furiously to keep the window clean but visibility is low and splotchy.

"I think Will might go to the same beach spot where we spent some time." The spot we went after he told me about his diagnosis. At the last bridge to the beach, a line of cop cars is blocking us. But opportunity waits for no man. I jump out of the truck and run up to the officer in charge of redirecting traffic away from the bridge.

Once again my law degree comes in handy, as I cite potential legal issues regarding a man who might be entering a psychotic state. I also do a fair amount of begging. When I slide back into the truck, soaked to the bone, my hair a wet hose dripping down my back, I can't help but smile.

"He says we have fifteen minutes to get back out." I shiver and Brinn cranks up the heat.

With the rain pushing against the truck in heavy sheets, it takes three minutes longer than the normal five to get to the turnoff to the beach.

"Look!" A motorcycle is parked behind a dumpster. It's Will's. I'm out and running toward the beach before Brinn can put the truck into park.

The wind is picking up and the rain is cold, cutting right to the bone. I come to a stop when I reach the sand, my hands flying to mouth to cover my horrified gasp. Brinn touches my shoulder and I jump.

Will is pacing the beach, barely seen through the curtains of rain. He looks to be ranting, his arms waving manically. His jeans are soaked; his boots lie scattered on the sand. His shirt is gone, and between rants he covers his ears and screams with an intensity that forces him to bend at the waist; his face contorts, shattering his features. The wind howls yet I can hear him between gusts.

"Hold back a second. I don't want you to freak him out," I tell Brinn before I take off at a run across the sand. Brinn follows further behind.

"Will," I cry.

I can barely hear anything over the waves and the rain. Much less my voice. But magically he hears me.

He turns to me. His large scar is red and appears to be pulsing. It gives him such a sinister appearance I involuntarily step back. He runs toward me, gets in my face, and starts screaming.

I try not to wince but he's so close. It takes every ounce of inner strength I have to stand my ground. I can't make out the words because they come out too fast and garbled. Suddenly, the wind stills in an eerie intermission, a pause before the next onslaught. Will stops screaming.

"Will, we have to go." I use the calmest tone I can muster under the circumstances. "A hurricane is coming." I try to grab his arm, a critical mistake.

He bucks like a bronco and pushes me with a force that sends me back yards. I get up, gesture for Brinn to wait as he's moving toward Will, ready to charge. He doesn't look very happy with standing back. But there's no time to explain.

I run to Will and try a new tactic. "You have to get out of here. Now." I gesture to where we parked the truck. "We have a ride waiting for you. It's totally protected and no one will know you're in it."

"You're lying," he screams. "They always know where I am. You told them. You do this to me. Why do you do this to me?" He lunges at me before turning back to the water and walking into it.

I have no option. He must be saved from himself. I run up behind him and take him out at the knees. He drops like a sandbag; the tide is high and briefly he's underwater. His arms flail madly in what I assume is panic from being submerged.

"OK, help now," I yell to Brinn, and for fear he can't hear me, cast him what I hope is a pleading look. I get my arms under Will. He's so freaking heavy that I only drag him a foot before I'm exhausted. The cold water must have shocked him into a state of paralysis, as he doesn't fight me.

Brinn pushes me aside, grabs Will under the shoulders, and starts running backward up the beach. We make it half way to the boardwalk when Will comes to his senses and begins protesting by kicking and thrashing. He pulls away, crawls through the sand like a crab for a few feet then scurries to his feet.

"You crazy bitch," he screams and lunges at me, arms swinging madly.

I block with my arms and sweep my leg wide, knocking him off his feet again. He's in the sand and continues to rant at me and the voices that only he can hear.

"Knock him out," I plead to Brinn. "Cold cock him, please."

"Seriously?" He steps closer to Will.

"Yes, it's the only chance we've got. Hit him," I scream before stooping to snatch up a handful of sand. I toss it in Will's face to distract him.

Will tries to deflect it. He sputters and rises up, his trunk coming off the sand. When he's at the right angle, Brinn clocks him. Catches him just right in the jaw, which snaps his head to the side and sends him into the sand, out cold.

"Come on, grab his feet," Brinn yells over the rain, as the wind's picked back up in a haunting howl.

I stagger under the weight of his feet and legs. We make it to the boardwalk and Brinn flips him up over his shoulder, fireman style. We fight the wind and powerful rain to make it to the truck. It's a mad dash to the hospital, where the adventure only gets started.

TWENTY-FIVE

THE HOSPITAL in Daytona is evacuating patients and the triage queue puts Will somewhere in the middle. I'm tempted to toss out my father's name, his financial status, and profession, but I know that'll only bring them into the loop and it's likely Will wouldn't want that. Instead, I have Daanya reach out to his physician, who has a brief conversation with the doc in Daytona. Will's given a shot that sedates him and we wheel him back to Brinn's truck to make the long drive to Gainesville, the hurricane chasing our heels.

I fret over Will, whose head lolls around in my lap as drool snakes out the corner of his mouth. I don't care that we were soaked to the core, dried partially while at the hospital in Daytona, got soaked again going back to the truck, and have dried to a stiff crispness, sand sticking to patches of our skin. Discomfort and pain is in watching Will suffer. Knowing that there's a beast within him and I can't even pretend to understand it or know how to handle it. I try not to think of him going through this before and wonder if he felt alone.

The ride is quiet. I focus on Will and Brinn on driving. I can still hear him screaming, a constant, high pitch ringing in my ears.

Trigger. The word is on a repeat in my head.

Did my presence cause this?

It takes us an hour longer than normal to reach Shands, where we get Will admitted and his treatment begins. Daanya pieces it all together for me as she works with many of Will's doctors. According to her, Will believed his current medicinal regime was starting to affect his quality of life through anxiety, increasing episodes of obsessive compulsion, and those repetitive jaw movements he calls Tardive Dyskinesia. That's why he switched to the new trial. Unfortunately, they're speculating the new drug wasn't as effective for Will as it had been for others.

If I voice my fears to anyone in the room, they'd tell me that today was about medication and not about me being here. But I have to wonder if the reaction to this new medicine would've been different had I not been around.

Regardless, talking to Daanya and the doctors introduces me to a different insight into Will's life and the obstacles he faces each day.

He once said, "Every day is chaos and a risk for me." Now I understand just how that is.

Daanya gives me the keys to their house and Brinn forces me to leave the hospital. There's nothing I can do but watch Will sleep. The ride is silent except for the brief directions the GPS gives. We pull into the driveway and I take one look at Will's house and burst into tears.

It's so normal, with its large yard, front and back, evenly trimmed shrubs, and oversized ficus in the front. It's an illusion. No one would look at this house and know it belongs to a person with a mental illness. There's no stereotypical sign of the betrayal of my brother's brain, no junk in the yard or shutters resting crooked against the house. I realize how even I was lured by what I wanted to see and what I expected to see.

"Hey, it's going to be OK." Brinn pulls me into his arms. I rest my forehead on his shoulder and hold tight as the sobs escape me.

"It's never going to be OK, at least not for Will. I know things could be worse. I know I should be thankful but I'm devastated all over again. I didn't know what to do out there. I feel helpless and ignorant—"

"You're the last thing from helpless. You faced several obstacles to find him and you did. He's getting great care because of you." He's rubbing my back and suddenly I'm exhausted. The rain continues to beat against the earth and small rivers run down the streets and through people's yards.

"But what about tomorrow or the days after that. How can I help him?" I ask the question I'm sure a million other families have asked a million times.

"I don't know the answer except to say that you have to take it day by day."

I nod, knowing this can't be riddled out with a book or one visit to the hospital. "Let's go inside," I say once I've pulled myself together. I exit on his side and use Daanya's key to let us in. Thankfully, the power is still on and after becoming familiar with the kitchen, I immediately make a fresh pot of coffee and find I'm famished.

"Do you want something to eat?" I ask.

Brinn's taking in the surroundings, the eclectic mix of Daanya's Hindu taste and Will's travels and science fiction bent. Books on Dr. Who and Buddhism rest on the coffee table, a mix of architectural sketches hang on the walls. Most are of doorways and windows. Some of arches. Books are stacked in corners but the place is clean and simply designed.

"Did you expect it to be different?" I ask, wondering how he now perceives Will. Remembering how I felt about the outside of the house.

I know I feared that maybe it wouldn't look...typical? Maybe I expected what I saw all those years ago in his closet. Tons of drawings pinned to the walls.

"I dunno. I suppose so," Brinn says and picks up the remote.

The TV is small and sits in the kitchen, resting on a counter, likely used for news and the occasional sitcom but not on longer than thirty minutes. Brinn turns it on and the Weather Channel pops up, the last channel my brother or his girlfriend was watching.

I open the fridge and take a quick assessment. "I can make us an omelet." But I don't wait for an answer because the weather reporter assigned to Daytona Beach comes on the screen. The station does a quick intro and I hold my breath. "The city of Daytona Beach and surrounding areas are the target of this storm. Currently, we're experiencing the calm of the storm's eye but cities as far north as St. Augustine and as far south as Sanford are feeling her effects. Spin-off tornadoes have been spotted inland in Winter Haven and Sebring. Hurricane Layla has left most of the Daytona Beach residents without power. We're told the intercoastal areas were hit the hardest. Flooding being their biggest problem at this moment. Inland, the speedway, and airport have taken a direct hit as well. Locals are anxiously awaiting word about the famous Daytona Beach Pier, which took a hit from

Sandy. Is it still standing? Only time will tell. For now, Volusia and Flagler County brace themselves for the worst as we wait for those Cat five winds to come ashore and for the eye of the storm to pass. Back to you, Tim."

I swallow and watch Brinn, who has done nothing but rub his hand over his chin, repeatedly.

"The insurance came through on the new plane, right? I know you said it did but tell me again," he says without looking at me. He stares at the footage of Hurricane Layla's winds as a tree bends at a ninety-degree angle in protest.

"Yes, it's in the paperwork folder. I even called to reconfirm earlier today before I came to see you." I step toward him, reach out gently, and take his hand, massaging the calluses on the pads of his palm. "It's gonna be OK."

Brinn nods but his face is pale and his lips are pressed into a thin line. He pulls his hand from mine and rests it on his knee. I hope I'm right. Screw hoping. I'll make sure it's going to be all right.

"I gave up my adjunct job. If this hurricane does serious damage, it'll leave me unemployed, but I could pick up more flight instruction time, I suppose. If there's a runway left, that is." He's talking more to himself than me.

I have no platitude that will ease his pain. Everything he's worked for might be gone and I can't help feeling partially responsible for that. If I have to sit the bar and become a lawyer, if I have to work for my parents, whatever the cost, I'll make this right for him. But for now, we'll get through this moment together.

"Why don't you take a shower and I'll make us something to eat. There's nothing we can do at this moment for Will or the office." I shift and try to tuck my hands in my back pockets but they're crusted shut.

"I'll run out and get my flight bag in a second." He glances at me before returning to stare at the television.

It worries me that he barely looks at me. "Brinn," I whisper.

He looks up and I understand now what I am seeing. He's afraid. Of what I cannot be sure until he says, but going against Mark's orders, losing the plane, possibly his house, not knowing about his brother, the list is endless. His phone vibrates on the counter and he snatches it up.

Briefly, his face visibly relaxes and his eyes meet mine. "It's Vann. He and some friends decided that west Volusia wasn't far enough and they drove to Tampa."

I smile and rub his arm. Salt from the ocean clings to his skin "The rest is replaceable."

"Yeah, but let's hope we don't have to replace anything. Did you mention a shower?"

"Come on." We find the guest shower and I get it started, heating up the bathroom while he runs out to get his bag. I sip at my coffee and watch the news as I wait for my turn. The mood is not one that fosters showering together, and I use the moment alone to steady my hands and fight back the urge to have a good cry. I constantly check my phone for any update from Daanya and further toy with the idea of calling my parents, but my best guess is that this might have happened before and they were never notified. So I wait.

"Anything new?" Brinn comes toward me. He's wearing a plain white undershirt and it accentuates the cut of his chest and the bulk in his arms, and he's paired it with low-slung jeans that fit all the right areas nicely. He's toweling his hair dry and when he finishes I hand him a mug of black coffee.

"No, just that the westerly winds are coming on shore now."

"Jeez, I hope I don't lose everything," he mumbles.

"It's going to be all right. It's a blip on the screen. These things help us appreciate the highs." I say it with the most convincing tone I can muster, but I'm not sure if either of us has any hope left to believe in those words.

"I can't afford to start over." He stares at the pictures on the screen, his jaw flexing.

"It's a stressful night," I say more to myself than to him. He's very clear on how stressful the night is for both of us.

He turns from the screen to look at me. "Let's just hope it's gonna be better tomorrow."

What are the odds of that happening?

"I'm going to take a shower." I shuffle to the bathroom and peel the scratchy clothes off. I step under the hot spray and expect to fall apart in this safe space. But as the water washes over me and I clean the sand out of the scratches Will left on my arm, I don't fall apart like I thought I would. Instead, I start making mental lists. Contingency plans of what we'll do if the hurricane does the unimaginable. Plans about Will and when or if I ever do bring our parents into the picture. Plans about how I can help Brinn if there's some loss at the shop. Plans that I know will require rebuilding of some sort. Plans to stay. The lists give me a sense of peace and control, and when I step out of the shower, I'm braced for the worst but feel armed and ready for the challenge.

We watch the news, drink coffee, and scarf down the spinach and Gouda omelets I made. I doze on the couch as we wait for some word about both storm fronts, Will's and Daytona's.

It's not until after midnight that Daanya texts me to say

Will's been stabilized and is resting peacefully. They're less worried he'll experience psychosis. It's not long after that when the scenes from Daytona Beach start to come across the airwaves and it's terrible. Worse than terrible, horrific. I've seen pictures of Katrina and Andrew. I helped with the clean up after Sandy and this new hurricane, Layla, appears to have joined their ranks. She's cracked Daytona like an egg and scrambled the city, leaving a debris field miles far and wide.

I reach for Brinn but he steps away, moving to put his coffee cup in the kitchen sink. Briefly, he looks out the window before resting his elbows on the counter and burying his head in his hands. The newscaster confirms that the airport's been leveled, including the airfield and surrounding hangars and businesses.

TWENTY-SIX

BRINN LEFT EARLY to go assess the damage at the airfield and I stay behind to follow up with Daanya about Will. But, discovering I'll be unable to get a visit with Will until further notice, I score a rental car and drive back to Daytona to see what I can do to help Brinn.

I pull over to take a call from Mark, who tells me everything is lost and he's cashing in. Not going to rebuild. I sit on the side of the road trembling long after the call is over.

What will Brinn do? The dream he's had since he was a kid is gone. He gave up teaching at the university to focus on buying into the school. Now that's gone too. I scroll through all the options I know of and mentally make a list of ideas to help him get back on his feet. He'll have a hard time seeing past all this devastation. Who wouldn't?

When I pull my car alongside the curb in front of their house, Vann gives me a wide-eyed look that almost makes me stay in the car. Almost. Their house managed to come out only requiring small repairs to the roof. Others down the street were completely wiped out.

Brinn gets out of his truck and hands Vann bags of take out. He doesn't look at me.

"Is there something you need?" he asks as he heads back to his truck. He pulls a sign and frame from the bed of his truck. *For sale by owner* it reads.

I flick my gaze to the sign. "You're selling the house?"

His face is dark, his anger barely checked. "Vann's moving away for his Master's program. He needs his half of the house to pay for school."

"Oh." I suppose I thought he was calling it quits.

"Why are you here, Josie?"

"I wanted to say I was sorry for the shop. Mark called. I know you're—"

"What is it you think you know?" He swings his gaze to mine and there's a steely glint found there.

So that's how it's going to be?

We face off in the driveway. I'm not in a good place. I've spiraled into a tenuous stream of thought where I'm questioning if I leave mass destruction in my wake. Does anyone I get attached to come out unscathed? I know Brinn well enough to know he's in a bad place too. Understandably so.

"Do you blame me for this?" My voice is low and the question is carried by my shock and confusion. I never told him to come with me.

"You should go. I've given it a lot of thought and it's time we call this quits. Whatever this is. We chalk it up to getting exactly what we both needed and walk away. But it needs to be over. And you should go. Now." He nods as if to give his words the exclamation point they lack.

"You do blame me." Anger sparks through me. I plant my hands on my hips and level him with a glare.

"I don't blame you. I blame myself for getting caught up

with you. For not staying focused." He holds the FOR SALE sign between us. Like I'm going to kick him in the knees or something.

Well, OK, there's some validity to that concern.

"But—"

"You're chaos. You're in the moment. That's how you live your life. It was a good thing while it lasted but it's time to end it. I need more than the moment. Especially right now. I need to focus on the future, and I don't even know what that looks like. Just move on with your plans and let me get about the business of figuring out mine." He steps away.

The term chaos leaves me breathless because right now I do feel like I bring turmoil. That Will might be sitting at his desk writing a book had I not come into his life. That Brinn might not have questioned his path had I not taken him to a psychic, told him Erik would be a good partner, said I thought he was more than a flight school owner.

Who cares what I think? While I was actively participating in their lives, I was also planning my exit route.

I look up at the sky and force my tears back. Holding them inside. The time for my pity party is not now.

"What about that start-up idea you had? That guy, Shawn Henderson, at the ball said he'd invest in something like that."

"Says the girl who could go home tomorrow, say she's sorry, take the bar exam, and slip into a cushy life without so much as breaking a nail." His tone is biting. His stance angry.

"But all you have to do is go talk to him—"

"No, Josie. I have to do far more than that. I have to have the capital or at the very least the credit for the capital. I don't have a job." He walks to the front yard and drives the sign into the yard with one powerful push. "And once this house sells, I won't even have collateral. Not that it's worth a whole lot anyway."

"Can't you buy Vann out?"

"Where does that get me? With collateral and a new debt. It doesn't work out."

"OK. You're in a shitty place. I get that. You need to make your next move. Do you have any idea what that might be?" I step toward him but he turns his back and walks to his truck.

"I'm gonna move. Maybe I'll join the military. I'll bounce around from place to place, not getting attached to anyone and never looking back at what I left behind. Sounds good. It's about time I do something selfish. Hell. Sounds easy."

I gasp. "That's a shitty thing to say." A tear leaks and falls down my face.

He turns, one hand on his hip. "You're right. It is. I'm sorry, but in case you haven't noticed, I've lost everything."

I square my shoulders. "You have so many options."

"Not from where I'm standing." He turns away, heading toward his house.

"Brinn, I can help." My voice quivers and I'm down to my last bit in reserves.

"That's all right, Josie. Thanks but no thanks." He walks into the house, closing the door softly behind him.

Shutting me out.

Part of me wants to cry. A different part of me wants to throat punch some sense into him. I unharness my anger—it's easier to control and predict—and tuck away my pain. Besides, I'm not going to sit in my car and cry over a guy whose head is stuck so far up his ass he can't tell whether it's night or day.

I peel away from his house and head toward my place. Suddenly desperate to check the state of my apartment. The clean-up will couple nicely with burning off my anger. I won't have any perspective until that happens. But cursing Brinn for being a pigheaded, stupid, goal-driven, tight-ass fool will feel good, for a few minutes at least and keeps me from becoming overwhelmed by the pain of my broken heart.

I'm such a fool to think I'd never fall for someone, to deny that it had been him.

"No, I'm not crossing some line, I'm just giving him good memories" had been a delusion of the highest grandeur.

Karma

Desperate to get home so I can lose my shit in privacy, I turn onto my street and am forced to stop three houses away. Debris is everywhere. Several trees are uprooted and lying across the road, the spiky ends of their trunks pointing to the sky. City crews, FEMA volunteers, and neighbors are out trying to pick up the pieces. I park the car and walk the distance to Mrs. Cramer's house. The shock of what's waiting for me brings tears to my eyes, my anger forgotten.

The house is still standing. Bits of the roof are missing and a neighbor is putting a tarp over the holes. But the garage and my apartment are gone. Not blown away to lands unknown, but the roof's gone, completely lifted off. The garage doors have blown out; a giant ficus tree is laying half on the driveway and half across the garage. The stairs to my apartment are gone. The only way up is through the interior of the garage, leading into the laundry room where the blue walls are intact but no ceiling, which means the only thing I have left is what I have on me. One outfit, my laptop, and the hematite stones Brinn and I bought in Cassadaga. I stand next to my car, leaning against the driver's side door, and remove my phone from my pocket to call Mrs. Cramer in Miami, where she fled in hopes of avoiding the hurricane. I look away from the house, down at my lap, and trace a pattern on my jeans. "Oh, Josie," she says when she answers.

"I'm so sorry," I say and try to control my tears.

"Oh, sweetheart. I'm the one who's sorry. You lost everything." Truer words were never spoken though what I lost in the apartment is nothing compared to what I just lost down the street.

"Is there anything I can do? How can I help with this clean up?" I ask as a tear lands on my thigh. I brush the few on my cheek away before I force in a deep, resolve steeling breath.

"No, dear. The city said the stairs in the garage are sound and the building is structurally safe, so you go on and take whatever you need. Stay in my house if you want, if you need someplace. I'm trying to find a construction crew to start clean up and rebuilding, but as you can imagine...I've lots of competition."

"OK. Thank you for the offer but I'll just... I have somewhere to go. Don't worry." My voice is weak, stretching thin with the tension of trying not to cry. I suck in another breath and the constriction of my chest makes the inhalation hurt. So much for my determination not to be weak.

We exchange a few other condolences before hanging up and I'm left quivering from the emotions of it all.

What do I do now?

I have two weeks before my cruise line job starts. It's unlikely I'll be invited back into Will's life considering I could be part of the cause of his recent episode. Brinn is done with me. Nothing else tethers me here except Jayne. Looks like a clear sign from the universe that I should move my shit along. Clearly, I've overstayed my welcome.

I do a quick walk through of the apartment just to make sure nothing else can be salvaged. The green chenille blanket, the one that reminds me of Brinn's eyes, is still in the dryer. Which, funny enough, sits right where it should be in the laundry room. The washer is who knows where.

Reaching in, I pause before taking it out. Perhaps this is the one time mementos aren't recommended. The memories will be hard enough to live with. The last thing I need is to fall apart and cry into a blanket over some rocks and a guy with green eyes. Speaking of the rocks... I dig them from my bag and after I collect a few shirts and a skirt that managed to weather the storm, I stand on the bank of Mrs. Cramer's backyard and stare out at the river. I chuck all the hematite stones at once, hoping to send my heartbreak with them. But all I'm left with is the continual burning ache in my chest and more room in my purse.

Without looking back, I drive away in my rental car. All that's left is saying goodbye to Jayne.

The Fox is open, as are a few of the other places that survived the hurricane. Many are not providing their usual service but instead a hot meal, cold drinks, and a place to forget. Temporarily.

I find Jayne in the storage room.

"There you are." She tosses her hands in the air, dropping the broom she was holding. It clangs on the floor and causes me to jump. "I've been trying to reach you for a day. Are you OK?" She comes toward me. "Josie?" She stops in front of me and snaps inches from my nose.

"I came by to say good-bye. I'm leaving. It's time for me to move on." I shrug one shoulder.

"What? Why? You can't mean to tell me you're still going to take that stupid cruise job. I thought for sure you'd see now everything you have here."

I shake my head. "I have nothing."

"Rubbish. You have everything: friends, your brother, Brinn, and job opportunities. Whatever might have been damaged by the hurricane can be repaired."

"I've lost it all," I say, crying. "Not that I deserved any of it." I fall into her arms and let go of all the tears I've been holding back.

"Why ever would you say that? You do deserve it all." She folds me in her arms and rubs my back.

I give her a derisive snort. "I've been given so much. Your friendship, a new connection with my brother, this thing with Brinn, and I pissed it away. Like law school. Like every-thing. I played it all fast and loose with no thoughts to the aftermath. Why would life ever reward me for that?" I push away, feeling caged in.

"Oh, love."

"I had everything. Even here I had everything, and I took it for granted. He's never had a single thing and now he's lost it all. No wonder he can't even look at me. I'd hate me, too." I cover my mouth with my hand, appalled.

Jayne's eyes widen as she pieces my words together and dip with sympathy when she comes to a correct conclusion.

"I'd hate me, too," I whisper, hoping the truth will harden me.

"He doesn't hate you. Maybe he just needs a few days," Jayne says.

"I don't deserve him," I whisper. "He's right. I brought chaos to his life, but I swear I thought I was just helping him live a little. I never meant to.... I just wanted to be a fond memory."

"I know this will be hard to hear, and I don't want you to answer me. Only that you know the answer yourself." She lowers her voice before she continues, "Are you upset because it's over between you and Brinn, or because he left you instead of you leaving him?"

I jerk my gaze to hers but she puts up her hand to stop me from saying anything.

"My biological dad left me and my mum when I was just a child. Went off and started a new family. Like we weren't good enough or something." She gestures between us. "I recognize a kindred spirit when I see one. You can keep running and wondering why you have no one in your life or you can try something different."

Her words leave me weak in the knees, scared. There are so many hurdles ahead of me.

Jayne sighs deeply. "So what are you going to do about it?"

I shrug and rub the space between my breasts, wrapping one arm around my waist. "I don't know. I've no idea how to start over here. I've always moved on."

"You still have a job at the Fox. You can start with that. Or you can take the job with Samantha. You know you're interested. You talk to her about it every time she comes into the bar."

"But then I could've just stayed home and been a lawyer. I could just go do that now." I drop my head, feeling that epic fail that Brinn mentioned.

"Yes, you could. But you weren't happy with that so you left and went after what you wanted." She wraps her arm around my shoulder.

"I might love him," I whisper.

"Is that so terrible?"

"I can't love him." I shake my head in denial.

"Why ever not?"

"Because it's stupid. Falling in love with him is stupid."

"Darling, no one ever said falling in love was smart. They say to fall in love with a good person. Someone you can see yourself with forever, through thick and thin, because everything about it is stupid."

"Wow, you're a real romantic," I say while drying my eyes.

"I'm a realist." She laughs. "You, my lovely friend, have been sideswiped by your own machinations. Your reticence to commit and desire to live in the moment has given you something wonderful. It's given you the experience of bliss. Something people rarely get." She points to herself. "If I had an experience like you've had with Brinn, I'd treasure it for always, hold it close and let the memories warm me on those cold nights. I'd be thankful for the gifts it's given me."

I place my palms over my heart and press. "But it hurts so damn bad."

"I imagine it does. Do you think if you left you could outrun it?"

I shake my head. "What do I do?" I lean against her, resting my head against her shoulder.

"You'll know when you know. You'll work it out."

I nod, hoping she's right. For now, I know nothing and it's disarming and humbling and I hate it.

TWENTY-SEVEN

MY FIRST MOVE is to change my Facebook status to Jayne's roommate.

Temporarily, of course, while I got my shit together.

My next move is to go see Will. Per his request.

Standing outside the hospital ward, I turn over my purse to the security guard and listen to the instructions about protecting myself. Not that I should be in any danger, he adds.

I face Daanya, "Are you sure this is OK?" The last thing I want is make my brother worse.

"It's perfect. He's looking forward to seeing you. Just be yourself." She takes my hands in hers. "Be his sister."

I nod.

"Have them page me when you're done." One last squeeze and she's off, down the hallway in her blue scrubs and shoes, so quiet I hear nothing but the pounding of my heart in my ears.

Inside the ward, behind the locked door, a guard points me toward an open day room full of tables, a TV, and a wall of windows. When I step inside Will's sitting by himself at a table with a chessboard in front of him. I slide into the chair, grip the seat, and smile.

"There's no way I'm playing you in chess. Especially since I've never won one game. Ever."

He's wearing sweat pants and a T-shirt and looks beat down. Dark circles reside under his eyes, and when he rests his arms on the table and leans toward me, I see he's chewed his nails drastically short and many are bleeding.

"That's because you were always trying to do what the manual said instead of trusting your instincts." His smile is small but sincere and it follows the tick of his wiggling jaw. A movement I'm quickly becoming accustomed to.

"I'm not sure I have instincts. If I do, they're...." I take a breath. "Jacked up."

"Your instincts are fine. You knew I'd be on the beach."

"Yeah, but had I just stayed away then you wouldn't—" I can't even look him in the eye, my guilt is so heavy.

"Stop. Stop right now." Taking my hands in his, he says, "Look at me, Jo. This has nothing to do with you."

I force myself to make eye contact. "That's generous, Will, but you're wrong. I'm a trigger. Our whole family is." I swallow hard. Hearing that I contribute to my brother's illness breaks me into pieces.

"Jo Jo, I swear this had nothing to do with you. But everything to do with me not wanting to have these stupid ticks anymore. I hate this." He gestures to his swinging jaw. "I was on those new meds and at first I thought they were going well. The ticks were decreasing, but Daanya says my compulsions were increasing." He shows me his hands.

"Look what I did to my nails. All because I couldn't get them clean."

I reach one hand out, palm up, and he places his hand in mine. I hold on tight.

"I should've listened to her, but I wanted these stupid ticks to be gone. I hate that she's seen with a guy who can't control his jaw." His laughter is heavy with a bitterness that would break most men.

"You know she doesn't care."

"I know. I also know she can do better than me, but I'm going to hold on to her as long as I can." His smile is sad and it takes every bit of willpower for me not to burst into tears. I'd give anything to make his life better.

"I want to help. How can I help? Please let me help."

Will lets go of my hand and tucks his in his lap before he shrugs. "You can come by and visit me every day before you leave. Maybe even play a game of chess." He nods to the board. "Or you could stay and come any day, every day."

I find my answer written on his face. His sincerity and absolute certainty that I'm not a trigger is all I need to accept what I have been so desperate for.

I shake my head. "I'm not leaving. I'm staying. And if it's OK with you, I'd like to be more a part of your life. I really want that."

Will raises a brow in surprise. "What about your cruise job and European experience?"

"There's nothing I want in Europe. Everything I need is here." I wait with bated breath for his response.

He leans forward. "If there's one thing I've learned, it's that I can't tackle this thing by myself. I really could use your help. I want you to stay."

I promptly burst into tears, covering my face with my hands.

"Jo Jo?"

His hand is on my wrist, so I drop mine and look at him through my tears of happiness. "I'm so happy, Will. I wasn't sure you'd want me to stay. And I really, really want to stay."

"I'll admit I'm surprised. When the shit hits the fan, you have a history of scurrying off and hiding. Like a…a…"

"Bunny?" Holy fuck. Seriously?

"Yeah, a scared little bunny. You tuck tail and run. Find a new burrow to hide in. Always have. Remember when Max fell out of the tree house? I found you hiding under the bed in the guest room. You missed dinner and everything."

I brush away my tears and laugh. "Well, I'm not a scared bunny anymore. Wait, that's not true. I'm scared but I'm not going to run." Maybe I should pay Madame Monica another visit. "I'm gonna make mistakes, Will. But I'm like a fly stuck to flypaper. Not going anywhere."

We laugh and I notice he takes in a deep breath just like me. Relief is a wonderful thing. Pushing back from the table, he stands and opens his arms for a hug. I step into them and hold on.

"What'll it be? Ebony or ivory?" he asks as we step away.

"What?"

He indicates the board. "Ebony or ivory. You pick your pieces, and I'll get a clock so we can time our moves." He swivels on his heel and trudges off in an annoying slap of slippers against linoleum.

"I'm not playing with a clock," I shout at his back but he just keeps right on walking. I swipe up the ivory pieces and start placing them on the board. I'll let Will be ebony. The color suits his dark, competitive chess-playing soul.

TWENTY-EIGHT

"I'LL WAIT HERE," I tell Jayne when she pulls into the parking lot of the Fox and Hound. We've spent half of the day and most of the evening out looking for Brinn and the failure has left me feeling light years past dejected. After my heart to heart with Will, I returned to Jayne's with a plan in mind. I wasn't going to walk away from Brinn without a good fight. I can't take the chance of running into him around town and always thinking what if. This way, if he rejects me again and I run into him in town, my what if will be more about him being a stupid, bull-headed moron who doesn't deserve me.

"Let's eat inside. You need to see something other than my place." She turns off the car and unfastens my seat belt.

"We've just seen most of Daytona, Flagler Beach, and Port Orange." I pull the belt back and click it in place. "I'd rather go home."

"Come on, mum makes a bread pudding that helps ease heartache," she says and unfastens my seat belt again.

"Just get it to go," I plead.

Yeah, I'm having a suck attack but this broken heart shit hurts and I'm not handling it the best. I'm moody and not fun to be around so there isn't any purpose to going inside. Why Jayne continues to invest time in me is beyond my understanding. But I love her for it. I owe her more every day.

Jayne levels a glare at me and presses her lips together making them a thin line. She won't let go of my seatbelt.

"Fine, but I'm not up for an all-nighter." She won't shut up about it so I might as well just give in now.

I pull my hoodie around me, though the breeze is slight, the chill in the air goes right to my bones as if I have no protective layer whatsoever. I'm exposed. Jayne's layered two T-shirts and is wearing skinny jeans, and she looks as if she's warm to my freezing.

I shuffle in behind her and automatically go to the bar, taking a seat on a corner stool. Jayne sits next to me and catches the eye of the bartender, Jake. A true asshat who has played around with the waitresses. He thinks man was created in his image.

"Hey, Jake, we're going to order food," Jayne says.

I stare ahead. I'm in a space that waffles between angry and sad and if someone looks at me wrong, like Jake might, I may just go on a good rage.

"Sure," he says and pulls out two menus. "Hey, Josie." He gives me a nod and his gaze lingers.

My palm itches to slap him upside the head, but instead I look away because it's not him but my urge to strike out at someone. I'm eager to see Brinn and say what needs to be heard. So much is unfinished and I'll be restless until that moment happens. I crave this like an addict craves their next fix.

Truth is, Brinn is my fix, and none of these emotions likely have anything to do with closure or saying my mind. So there's that.

"Relax," Jayne says.

Forcing my shoulders back, I roll them to release the tension. Doing so makes me think of Pippa and her yoga, and I hope she's living it up in India.

I smile. "You were right," I tell her. "Getting out was a good idea."

"You have very intelligent friends," she says.

"Maybe I'll have a drink. Jake, can I get a whiskey sour?"

"Same for me," Jayne says and signals for Jake to take our orders. She looks over my shoulder and her eyes go wide and instantly I know.

I jump off the stool and spin to face the booths, finding the back of Brinn's head in one. It's bent over and I realize he's on the phone. I'm halfway across the room when Vann sees me, nudges his brother, and indicates in my direction. I'm at the table before he hangs up the phone.

"Never mind, I found her, Erik. I'll call you back," he says and disconnects without looking at the phone, his eyes laser focused on mine, a broad smile across his face. "Josie." He says my name in a deep, rough voice, and I swear that if these were different circumstances I might think he sounds happy to see me.

"Shut up," I say and push him back into the booth when he tries to stand, blocking him with my body. I lean forward, my face close to his. "Now it's your turn to listen to me, Brinn McRae. You said some shitty things to me and I never deserved that. You said I would run; yet here I am. You said I was chaos, destruction, yet you never accepted any responsibility for your own actions. I'm solely to blame. Yes, I have a past. I'm embracing spontaneity and willing to try new things, but that's because I was where you are and I wanted more for my life. I dared to dream and hope and live—"

"I—"

"Stop." I put my fingers to his mouth, pinching his lips together. "Listen to me. I believe you can do anything. That you've lost nothing but you're dangerously close to losing me and I have to know—are you OK with that?" I search his face, looking for something, anything to jump-start my heart as it's stopped, waiting for a sign.

He places his hand over my wrist and removes my fingers from his lips. "You need to understand something." His hand curls around my wrist and holds tight.

"I already know—"

"I can't change directions as quickly as you can. I've worked so hard to get control of my life." His eyes flick toward Vann. "Our life. I forgot to enjoy the moments. Guys get scared too, you know." He lets go of my wrist and places his hands on my hips; pushing me back, he stands and leans toward me.

"I look at you and I'm afraid to want you. Because then I'll need you and what if you don't feel the same way?"

"But I do, and I'm scared, too. I don't know how to do this." I step into him, our bodies slowly pressing against each other. "I left my family and life as I knew it to find something more and ended up falling in love with a guy who's like my father. How's that for irony?" I slide my hands up his chest, slowly. Hesitantly.

"You love me?" He cups my face between his hands.

"Well, either it's you or this city. There's something here I love. Could go either way." There's a crinkling of tape and what feels like a bandage under his shirt. "Are you hurt?" I pull up his T-shirt and see the taped gauze over his left breast. "Oh my God, what happened?" I step back and try to push his shirt up further, not caring that we're in a public place.

"It's nothing," Brinn says and reaches for me. "About this love thing."

"It's a tattoo. He just got it today," Vann says.

Over Brinn's shoulder, Vann tips his beer to me before he takes a pull.

I look back at Brinn, "A tattoo? Are you serious?" I peel away the ouch-less tape and pull the gauze back.

I burst into tears when I see the design. It's born for henna and looks like something I'd paint on my body.

"Don't cry, baby." He wraps me in his arms, crushing me to him. He kisses me with all the longing I feel and the salt from my tears makes it all that much sweeter.

"Do you mean it?" I whisper after we pull apart, my fingers tracing the tattoo.

"Babe." He cups my face.

"Are these flower buds?"

"Yes, it means new growth, new life."

"I know. I also know that the sun, moon, and stars woven among the vines and leaves signify a deep and lasting love."

"It's how I feel about you. It's just as much a declaration of love as it's a touchstone. You know how people get symbols for peace or harmony?"

I nod.

"This henna design is my reminder of how tenuous each day is. How valuable the simple things are. How much I can achieve, and about the girl who showed me how much I needed these reminders. How much I want and need her."

"I'm scared." I confess. "I know. Me too. But we'll do this

together. I'm right here with you." He dries my tears with the pad of his thumb.

"I'm not ready to be married and have kids." I kiss his palm.

"I can wait. Besides, it might be a good idea to not rush things considering I don't have a job and am selling the place where I live. Right now I'm not looking like a good prospect." He kisses the tip of my nose.

"Hmm, well. When you put it like that." I grimace, which results in both of us laughing. I reach up and he bends to meet me half way. Our lips touch and all will be right with the world once again.

EPILOGUE

I SMILE at the lady sitting across from me. Though, lady might not be the right word as she's likely the same age as me. She uses the tissue I gave her to swipe at her red-rimmed eyes.

I reach out and squeeze her hand. "Take your time. It's going to be OK."

"I know," she says and sucks in a ragged breath. "I think that's why I'm crying, because I'm relieved."

She breaks down again and I hand her the box of tissues.

"I'm sorry. What was the question again?" she asks.

"I asked if you wanted to take your maiden name back. We can petition the court while we finalize the divorce. If you do it all at once, you won't have to pay for the name change."

She's a pretty thing with curly red hair, the kind of red that's more orange-red than brownish red. Her freckles make her look too young to be married, and I flip through the intake sheet until I find her birthday. I'm only three months older.

She nods. "Yes, I want my maiden name back. I want nothing from that jackass. Especially not his name."

"That's the spirit," I say. "Good for you. But you do want some things. Like your half of the house. Do you want alimony?" She shakes her head.

"Here's a list of common assets. Do you mind reading through this and circling any of these that you all had?" Turning the paper to her, I hand her my pencil.

The door to the office buzzes the arrival of someone and a second later Brinn peeks in the door of the conference room. Instantly my heart leaps. He's been out of town the last four days and I've missed him desperately. I can't wait to get him home and get my hands on him; though it's not likely we'll make it past the truck.

"Ten minutes," I mouth over the client's head.

He gives me a sad shrug as if asking him to wait ten minutes is a lifetime then taps his watch before setting the stopwatch.

I roll my eyes and focus on the girl before me. We could be friends, she and I. We're the same age and as she sits here trying to rebuild a new life, she's not feeling sorry for herself at her circumstances, but more that she waited so long to get here.

"OK," she says. "This is everything." And hands the paper to me. "I just want him out of my life. I want a fresh start and to be left alone."

"We'll help you get that. You've come to the right place. Samantha is amazing and we know this isn't an easy experience, but we're here to try to make it as painless as possible. You worry about the healing and we'll take care of the dealing."

She laughs. "Please tell me that's not on the business card."

"It's not. I just made it up. Don't hold it against me."

"Thanks," she said. "I needed that laugh."

"Anytime. Hey, you should come down to the Fox and Hound sometime. My friend Jayne and I hang out there. We're always good company for a little man bashing." Though I don't tell her it's usually Jayne doing the bashing because I'm so blissfully in love with the best man in the entire universe.

"I might just do that. Thanks. My friends Kenley, Heather, and I meet on Wednesday's at the Ale House. You should pop over there sometime."

"Oh, I will, and then you'll be sorry you ever said anything." I scan the paper, making sure it's complete.

"Ha, I doubt that. I've learned that in the wake of this, there's very little I regret in comparison."

"We're done here, unless you have any other questions?" I say as she gathers up her purse.

She shakes her head.

"Oh, wait. Your maiden name. I forgot to fill that in. If we're going to petition the court for it, maybe we should know what it is."

"McAllister. My maiden name is McAllister."

"It's nice to meet you, Paisley McAllister," I say and offer her my hand.

She shakes my hand and laughs. "I like the sound of that. I'm looking forward to being Paisley McAllister again."

I hold the door open for her then quickly make a date reminder in my phone to pop in on her at the Ale House.

Brinn watches her leave before he slips behind the door, turns the lock, and pulls the blind downward. We've come a long way since the hurricane. First living in his place until it was sold and then renting a small apartment until the construction was complete at Mrs. Cramer's place. She rebuilt the apartment and I love it just as much if not more. Sharing the place with Brinn makes it even more perfect.

I stand in the doorway of the conference room and take in the sight of him. This start-up he's got going with Erik and Erik's math genius and former college roommate, Stacy, really eats into our time. I get that it requires hard work and dedication and Brinn is nothing if not those, but between studying for the bar, working as a paralegal for Samantha, and helping him with the business as much as I can, we're spread thin. Yet, it's a wonderful place to be because we're making our happiness and dreams happen. It's thrilling and exhausting.

Brinn moves toward me, and I step back into the conference room and wait.

"Hello, my love," he says. "I missed you." His eyes turn a darker shade of green and his pupils dilate. Thank God I'm alone in the office because it was wishful thinking we'd make it to the truck.

"Not nearly as much as I missed you." I dim the lights.

It's insane how being apart from him for even the shortest period feels as if an eternity has passed. As if I fear I've forgotten how he feels. I want to press him to me, feel his body against mine, leaving an imprint on me like a tattoo.

He opens his arms and I leap into them.

Ready to read more? Time to meet Paisley. Recently divorced, she finds herself waking up in her best friend's childhood bedroom. Sleeping naked next to her best friend's older brother. Did her one night just ruin two friendships? Ever had a crush on your best friend's hot brother?

Grab your copy and find out!

Amazon

Google

Nook

Apple

Kobo

BOOKS BY KRISTI ROSE

<u>The No Strings Attached Series-</u>

(Romance) The No Strings Series has a chick lit vibe and some are available in audio.

The Girl He Knows

The Girl He Needs

The Girl He Wants

The Girl He Loves

<u>Like cowboys?</u>

<u>The Wyoming Matchmaker Series</u>

(Romance) Sweet and sexy romances on the ranch. There's action, adventure, and heartbreaking angst paired with feel good rewards.

The Cowboy Takes A Bride

The Cowboy's Make Believe Bride

The Cowboy's Runaway Bride

<u>Samantha True Mysteries</u>

<u>Also in audio</u>

(Mystery) These laugh out loud, action pack books take place in the Pacific Northwest. Join Samantha, an adult with dyslexia who's hid behind photography, on her adventures in her new life as a Private Investigator. A job she inherited when her new husband died unexpectedly and left behind a mess and another wife.

One Hit Wonder

All Bets Are Off

Best Laid Plans

Caught Off Guard

Two Time Loser

Dodged A Bullet

The Meryton Brides

(Sweet romance) The Meryton Brides is a complete series (for now) that is a light, pleasant modernization of Jane Austen's Pride and Prejudice with a twist on the characters. These sweet contemporary romance books are full of love, friendship, trust, and family. Darcy and Elizabeth's story spans the series and ends in book 5, but each book provides the happily ever after we seek.

To Have and To Hold (Book 1)

With This Ring (Book 2)

I Do (Book 3)

Promise Me This (Book 4)

Marry Me, Matchmaker (Book 5)

Honeymoon Postponed (Book 6)

Matchmaker's Guidebook - FREE

The Coming Home Series

(Sweet Romance) A collection of small-town short stories that take place in Lakeland, Florida where Kristi grew up. These sweet romances are bite sized stories of happiness, wit, and laughter and invite you into the lives of 5 women and leave you happy because of the feel, good endings.

Second Chances

Once Again

Reason to Stay

He's the One

Kiss Me Again

or purchased in a bundle for a better discount.

The Coming Home Series: A Collection of 5 Second Chance Short Stories (Can be purchased individually).

Love Comes Home

Standalone Mysteries:

Campus Murder Club

Perfect Place (Using pen name Robbie Peale)

MEET KRISTI ROSE

Hey! I'm Kristi. I write romances that will tug your heartstrings and laugh out loud mysteries. In all my stories you'll fall in love with the cast of characters, they'll become old, fun friends. **My one hope** is that I create stories that *satisfy any of your book cravings* and offer a get-away from everyday life. When I'm not writing I'm repurposing Happy Planners or drinking a London Fog (hot tea with frothy milk).

I'm the mom of 2 and a milspouse (retired). We live in the Pacific Northwest.

Here are 3 things about me:

- I lived on the outskirts of an active volcano (Mt.Etna)
- A spider bit me and it laid eggs in my arm (my kids don't know that story yet)
- I grew up in Central Florida and have skied in lakes with gators.

I'd love to get to know you better. Join my Read & Relax community and then fire off an email and tell me 3 things about you!

Not ready to join? Email me below or follow me at one of the links below. Thanks for popping by!

You can connect with Kristi at any of the following:
www.kristirose.net
kristi@kristirose.net